ALSO BY CALEB CARR

The Alienist

The Devil Soldier

America Invulnerable (with James Chace)

Casing the Promised Land

The Angel of Darkness

KILLING TIME

Random House / New York

KILLING TIME

A Novel of the Future

CALEB CARR

Published in the United States by Random House, Inc., New York, and simultaneously in Canada by Random House of Canada Limited, Toronto.

RANDOM HOUSE and colophon are registered trademarks of Random House, Inc.

A portion of this work was serialized in *Time* magazine in slightly different form.

Library of Congress Cataloging-in-Publication Data

Carr, Caleb

Killing time: a novel/Caleb Carr.

p. cm.

ISBN 0-679-46332-1 (acid-free paper)

1. Presidents—Assassination—Fiction. 2. Twenty-first century—Fiction. 3. Psychology teachers—Fiction. I. Title.

PS3553.A76277 K55 2000

813'.54—dc21 00-59112

Random House website address: www.atrandom.com

Printed in the United States of America on acid-free paper

2 3 4 5 6 7 8 9

First Edition

Book design by Caroline Cunningham

This book is dedicated to

SUZANNE GLUCK

Anyone who has a problem would do well to

take it up with her.

I have but one lamp by which my feet are guided, and that is the lamp of experience. I know no way of judging the future but by the past.

—PATRICK HENRY, 1775

KILLING TIME

CHAPTER 1

SOMEWHERE IN THE MITUMBA MOUNTAIN RANGE OF CENTRAL AFRICA,
SEPTEMBER 2024

We leave at daylight, so I must write quickly. All reports indicate that my pursuers are now very close: the same scouts who for the last two days have reported seeing a phantom airship moving steadily down from the northeast, setting fire to the earth as it goes, now say that they have spotted the vessel near Lake Albert. My host, Chief Dugumbe, has at last given up his insistence that I allow his warriors to help me stand and fight, and instead offers an escort of fifty men to cover my escape. Although I'm grateful, I've told him that so large a group would be too conspicuous. I'll take only my good friend Mutesa, the man who first dragged my exhausted body out of this high jungle, along with two or three others armed with some of the better French and American automatic weapons. We'll make straight for the coast, where I hope to find passage to a place even more remote than these mountains.

It seems years since fate cast me among Dugumbe's tribe, though in reality it's been only nine months; but then reality has ceased to have much meaning for me. It was a desire to get that meaning back that originally made me choose this place to hide, this remote, beautiful corner of Africa that has been forever plagued by tribal wars. At the time the brutality of such conflicts seemed to me secondary to the fact that the ancient grievances fueling them had been handed down from generation to generation by word of mouth alone; I thought this a place where I might be at least marginally sure that the human behavior around me was not being manipulated by the unseen hands of those who, through mastery of the wondrous yet sinister technologies of our "information age," have obliterated the line between truth and fiction, between reality and a terrifying world in which one's eyes, ears, and heart can no longer be trusted.

There are no newspapers here, no televisions, and above all no computers, which means no damned Internet. Dugumbe forbids it all. His explanation for this stance is simple, though no less profound for its simplicity: information, he insists, is not knowledge. The lessons passed on from one's elders, taught by the wisest of them but recorded only in the mind, these, Dugumbe has always said, represent true knowledge. The media I've mentioned can only divert a man from such wisdom and enslave him to what Dugumbe calls the worst of all devils: confusion. There was a time when I—a man of the West, the possessor of not one but two doctorates—would have laughed at and disdained such beliefs; and in truth, during the time I've been here the laws and folklore of these people have come to trouble me deeply. Yet in a world stuffed full of deliberately warped information, of manufactured "truths" that have ignited conflicts far greater than Dugumbe's tribal struggles, I now find myself clinging to the core of the old king's philosophy even more tightly than he does.

There—I've just heard it. Distant but unmistakable: the thunderous rumble that heralds their approach. It'll appear out of the sky soon, that spectral ship; or perhaps it will rise up out of the waters of Lake Albert. And then the burning will begin again, particularly if Dugumbe attempts to forcefully resist the extraordinary brother and sister who command the vessel. Yes, time is running out, and I must write faster—though just what purpose my writing serves is not quite so clear. Is it for the sake of my own sanity, to reassure myself that it all truly happened? Or is it for some larger goal, perhaps the creation of a document that I can feed out over what has become my own devil, the Internet, and thereby fight fire with fire? The latter theory assumes, of course, that someone will believe me. But I can't let such doubts prevent the attempt. *Someone* must listen, and, even more important, someone must *understand* . . .

For it is the greatest truth of our age: information is not knowledge.

CHAPTER 2

In retrospect, the pattern was there to be seen by anyone attentive enough to trace it. A remarkable series of "discoveries" in history, anthropology, and archaeology had made headlines for several years; but they were all, on their surface, attributable to the great advances made possible in each of those fields by the continued march and intermingling of bio- and information technology, and so those of us who might have detected a controlling presence at work simply got on with our lives. Our lives; yes, even *I* had a life, before all this began . . .

In fact, by the standards of modern capitalism I had a good life, one graced by both money and professional respect. A psychiatrist by training, I taught criminal psychiatry and psychology in New York (the city of my birth and childhood) at John Jay University, once a comparatively small college of criminal justice that had grown, during the movement toward privatized prisons that gained such enormous momentum during the first two decades of this century, to become one of the wealthiest educational institutions in the country. Even the crash of '07 and the resultant worldwide recession had not been enough to stop John Jay's expansion: the school has always produced America's best correctional officers, and by 2023, with mandatory drug and quality-of-life punishments so stringent that fully two percent of the nation's population was behind bars, the United States needed nothing so much as prison guards. All of which allowed those who, like me, taught the headier subjects at John Jay to be paid a more-than-decent salary. In addition, I'd recently written a best-selling book, *The Psychological History of the United States* (the second of my degrees being in history), and so I could actually afford to live in Manhattan.

It was those two areas of expertise—criminology and history—that brought a handsome, mysterious woman to my office on September 13, 2023. It was a grim day in the city, with the air so still and filthy that the mayor had asked the populace to venture outside only if their business was urgent. This my visitor's certainly seemed to be: from the first it was obvious that she was profoundly shaken, and I tried to be as gentle as possible as I led her to a chair. She asked in a hushed tone if I were indeed Dr. Gideon Wolfe; assured that I was, she informed me that she was Mrs. Vera Price, and I recalled instantly that she was the wife of a certain John Price, who'd been one of the movie and theme-park industry's leading special effects wizards until he'd been murdered outside his New York apartment building a few days earlier. Murdered, I might add, in a particularly unpleasant way: his body had been torn to such tiny pieces by some unknown weapon that only recourse to his DNA records had made identification possible. I offered my condolences and asked if there'd been any progress on the case, only to be told that there hadn't been and probably never would be—not unless I helped her. "They," it seemed, wouldn't permit it.

Wondering just who "they" might be, I continued to listen as Mrs. Price explained that she and her husband had had two children, the first of whom had died, like forty million other people worldwide, during the staphylococcus epidemic of 2006. The Prices' second child, a daughter, was now in high school in the city, and even she, Mrs. Price claimed, had been threatened by "them."

"Who?" I finally asked, suspecting that this might be a case of hysterical paranoia. "What do they want? And why come to me about it?"

"I remembered a television interview you did last year," she answered, rummaging through her bag, "and downloaded it. Crime and history—those are your fields, right? Well, then, here—" She revealed a silvery computer disc and tossed it onto my desk. "Take a look at that. They confiscated the original, but I found a copy in my husband's safe-deposit box."

"But—"

"Not now. I just wanted to bring you the disc. Come to my house tonight if you think there's any way you can help. Here's the address."

The flutter of a slip of paper, and she was back out the door, leaving me nothing to do but shake my head and slip the disc into the drive of my computer.

It took all of one minute to look at the images that were burnt onto the thing; and then I found myself grabbing for the wireless phone in my wallet in a state of agitated shock. I began punching a familiar sequence of numbers, until Vera Price's words about "them" came back to me. I ended the wireless call and picked up the land line on my desk. Whoever "they" were, they couldn't have tapped it—not yet.

I redialed the number, then heard a disgruntled voice: "Max Jenkins."

"Max," I said to my oldest friend in the world, a former city cop who was now a private detective. "Don't move."

"What do you mean, 'don't move'? What the hell kind of a way is that to talk to people, you bloodless Anglo-Saxon bastard? I'm going out to lunch."

"Oh?" I countered. "And suppose I told you I'm looking at possible evidence that Tariq Khaldun didn't shoot Forrester?"

Silence for an instant; then: "Is that insane statement supposed to make me less hungry?"

"No, Max—"

"Because it isn't—"

"Max, will you shut up? We're talking about the murder of the president."

"No, *you're* talking about it. *I'm* talking about lunch."

I sighed. "How about if I bring the food?"

"How about if you bring it *fast*?"

CHAPTER 3

Twenty minutes later, Max and I were sitting in front of a bank of computers that nearly covered an old desk in his office on Twenty-second Street near the Hudson River. As we stared at his main screen, we did our worst to a couple of vegetable burgers I'd picked up from the deli downstairs, so engrossed in what we were seeing—even the jaded Max—that we didn't even have time to engage in our usual nostalgia for the days before the devastating national *E. coli* outbreak of 2021, when you could still get a real hamburger at something other than the most careful (and expensive) restaurants in town.

On the screen in front of us was the by then deathly familiar scene of three years earlier: the podium in the hotel ballroom in Chicago; the impressive figure of President Emily Forrester striding up, wiping a few beads of sweat from her forehead and preparing to accept the nomination of her party for a second term; and, in the distance, the face, the assassin's face that had been enlarged and made familiar to every man, woman, and child in the country since the discovery just a year ago of the private digicam images taken by some still anonymous person in the crowd. It was a face that, after only a two-month search, had been given a name: Tariq Khaldun, minor functionary in the Afghan consulate in Chicago. Justice had been swift: Khaldun, constantly and pathetically shouting his innocence, had been convicted within months and had recently begun serving a life sentence in a maximum-security facility outside Kansas City. As a result, diplomatic relations between the United States and Afghanistan, always fragile, had been strained almost to the breaking point.

But Max and I had other problems to worry about that day, specifically the fact that on the disc given to me by Mrs. Price the images, instead of proceeding on to the scene of panic that usually followed the assassination, suddenly disappeared; the screen went black for a few seconds, then came alive again with a replay of the crime, one in which the area where the eye was accustomed to seeing Khaldun's face was a carefully delineated blank. Next the screen went black a second time, and finally a third version of the same sequence appeared; but in this go-round, the man wielding the gun in the background was someone entirely different: Asian, maybe Chinese, certainly not Afghan.

I turned to my bearded friend. "What do you think?"

Eyes on the screen as he chewed on a sliver of potato, Max answered, "I think they cook these fries in llama dung." He tossed his paper dish aside.

"The disc, Max," I said impatiently. "Is it evidence of a forgery or not?"

Max shrugged. "Could be. Nobody was better than Price when it came to image manipulation—and we all know that you can't believe a goddamned thing you don't see firsthand anymore. But this isn't setting off any alarms in *my* software."

Which was significant. Max, like most private detectives of our day, had come to rely almost exclusively on computers for everything from forgery identification to DNA analysis. If his programs—and they were the best—weren't catching any evidence of deliberate manipulation in what we were watching, then something very confusing was going on. And as that something concerned one of the seminal acts of political violence of our time, the implications of the disc, along with the cause of Vera Price's desperate behavior and statements in my office, became uncomfortably apparent.

"If Price *was* mixed up in something," Max mumbled, "then we should get a look at the spot where he was killed."

"The police went over it pretty thoroughly."

"I used to *be* the police, Gideon," Max answered, stroking his beard. "We ought to take a look for ourselves. And there's one other thing . . ." He squinted, moving his fat frame closer to the computer. "I'm picking up something else on this disc. Something encrypted, and I mean but *encrypted*. It'd take a while to unlock it, but—I'd swear it's there . . ."

"One step at a time," I said. "If this isn't just some special effects genius's idea of fooling around, we've opened up one very ugly can of worms already. We don't need two."

"Hey, *you* brought this crap to *me,* Sherlock." He belched once and frowned as he went to work on his keyboard. "Damn it. I should've known better than to let you get the food . . ."

CHAPTER 4

That evening Max combed the sidewalk outside the Prices' building on Central Park West while I went up to the penthouse to see the recently bereaved. I found her huddled with her daughter in a huge living room that overlooked the park and informed her that, given what I'd seen on the disc, I did understand her fears; but I still needed to know just who the "they" she'd talked so insistently about that afternoon were. She explained that her first move on finding the disc among her husband's effects had been to go to the FBI; but they had only confiscated the thing immediately and hinted not so subtly that any discussion of it on her part could prove very risky for both her and her daughter. When Mrs. Price had found the backup copy, she'd figured she had nowhere to turn, and had been on the verge of destroying it when she remembered the interview I'd done on public television.

I asked her if she was aware that there was apparently a second batch of information on the disc, to which she said that she wasn't, but that it didn't surprise her; nor did her husband's evident encryption of it. He'd apparently been doing a lot of contract work for a private client lately, and although he'd kept her in the dark about its nature, she had discovered that he was being paid an astronomical fee for it. "Astronomical," for somebody whose day job already brought down enough to cover a penthouse on Central Park West, a century-old mansion in L.A., and one of the few waterfront houses in the Hamptons that had survived the hurricanes of '05, obviously meant quite a bit; but though my curiosity was piqued, Mrs. Price could tell me nothing more. So I left the grieving wife and daughter after receiving the promise of a fee that, by my own humble standards, was itself pretty damned astronomical.

As soon as I was back on the street, Max urgently yoked my neck into one of his heavy arms. "Let's get the hell out of here," he said, eyeing the building's doorman and then the darkened expanse of Central Park across the street.

"Why?" I asked, stumbling as he pulled me down the block toward a free taxi.

"Because," he answered, opening the cab's door and shoving me in, "you have gotten me involved in some very bizarre crap, Wolfe." At that he jumped in beside me and ordered the Indonesian driver to take us back to his office.

Max pointedly refused to do anything more than discuss take-out options for dinner that night as we rode downtown, prompting our sour-faced driver to extoll the virtues of his native cuisine. These uninvited comments inevitably led to a diatribe about the injustice of his country having become, since its total degeneration into anarchy and violence after the '07 crash, a United Nations protectorate. Max told him to just shut the hell up and drive, inspiring the bitter little man to handle both steering and brakes in a fashion unquestionably designed to induce nausea. All in all, I was confused, sickened, and fairly irritated by the time we got back to Max's building; and my mood wasn't improved when my friend jumped out of the vehicle, closed the door before I could follow, and said:

"This is gonna take a few hours. Go home, I'll call you."

Before I could argue he was inside, leaving me alone with the Indonesian zealot. I elected to pay off the driver and try my luck in another cab for the trip down to Tribeca. But the world is full of people with axes to grind, and an inordinate number of them have always ended up driving New York City cabs; and so my journey down the upper level of the West Side Superhighway was no more pleasant than the trip from Central Park had been.

I was still thinking about all those grinding axes when I got back to my loft. Procrastinating until Max's phone call, I switched on my computer, printed out the first section of the late edition of *The New York Times,* then settled into my couch with a bottle of Lithuanian vodka and started leafing through the paper, the experiences of the day and evening making me see the stories it contained in other than the usual trusting light. Suddenly no piece of information seemed entirely reliable, and I was reminded of Thomas Jefferson's admonition that a citizen can be truly informed only if he ignores the newspapers. Specifically, the *Times* reported the details of half a dozen hot spots around the world in which the United States was either diplomatically or militarily involved; and it seemed increasingly possible that because of the Khaldun business, Afghanistan would shortly be added to the list. I found myself wondering if computer discs containing bizarre, undiscovered information about all those other crises existed; and in that unsettled state of mind I drifted off to sleep.

Several hours later, I was woken by the sound of my vacuum cleaner charging out of the hall closet and then following a series of electronic sensors under the carpet in an effort to carry out its cleaning program. This sort of thing had been happening with increasing frequency lately: never much of a housekeeper, I'd dropped a bundle on one of those "smart apartment" setups, only to watch it go mad over the ensuing weeks and try to clean up, make coffee, adjust the lighting, and God only knew what else at all hours of the day and night, generally with stunning inefficiency.

Cursing the brilliant soul who'd shrunk microchips to the size of molecules and made such supposedly "smart" systems possible, I began unsteadily pursuing the vacuum cleaner around the loft. I'd no sooner corralled the thing and shut it off than the phone began to ring; and I just managed to get to it before my answering service, which was almost as brilliant as my vacuum cleaner, had time to route the call to my wireless phone.

On answering I once again heard Max's voice: "Get up here—I broke the encryption, and I've got a crapload of other stuff, too. Jesus, Gideon, this deal is getting spooky."

CHAPTER 5

Another lousy cab ride later, and I was back at Max's. I found him switching on the various systems he used to jam and otherwise thwart listening devices, after which he guided me over to a stack of DNA sequencing and identification equipment near a window that had a beautiful view of the river.

"I found a few hairs embedded in the brick wall at the murder scene," Max explained, indicating the buzzing equipment. "I ran them through my remote terminal while we were there, but what I got back didn't seem to make any sense, so I wanted to try it again on the big rig. Results came up the same. A few of the samples belong to John Price, but the rest? The rest match a guy who's in jail."

"In jail? Then how—?"

"Don't start asking questions yet, Gideon, or we'll be here the rest of the night. So while I'm trying to figure out how somebody who's already locked up could off our boy, I find these." He dropped a few metal pellets about the size of mouse feces into my hand. "Any idea what they are?"

"No," I answered dimly.

"I didn't either, until I ran them for stains. Price's blood was there." Max took a deep breath. "You know what condition his body was in?"

I nodded. "Almost disintegrated, the cops said."

"By these," Max went on, taking one of the pellets and studying it. "Any idea how fast they'd have to be traveling to do that to a human body?"

"*Could* they do that to a human body?"

"Sure. Theoretically. If I toss a little lump of lead at you, it isn't gonna kill you. I shoot it out of a gun, that's a different story. Fire a bunch of these jobs at a high enough velocity, and yeah, your body would almost vaporize. But that's a hell of a velocity. And nobody heard any gunfire, not even the doorman. Or so he says."

"So what could—?"

"Gideon, I told you—wait with the questions. Now—" He walked purposefully back over to his main bank of computers. "It took me a while, but I finally busted Price's encryption of the second batch of information on the disc—though why he worked so hard to hide *this* is beyond me."

Touching a keypad, Max called up an image on his main screen: an old piece of grainy film that offered a glimpse of what appeared to be—of what, I soon realized, in fact *was*—a mid-twentieth-century German concentration camp. There was a shot of some starving, laboring prisoners, a pan off to some SS officers, and then a further pan to reveal . . . a silhouette. A grayish human silhouette, moving, yes, but as unidentifiable as the similar blank spot in the second of the three versions of the Forrester assassination we'd seen had been.

"Okay," Max said, watching my dumbstruck face. "Now you can ask questions."

I took a deep breath. "Dachau?" I asked.

"Good call, Professor," Max answered. "I downloaded some matching footage half an hour ago. It's pretty stock stuff. Except for the mystery guest there."

I kept staring at the silhouette. "Something about that general outline looks familiar," I said. "There—when he turns in profile . . ."

"Okay. So maybe then you can tell me how this connects to some hairs from a guy who's already in prison and some kind of supergun that apparently turned John Price into so much jelly without making a sound."

I found it hard to take my eyes off of Max's computer screen, which kept replaying the same snippet of film footage over and over. "What's the guy's name? The one who's in jail?"

Max crossed the room to a table. "Got that, too—hacked into the correctional banks. Here—Kuperman. Eli Kuperman."

My head snapped around. "Eli Kuperman the anthropologist?"

"The same. Know him?"

I shook my head. "But I know his work. Controversial stuff—brilliant, though. The origins of primitive cultures."

"That's what they nailed him for. Down in Florida, he was in some Indian burial ground. Digging up graves, or so the folks who run the reservation say. Kuperman never contested it. Tribe agreed to the government's sentence—five years in the local state pen." Max's face grew even more puzzled, and his voice softened. "Strange thing is, the day after he went up, just last week, the Indians laid concrete over the whole burial ground. So much for sacred . . ."

"Maybe they didn't want any more desecrations."

"Maybe," Max said with a shrug. "Point is, what's this guy Kuperman's hair doing at our murder scene?"

"You're sure it's his?"

Max shrugged again. "The universal DNA database doesn't lie. So unless he's got an identical twin—"

"That's what I'm talking about."

"What's what you're talking about?"

"Kuperman," I said, not quite believing Max's confused look. "He's got a twin brother."

Max swallowed hard. "Screw you, Wolfe."

"He does! *Jonah* Kuperman—he's an archaeologist, just as famous as his brother."

"Well, it wasn't in any of the hits that *I* pulled up."

"Jesus, Max," I said, going back to the DNA analyzer. "The sum total of human knowledge is supposed to be on the damned Internet—you mean they missed something as basic as *that*?"

"Hey, don't start with me about the Net again, Gideon, a few occasional screwups do not mean—"

Suddenly the window with the beautiful view in front of me shattered into hundreds of crashing shards. Instinctively, I went for the floor; but when I looked up, I saw Max—foolishly, I thought at that instant—still standing. I screamed for him to get down, but he only swayed strangely in the half-light of his computer. Then I noticed a bead of blood on his forehead; and looking past him I could see that his computer screen was splattered with something a good deal more vital and substantial than blood. I crawled like a pathetic crab across the floor while he crumpled with grim grace to his knees. He fell forward just as I reached him, allowing me to see that the missile that had entered his forehead so neatly had, on exiting, taken much of his brain and a good deal of his skull away with it.

CHAPTER 6

It wasn't until two days later, while I was on a filthy, packed old 767 flying from Washington to Orlando, that the full impact of Max's death descended on me. Up until that time I'd been too preoccupied with police reports and hiding all traces of what we'd been doing to really let it sink in. But when I caught sight of a large man who might have been Max's double sitting three rows in front of me on that flight, I suddenly felt like I'd been hit in the chest with a mallet. To lose one's last living connection to childhood is not an easy thing; to lose him in the way I had is the kind of event that makes you want answers—and makes you capable of doing almost anything to get them.

My first stop on the road to what I was determined would be an explanation had been the offices of several acquaintances at the FBI's national headquarters in D.C. What I heard there, along with the manner in which my contacts delivered it, was unnerving: couched in ostensibly friendly terms was a firm warning to back off of any investigation having to do with the deaths of John Price and Max Jenkins. Apparently both the attorney general and the head of the Bureau didn't much like me to start with, given that I'd had the temerity, in my book, to put some of the leading figures of American history under the psychological microscope and make a modest pile of money in the process. But there was more than just personal animosity conveyed during the meetings, and by the time they were over, I was feeling disoriented and isolated. In my line of business you come to expect idle threats from local police forces, which have always viewed profilers with deep suspicion; but to have the rug pulled out from under you by the feds—well, that's a lonely feeling.

Nonetheless, I pressed on to Florida to attempt an interview with Dr. Eli Kuperman, anthropologist and convict. He was incarcerated in the Belle Isle State Correctional Facility outside Orlando, which was yet another of the country's new corporately operated prisons. The structure had originally been intended as a high school; but given the remarkable levels of violence that had come to characterize teen behavior in the increasingly ghettoized suburbs of nearly every American city, the design of high schools was not all that different from that of prisons. Thus when Florida fell into line with the rest of the country by giving the people's mania for punishment precedence over education, converting the sheer stone and nearly windowless mass at Belle Isle into a penitentiary hadn't been much of a trick.

I arrived at midday, made my request, and found, much to my surprise, that Dr. Kuperman was not only willing but anxious to see me. He insisted, however, that he would do so only during evening visiting hours on the following day. By the time I took my seat at a clear, bulletproof panel on the second floor of Belle Isle's visitors' building at seven the next evening, it was nearly dark. A guard soon appeared through a door in the room on the other side of the transparent divider, followed by a man of moderate height and similar weight who had dark features and curly brown hair and wore delicate tortoiseshell glasses: Eli Kuperman. He recognized me as quickly as I did him and proceeded to sit eagerly opposite me. The guard switched on an intercom that allowed us to talk.

"Dr. Wolfe," Kuperman said with a smile. "It's an honor. I've read your book—fascinating, really." The fact of imprisonment seemed to be having no effect on him at all.

"Dr. Kuperman," I said, acknowledging his compliment with a nod. "I've read a great deal about your work, too—though I'll admit I can't quite figure how it's landed you in *this* place."

"Can't you?" Kuperman asked, again very pleasantly. "Well, you'll find out soon enough. Oh, that reminds me—" He unbuttoned the cuff of his sky blue shirt, revealing a small, flexible keypad adhered to his skin. Touching a few of the keys, he then rebuttoned his cuff with another smile and looked back up. "There. We have a few minutes yet. How would you like to pass them?"

I assumed that the "few minutes" he was referring to was the balance of the time I'd been allowed with him, and so I put my query bluntly: "Suppose you tell me what your brother had to do with John Price's death."

Kuperman waved me off cordially. "Oh, plenty of time for that later. And Malcolm will be able to explain it much more thoroughly than I can."

"Malcolm?"

"Don't worry, you'll understand. I'm sorry about Mr. Jenkins, by the way. We'd hoped he'd come along, too."

"Come along?" I said, now completely at a loss.

"Yes." He moved closer to the glass. "I know you're confused, but try to keep up some kind of a conversation, will you? Otherwise the guard—"

Kuperman suddenly stopped talking when we began to hear an

extraordinary noise: a deep, rumbling hum that seemed to come from all directions at once, even from inside my own head. It grew in volume and intensity at a quick but steady rate, until the metal chairs and tables in the room began to vibrate noticeably.

Looking up at the ceiling, Kuperman checked his watch again. "Well," he said, strangely unconcerned. "*That* was quick. They must have been closer than I thought . . ."

As the hum grew louder, I dashed to the only window in the visiting room and looked out into the darkness. There was precious little to be seen save the lights atop the prison walls, and then something appeared to blot even those beacons out. Moving above and across the walls was a dark mass, perhaps as long as a pair of train cars and twice as high.

"What the hell?" was all I could whisper; and then I noted Kuperman's shouting voice coming over the intercom and just cutting through the ever-intensifying hum:

"Dr. Wolfe! Dr. Wolfe, move away from the window, *please*!"

I did as he said, and just in time, too; for the bars outside the window, loosened by the mounting vibration, suddenly broke free of their anchors and flew away, while the wired glass panes did not so much shatter as explode. I ran back to the partition and saw that Kuperman's guard, clutching his ears, was screaming in terror.

"What is it?" I shouted through the intercom. "Kuperman, what's happening?"

Kuperman smiled; but before he could give any explanation the wall behind him began to shake violently. In just a few seconds it collapsed, the stone falling away and revealing a ten-foot-square passage into the night air. Once the dust had cleared, I could see, outside this gaping hole, what appeared to be a metallic wall about three feet from the violated stone edifice of the visitors' building; and over the insistent humming I began to make out the sound of gunshots coming from the prison yard below.

"It's all right, Dr. Wolfe!" I became conscious of Kuperman saying through the amplified intercom. "Don't worry! But try to get under one of those tables, will you?"

Once again my prompt observance of Kuperman's order saved me from being severely injured, this time by flying fragments of the transparent partition that had divided us. When I emerged from under the table and returned to Kuperman, I found him waving an arm and urging me to climb over the remains of the partition and join him. I did so, only to find myself faced by Kuperman's guard as well as a second officer. Both had their guns drawn, prompting Kuperman to turn to his man and cry out earnestly:

"Mr. Sweeney! Please! You don't really think that's going to do any good, do you? If you and Mr. Farkas leave now, I promise no harm will—"

Before Kuperman could finish we were presented with yet another extraordinary sight: the sudden delineation, by a series of small green lights, of a doorway in the metal surface outside the hole in the building's wall. Then, with a decompressing hiss, the door opened rapidly; in fact, it seemed to my eyes to almost disappear. Beyond the vanished portal was a dimly lit corridor in which stood a group of figures: four male, one quite distinctly female. The men wore coveralls; the woman was sheathed in a gray bodysuit that clung to her with what I might, under other circumstances, have called enticing tenacity.

With marvelous agility the young woman leapt through the three feet of open air and into the prison, the light of the room making two extraordinary things immediately apparent: first, the straight, chin-length hair that framed her delicate features was a strange silver color; and second, she held in her hands a device—presumably a weapon—that was obviously more complex and sophisticated than any handgun I'd ever seen.

The woman trained the device first on one officer and then on the other. Kuperman's man, Sweeney, had the good sense to drop his gun and head for the still intact doorway out of the room. But the second guard, Farkas, was foolish enough to let off a round from his pistol, even though his apparent fear made an accurate shot impossible. The bullet struck the wall above the woman, and she ducked for an instant; then she fixed her dark eyes on the guard with what seemed as much amusement as anger. Leveling the device in her hands at the man, she appeared on the verge of firing; but then she suddenly turned and trained the weapon on a desk that sat near the room's exit. She pulled what looked like a trigger, and then, without much of a sound, the desk was bombarded by a series of high-speed projectiles, reducing it to mere bits.

Had it been the guard's body she'd targeted, it would have completely disintegrated—just as John Price's had done.

Sensibly accepting this warning, the guard Farkas dropped his automatic and raced for the exit. Once he was gone, the woman pointed her weapon in the air, shifted her shapely weight to one side, and smiled at Kuperman and me.

"Doctors," she said with a nod. Then she touched the high collar of her bodysuit. "It's all right," she said, looking at the ceiling. "I've got them." Turning to us again, she nodded toward the hole in the wall. "I hate to rush you, Eli, but—"

"Rush me all you want, Larissa!" Kuperman shouted, bolting for the broken wall and then leaping through it and into the metal doorway beyond. "Hurry, Dr. Wolfe!" he called once he was safely aboard what I now realized must be some sort of vehicle or vessel.

"Yes, do hurry, Dr. Wolfe," the woman said, approaching me coyly. "My brother's been anxious to meet you—and so have I." She studied my face and smiled in a puzzled, slightly amused way. "You're not quite as attractive in person as in your author's photo, are you?"

Still stunned, I could only say, "Who is?" which prompted the woman to laugh delightedly and seize my hand.

"Can you make the jump?" she said. "Or do you want us to maneuver closer?"

I shook my head, finally getting a grip on myself. "I can make it," I answered. "But what—?"

"The jump first," she answered, pulling me at a run toward the hole in the wall. "After that, everything will make a *lot* more sense!"

And with her delicate but strong hand holding mine, I leapt out over the narrow corridor of open air beyond the prison wall, leaving the world and reality as I had always known them behind me forever.

CHAPTER 7

It was cold inside the vessel, a chill made all the more cutting by its contrast to the muggy Florida night and the stale closeness of the visitors' room in the prison. Even before I'd straightened up after landing on the gently heaving deck of the ship, I began shivering; and just as I became aware that I was, the same hand that had guided me through the jump began to rub my back.

"Bit of a shock, isn't it?" said the young woman Eli Kuperman had called Larissa. I stood and looked into her enormous black eyes, which formed such a distinct contrast to the oddly beautiful silver of the hair above and around them; already a bit smitten, I could only nod agreement to her assessment. Unspoken curiosity must, however, have been all over my face—why, I was thinking, would anyone capable of building such a vessel choose to exist in such an uncomfortable atmosphere?—because the woman quickly went on to explain: "My brother's gotten closer than anyone to creating superconductors that can operate at living temperatures—but we still have to keep most of the ship below forty-five Fahrenheit." She tucked her remarkable weapon into a holster that was slung on her left side, gave me that bewitching smirk, then looped an arm through one of mine. "You *must* try to stay warm, Dr. Wolfe . . ."

Before I could find the words to ask just where we were, Eli Kuperman stuck his engaging, bespectacled face between us, grinning wide and then tugging at one of the men in coveralls who'd been waiting in the hatchway during our escape. The second man's face was nearly identical to Kuperman's, although he wore steel-, rather than tortoiseshell-, rimmed spectacles: this, apparently, was the archaeologist twin brother of whom Max's Internet search had failed to produce any mention.

"Dr. Wolfe," Eli Kuperman said happily. "I see you've met Larissa already. And this is my brother, Jonah—"

Jonah Kuperman extended a hand, his manner every bit as engaging at his brother's. "Dr. Wolfe, it's a pleasure. We've been looking forward to your coming. Your book's been all the talk aboard ship for the last few weeks—"

"And back there," Eli said, indicating the two men farther along the corridor, "are Dr. Leon Tarbell, the documents expert"—I shook the hand of a small, wiry man in his middle years, whose red eyes glowed hot even when he smiled—"and Professor Julien Fouché, the molecular biologist." At that a well-built, gray-bearded man of sixty or so stepped forward, causing my heart to skip one or two beats: an understandable reaction on meeting a man who not only was one of the seminal minds of our era but was supposed to have been killed in a plane crash four years earlier.

"It can't be," I whispered, shaking his big, very vital hand. "You—you're dead!"

"Not so dead as all that," Fouché answered with a gruff laugh. "A necessary ruse to explain my sudden disappearance. My work with

Malcolm and Larissa was becoming quite exclusive, and uncomfortable questions were being asked—"

"All right, gentlemen," Larissa said. "You'll have time for mutual admiration later. Right now we'd better be on our collective toes." The others nodded and began to move purposefully away. "Prep the turret, Eli!" Larissa called after them. "I'll be right up! Leon—we'll want full power for combat maneuvers!"

Leon Tarbell's head reappeared for an instant. " 'Combat,' Larissa?" he asked with a knowing look. "Don't you mean *evasive maneuvers*?"

Larissa smiled deviously, and then Tarbell dashed off, looking for all the world like one of Satan's merrier minions.

As the men moved to attend to their tasks, each of them began shouting orders and answers, the whole producing an excited and exciting chorus such as might have accompanied the launch of an old seafaring ship. I turned when I heard a slight hissing noise and saw the doorway through which we'd jumped being sealed from above by a hatch that moved quite smoothly, especially given its considerable speed. Once it was in place, some gentle lights came up along the base of the corridor, revealing a surprising sight: rather than the usual plastic and polished metal that one was accustomed to finding in high-tech environments, the walls of the passageways were lined with fine wood paneling, and in every third or fourth panel hung a small painting, elegantly framed and subtly lit.

My mouth fell open. "Beautiful," I whispered.

"Thank you, Doctor," Larissa answered in a charmingly self-involved way, looking down and running her hands along her hips and thighs. Her face dropped a bit when she glanced up and saw what I meant. "Oh. The *ship*." She took my hand again, and we started down the corridor. "Yes, that's Malcolm for you—he *adores* the incongruous."

"*You're* not exactly what I would have expected either, Larissa—that is, if I may call you—"

"You may," she answered, striding purposefully along. "Larissa Tressalian, to be exact. You may also remark on the lovely sibilance of the name, through I warn you, it's a pretty stale line." For an instant I attempted to determine why her name, while indeed pretty, had a familiar ring to it; but then I was distracted when she touched the collar of her bodysuit with her free hand, indicating that she was receiving another communication. "Yes, brother dear? . . . Yes, I'm just taking him to his quarters to—freshen up . . ." She looked at me in a way that seemed more than a little suggestive; then she suddenly turned away, standing still. "Where? . . . Land and air units? . . . All right, I'm on my way to the turret." When Larissa looked at me again her expression had changed: the coy cat had become a gleeful predator. "Freshening up will have to wait, I'm afraid, Doctor." She gripped my hand tighter and broke into a trot. "A different sort of amusement's been lined up!"

CHAPTER 8

We proceeded along the narrow passageway to an intricately carved and richly carpeted wooden staircase. As we climbed the stairs, the humming of the ship's propulsion system—driven, as Larissa had just told me, by superconductive magnetic generators capable of producing unimaginable (not to mention clean) levitating and propulsive power—began to soften, and I could feel that we were moving forward. There were occasional dips and swells in the motion—not unsettling but noticeable—and when we reached the upper deck, I found myself facing a round transparent panel in the fuselage or hull. Looking out, I saw that we were traveling about a hundred feet off the ground, hugging the contours of the suburban landscape like some enormous cruise missile.

Larissa tugged at my arm. "No time for astonishment now," she said, pulling me forward along the passageway. "There's a small task force of local and state law enforcement on the way, and the federal boys won't be far behind."

"But," I stammered as we reached a ladder that led up through the ceiling of the passageway, "you've only got this one ship, can it really—"

Larissa spun around and put a finger to my lips, her eyes now positively shimmering. "Take a peek up there." She indicated the ladder, and I ascended.

Above was a circular space about fifteen feet in diameter, not unlike the turret of some fantastic tank, except that its shell was transparent. There was an enormous gun fixed in the center, on which was mounted an empty seat. To one side of the turret was a bank of tracking equipment, before which sat Eli Kuperman, carefully monitoring the many readouts. Glancing at the gun again, I noted that it looked somehow familiar; in fact, it seemed a giant version of Larissa's sidearm.

"They're both rail guns," she said, again reading my face as she climbed up, squeezed tight against me on the ladder, and drew out her smaller weapon. "It's a simple concept, really: the projectiles are propelled by completing a circuit between two conducting bars, instead of by a gas explosion. The electromagnetic field behind the projectiles multiplies the acceleration—you've seen the effect. Now, then—" She reholstered her weapon and gave my face a last touch. "I could stay here talking killing power with you for hours, but Malcolm really is anxious to meet you."

"Look, Larissa," I said, her closeness making me comfortable enough to reveal how uncertain I felt. "What *is* all this? Why am I here?"

She smiled gently. "Don't worry. All appearances to the contrary notwithstanding, you're in one of the last sane places on Earth. And you're here because we need you." She slipped by me into the turret, settling into the seat on the big rail gun. "Just keep going forward—you'll know the right door when you see it."

Eli Kuperman turned, his face all business. "The first of them are moving in fast, Larissa."

Larissa gripped two hand controls in front of her seat. "Better get going, Doctor," she called to me with another smile. "I'd hate to take your head off so early in our—acquaintance."

She tilted the controls to the left, and suddenly the entire floor of the turret began to rotate; in seconds it would close off the hatchway in which I was standing. I scrambled below, landing on the corridor floor with a jarring bump. Then I pushed on forward, past more wood paneling, more paintings, and more doorways, until I arrived at a portal that I took to be the one of which Larissa had spoken, as it was more elaborate than the rest and bore a legend painted in elegant gold and black:

MUNDUS VULT DECIPI

I ran through the medical Latin I'd learned years before, but to no avail; and so I was left with nothing to do but head on in and meet my host, a prospect that I found not a little daunting. Given the vessel I was in, the sister I had met, and the actions for which I knew he was responsible, I calculated that this Malcolm Tressalian—and again there was something very familiar about the name—must be an intimidating, perhaps overpowering, character, both physically and personally. But the encounter was now inevitable, and so I resignedly knocked on the door and stepped inside.

The nose of the vessel was a conical superstructure sheathed entirely in the same transparent material I'd seen in Larissa's turret, and the three levels of the space it housed—an observation dome up top, a helm and guidance center in the middle, and a small conference area below—were connected by bare metallic staircases. In fact, the fittings generally were in the high-tech mode I had originally expected to find on boarding; but coming as it now did on the heels of the rather anachronistic decor outside, the style was unexpected and even jarring.

The doorway through which I'd come was to the rear of the nose's control level. Though there was little to see by, I could tell that there were two men sitting before the guidance panel, and beyond them the decaying malls and decrepit housing developments of suburban Florida spread out before us. I began to move forward with trepidation; and then the man on the left spoke, cheerfully enough but without facing me:

"Dr. Wolfe! Excellent, you managed to escape Larissa—which is far more, I suspect, than our pursuers will do."

And then he turned, or rather the entire seat he occupied did: for it was in fact a wheelchair, one that even in the near darkness I could see contained not the formidable physical specimen I'd anticipated but a frail, somewhat pitiable form that did not seem to match the vibrant voice it produced.

"I suppose I should offer you some melodramatic welcome," the voice continued in the same amiable tone. "But we're neither of us the type, eh? No, I suspect that what you'd really like is some answers."

CHAPTER 9

"My name's Malcolm Tressalian—did my sister manage to relay that much to you, or have you endured uninterrupted flirtation since you came aboard?"

"Yes—I mean no—I mean, she did—"

Tressalian laughed and rolled closer to me, his face becoming fully visible for the first time. "You must understand that she almost never takes any interest in men—but when she does, my God . . ." I smiled at this statement, though I was paying more attention to his face than to his words. The features were not unlike Larissa's—handsome in a fine-boned way—and the hair was the same silvery color. The eyes, however, were quite different, being of a peculiarly light, rather otherworldly blue. Yet there was something far more important than any of this in the face, a look I had seen many times in children who'd served harsh prison terms, as well as in schizophrenic patients who had lived for too long without treatment:

It was the imponderable depth brought on by compressed, relentless mental and physical torment, a brand as unmistakable as any birthmark.

"And I do apologize," Tressalian continued amiably, "for the way you were brought aboard." As he said this he shifted into position to try to stand up, something that he apparently felt it was important to do at that moment, given the pain that it evidently caused him. He reached for a pair of aluminum crutches that were mounted on either side of his chair, clipped them to his upper arms, and then managed to get to his feet. I didn't know quite what move to make to assist him, especially since I guessed that he desired none; and indeed, once upright he looked very pleased that he was able to approach me and shake hands on his own. "However," he continued, "I'm sure you appreciate that we couldn't just leave you behind to suffer a fate like Mr. Jenkins's." His expression grew earnest. "I trust Eli expressed his condolences—let me add my own. It was a sickening thing to do, even for that unkillable beast we call Central Intelligence."

"Then it *was* the government," I said quietly, Max's face flashing across my mind for an instant.

Tressalian nodded sympathetically. "The pair of you were getting too close on the matter of John Price's death."

"The matter of his death?" I asked carefully. "Or the matter of the images he'd tampered with?"

Tressalian's smile returned. "The two are one, Doctor—surely you've guessed that much. *Your* death, however, would have caused an inconvenient public stir. Still, had you persisted they would almost certainly have found a way to quietly eliminate you."

"But why?" I asked involuntarily. "What the *hell* is going—"

I was cut off by the man seated at the piloting console, who spoke in a steady yet forbidding tone: "Larissa's preparing to engage. They're within range, and she's routed helm control to the turret station."

Tressalian sighed, though his concern did not appear deep. "Well,

Colonel, since that leaves you with nothing to do for the moment, come and meet Dr. Wolfe."

The man at the now-usurped guidance panel stood up, and even before he turned I could see that he had an eminently military bearing, one that was complemented by a high-collared suit of clothes that was really more of an unembellished uniform. When he did turn it was in a quick, wheeling motion, and what I saw next caused me to take in a quick and rather rude gasp of air.

Heavy brows loomed low over penetrating dark eyes amid the deep brown skin, and the jaw, had it been any more set, might well have shattered; but what prompted my extreme reaction was the sight of one of the most horrific scars I'd ever encountered, running the length of the right side of the head, tugging at one eye and pulling a corner of the mouth down into a perpetual frown. A streak of snow white followed the line of the scar up into the otherwise jet black hair.

"Dr. Wolfe," Tressalian said, "this is Colonel Justus Slayton."

"Retired," the colonel added in that low, almost ominous voice that made it plain I'd be well advised to tread carefully during any contact with him.

I did. "The same Colonel Slayton," I asked, offering a hand, "who almost changed the course of the Taiwan campaign?" That seemed to take just a bit of the steel out of the man's demeanor, and he actually accepted my hand, encasing it in his own with a force that was impressive.

"No one could have changed the course of that campaign," Slayton answered. "My men and I were a token resistance—sacrificed animals, nothing more."

"Offered on the altar of expanded trade with the commu-capitalists in Beijing," I agreed with a nod. "Still, you put up a hell of a fight."

"Excellent again, Doctor," Tressalian said. "Not many people understand the facts of that campaign. What you may *not* know about the colonel, however, is that after being wounded on Taiwan he became one of the Pentagon's top men in weapons development. That, of course, was before I persuaded him to—"

"Malcolm," Colonel Slayton interrupted. "Before we go any further, there's the matter of the doctor's DNA disc."

Tressalian became slightly embarrassed. "Oh, yes, exactly right, Colonel. I must apologize once again, Doctor. But recent events have forced us to become a little more circumspect in our dealings. Do you mind?"

"Oh—no, of course not," I said, going for my wallet and removing my DNA identification disc. "Hell," I went on as I quickly plucked a hair from my head and handed both items over, "during the last few days *I* wouldn't have been able to swear that I was me."

Tressalian and I watched as Slayton produced a handheld DNA reader (much like the one Max had carried nearly everywhere he went), then popped in the disc and the hair. After a few seconds he took them out again, nodding as he handed the disc back to me. "Ah, good, that nuisance is out of the way," Tressalian said, heading for the metal stairs that led up to the observation dome. "Now, Doctor, I'll be happy to answer any questions you have—though I think you might enjoy watching Larissa in action while we talk."

I mounted the stairs next to Tressalian, whose slow movements were practiced if not easy, while Slayton stayed a few steps behind us, either to make sure Tressalian didn't fall or to keep a careful eye on me; in all probability a bit of both. One felt the colonel's presence keenly no matter where he was, not least because of the disturbing and mysterious scar on his face. In an age when almost any organ or tissue in the human body save the brain could be fabricated in medical laboratories—when the colonel's own skin could have been duplicated and run off like so much cloth and then grafted onto his injury—the fact that he left the disfigurement unaddressed was certainly indicative of the man's character. The question was, what was such a character doing in the service of the strange, remarkable man who was hobbling along beside me?

All such cogitations left my head when we reached the observation dome, which offered an unobstructed view in every direction—a view that stretched the limits of my credulity even further.

CHAPTER 10

Surrounding us was the panorama of the night sky, though I didn't have an opportunity to enjoy it: I could see at least five Geronimos—Apache Mark V military helicopters that had been adapted for use by local law enforcement as well as the FBI—in pursuit of our ship, their cannons spinning as they blasted glowing tracer rounds at us. In addition, there was a fleet of late-model Hummers coursing through the streets below, lights flashing and large-caliber mounted guns ablaze. From the look of things, I quickly calculated that we had only a few moments to live—especially as we weren't yet returning fire.

But then I noticed that as the multitude of bullets being fired at us reached the tapering, rounded fuselage of the ship—its pair of foldaway wings and its glowing "head" resembling nothing so much as a giant flying fish—most of them swerved badly off target. Tresalian read the puzzled look on my face (he was evidently as perceptive as his sister), then touched the collar of his own shirt and began to speak to Larissa through what I realized was a surgically implanted communications system that provided the two with a secure link to each other.

"Sister? . . . Yes, Dr. Wolfe's right here, and watching anxiously. But remember, we're making directly for the coast, so there's no need for excessive—Larissa?" Tressalian took his fingers from his throat with an indulgent shake of his head, then held a hand toward the scene being played out around us. "I suggest you observe, Doctor—this seems to be for *your* benefit."

With that, the large rail gun in the ship's turret opened fire, expelling flights of projectiles that were proportionately larger than the ones fired by Larissa's handgun. The varied pattern of destruction wrought by the gun as it spun from pursuer to pursuer was awesome to behold: a finely focused burst could removed a Hummer's wheel or a Geronimo's mounted gun, while a wider pattern could reduce both land and air units to so much shrapnel—and human body parts. All of this, or so Tressalian had said, was for my benefit: an effort by Larissa not only to impress me with her flying and combat skills but also, it seemed, to let me know that what I had stumbled onto was some kind of mortal struggle. But over what?

Excitement, horror, and, yes, some satisfaction (given that our pursuers were doubtless ultimately controlled by the same people who had killed Max) were registering inside me; yet I was still clearheaded enough to be curious. "Their bullets," I said. "They're not reaching us."

"It has been said," Tressalian explained, "that the man who controls electromagnetism controls the known forces of our universe. I don't pretend to have *mastered* the area yet, but we have enough insight to be able to project fields that will cause far more complex forms of matter than bullets to change their behavior. Even without the fields we'd be in little danger—the ship's superstructure and sheathing, even its transparent sections, are constructed of advanced composite resins. Stronger than high-quality steel of a much greater thickness and far lighter." Tressalian paused a moment, still watching me. "You're appalled, no doubt," he finally said. "But believe me when I say that if the governments of the world left us any choice—"

"Of the *world*?" I echoed in a whisper. "But I thought—"

"Oh, our efforts are quite global. Here, come and look at this, Doctor." Tressalian turned and hobbled over to a bank of monitors that was installed on a low table at the center of the observation dome. "It may help you understand."

I soon found myself staring at half a dozen images of a considerable military force on the move. There were ships at sea, remote-piloted fighter-bombers in flight, their ghostly cockpits empty of anything save computer equipment, and carrier crews loading still more warplanes with bombs and missiles.

"What is it?" I asked.

"The reason your friend Mr. Jenkins was killed," Tressalian replied. "An American task force, on its way to inflict what will certainly be a massive attack."

"On whom? Where are they going?"

"The same place we are—Afghanistan."

CHAPTER 11

"Afghanistan . . ." I said, thunderstruck. "But why? And how in hell are you getting pictures of all this?"

"By satellite," Tressalian answered simply. "Our *own* satellites."

My mind made a sudden connection. "Satellites . . . satellites! *Tressalian*—Stephen Tressalian, the man who devised the four-gigabyte satellite system, who created the modern Internet!"

"He was my father," my host acknowledged with an ambiguous nod. "And that sin *was* indeed his, along with many others. But he paid for his transgressions in the end—and his money did allow us to undertake all this."

"But what in God's name are you *doing*?"

"The more important question right now," Tressalian answered evasively, "is, what is your government doing?"

" '*My*' government? Isn't it *your* government, too?"

Tressalian, slightly amused, shook his head. "Not for many years.

Those of us aboard this ship have renounced all nationalities—largely because of these sorts of *national* behaviors." He indicated the screens.

"What do you mean?" I asked. "What are they doing?"

"It would *seem* that they intend to finally eradicate the very impressive underground complex that has been the principal training ground for Islamic terrorists during the last two decades."

I looked at the busy screens again. "Retaliation for Khaldun killing President Forrester?" I asked.

Tressalian nodded. "Your country is, after all, nearing a national election. But there's a slight problem with the government's decision, one that I have reason to believe it has begun to suspect but which it cannot, given the political rhetoric that led to this launch, allow anyone such as yourself to discover. You see, Tariq Khaldun wasn't a terrorist—and he certainly didn't kill President Forrester."

"But the disc—"

"The man on that disc"—Tressalian touched a keypad on the table and brought up the assassination images that Max and I had studied for so many hours—"was in fact an actor of Afghan origin who enjoyed some slight success in the Indian film industry during the last part of the twentieth century. We—*borrowed* his image." Tressalian shrugged with a smile. "How could I know that there was a minor Afghan diplomat in Chicago who might be the man's double? Don't worry, though, we've arranged for Mr. Khaldun's escape. At any rate, the actual killer of the late, lamented President Forrester was"—another touch of a keypad, and the image before me changed to the second version of the event that I'd seen, the one in which the assassin's face was Asian—"this fellow. Hung Ting-hsin, a major in the Chinese external security force."

I paused, now wholly unaware of the dance of fire and death that was going on beyond the transparent shell around us. "You deliberately distorted what happened?"

"I'm afraid so."

"So Price created those images for *you*—you were the 'private contractor' his wife told me about."

"Correct again. None of us was happy about Mr. Price's death, Doctor—but he'd decided to try to blackmail us. Then, when Larissa and Jonah went to warn him against such a course, he became violent. Actually knocked Jonah against a wall, and would have done worse, but—well, *Larissa* . . ."

All the pieces surrounding the mysteries of John Price's and Max's deaths were falling into place—but none of them explained why in the world Tressalian was doing any of this, and so I asked him straight out once more.

"Oh, I have my reasons," he said, sighing again; but the sound was heavier this time, and as it came, Tressalian suddenly winced. "I have my—" His eyes opened wide as the apparent attack of pain seemed to rapidly worsen. "You must—forgive me, Doctor. I seem to—" Suddenly he clutched his head and pitched over with a muted cry, bringing Colonel Slayton to his side even before I could offer any help. "I—think, Colonel," Tressalian said through gritted teeth, "that I'd better rest for a bit. If our guest will excuse me . . ." His breathing became labored as Slayton pulled one of his arms around his own neck and lifted his disabled body as if it were weightless. "I'm sorry, Doctor, I know you want answers," Tressalian gasped. "Dinner—we'll talk at dinner. For now—remember—" He brought his head up and, through his agony, gave me a look that I will never forget: it was full of all the mischievousness of his sister but at the same time conveyed a dark, terrible urgency. "Remember," he went on, "what you saw on the door . . ." And with that, Colonel Slayton whisked him away.

Tressalian's sudden attack, combined with the images on the screens at the table as well as the ongoing combat outside—not to mention the fact that I was now alone—served to turn my growing anxiety into the beginnings of what I feared would soon become panic. I tried to calm myself by focusing on what Tressalian had said, by forcing my mind to delve deeper into the Latin I'd learned so long ago in order to come up with an answer to the riddle of the legend on the door.

I don't know how long I stood there, watching Larissa decimate our pursuers and mumbling to myself like an idiot. *"Mundus vult decipi,"* I repeated over and over, as bullets streamed around the ship. "*Mundus,* 'the world,' yes. *Vult,* 'wills'? 'Wants'? Something—"

And then I froze at the sudden sound of a pulsing alarm that echoed throughout the vessel: not a harsh tone, exactly, but enough to let me know that something big was happening. I scanned the horizon in all directions, trying to catch sight of what might be prompting it—and looking forward, I got my answer:

The wide expanse of the Atlantic Ocean had appeared on the horizon.

I spun around when a voice I recognized as Julien Fouché's began to speak over some sort of shipwide address system:

"Thirty seconds until system transfer . . . twenty-five . . . twenty . . ."

We showed no sign of slowing our approach to the water as Fouché continued to count down, in five-second increments, to "system transfer," whatever that might be; and then I experienced a startling chill as, in the midst of my mounting fear, I succeeded in translating the legend.

"Mundus vult decipi," I said aloud. " 'The world wants to be deceived'!"

Not yet realizing the potentially threatening connotation in the words, I felt a sense of triumph—one that quickly reverted to terror as the ship sped over the shoreline and dived into the open sea beyond.

CHAPTER 12

As soon as the vessel was completely submerged, a series of powerful lights on her hull's exterior came on, offering an extraordinary view of the coastal Atlantic depths as we turned north along the line of the continent. What I saw outside, however, was not an idyllic scene of aquatic wonder such as childhood stories might have led me to expect but rather a horrifying expanse of brown water filled with human and animal waste, all of it endlessly roiled but never cleansed by the steady pulse of the offshore currents. Sometimes the trapped filth was identifiable—great stretches of medical waste and the detritus of livestock husbandry were particularly disturbing—but for the most part it all blended into one indistinguishable mass that I, left alone to watch and ponder, found utterly disheartening. I knew, of course, that in the years since the '07 financial crash, environmental cleanups had been deemed unaffordable luxuries in most countries; nevertheless, to be presented with this sort of firsthand evidence was shocking.

After what seemed a very long time, I was escorted to my quarters not by Larissa Tressalian (who I assumed had joined her mysteriously stricken brother) but by the curious little man called Dr. Leon Tarbell. Alone among the crew, the "documents expert" Tarbell was unknown to me by either sight or reputation, a fact that made him all the more intriguing; for he was certainly treated as an equal by the others and behaved entirely as such.

"Do you enjoy the decor?" Tarbell asked pleasantly as we walked down the carved wooden staircase to the ship's lower deck. His accent was hard to pinpoint, and his manner was equally ambiguous: though clearly friendly, he seemed to enjoy my lingering uneasiness. He pulled out a pack of the new, smokeless, and supposedly "safe" cigarettes that the American tobacco industry, after a generation of pressure and lawsuits by a combination of East Asian nations, had recently started to market and offered me one. I declined, and as he lit his he said, "It is not to my taste, this particular area. I prefer the modern. Minimalist, athletic—sexual."

"Some might simply say 'ugly,' " I offered quickly, before bothering to consider whether Tarbell might take offense.

But he only laughed. "True! It can be very ugly. But ugly"—his fiery eyes grew even more agitated—"with sexuality!"

I would soon learn that the entire world, to Tarbell, was divided between people and things that were not "sexual" and those that had "sexuality!" Though a simple formula, it seemed as valid as any and a good deal more amusing than most, given the way he made his pronouncements with near-comic vigor; so I laughed along with him, relaxing a bit as we arrived at the door to what were to be my quarters.

Inside was a small stateroom that recalled images I'd seen of early-twentieth-century transatlantic ocean liners. The temperature was well above the forty-five degrees of the corridor, creating a welcoming atmosphere that was complemented by more wood paneling, a small, porthole-shaped transparent section in the hull that could be chemically tinted at the touch of a nearby button, finely crafted glass light shades, and marble-and-ceramic sanitary facilities that appeared to be genuine antiques. It was even more unlike the very high tech nose area of the ship than were the corridors, a fact that caused my confusion to spike once more.

"Past and future, side by side," Tarbell said with a nod. "You could say that time does not exist aboard this vessel. Such is Malcolm!"

I turned my thoughts to my host. "Is he all right?"

Tarbell nodded confidently. "They pass, these attacks."

"But what's wrong with him?"

"I am not entirely comfortable speaking about such things. Perhaps he will tell you. Or perhaps Larissa." Tarbell gave me his demonic grin. "She has fastened her eye on you—lucky man. A woman of rare brilliance, beauty—and sexuality!" As he barked the last word, he clapped a hand on my shoulder. "Yes, you will join our little company, I think!" Turning to go he added, "You will find everything you need—even fresh clothes. We dine forward, in one-half hour. Malcolm tells me that you enjoy vodka—come soon, and I will share my private stock!"

It was evident that these people already knew almost everything about me, from the size and preferred style of my clothing (there was nothing in the closet of my quarters that I could not or would not have worn) to my taste in liquor. I didn't wonder how they had attained such knowledge, any more than I wondered about the cost of building the ship on which we were traveling. Malcolm and Larissa Tressalian's father, Stephen, whose satellite system had made the modern Internet possible, had been one of the wealthiest men in the world. He'd also been a leader of the group of information technocrats who, during the '07 crisis, had put up their collective private and corporate assets to guarantee the solvency of the American government, just as the financier J. P. Morgan and his associates had done a century earlier. Tressalian and his allies had then used this timely support as a club with which to beat Washington into dropping any and all attempts to regulate information commerce, thus dealing the deathblow to, among other things, the already wounded concept of personal privacy.

There would have been few things beyond the reach of such a man's heirs, yet that fact alone did not explain the most urgent questions at hand, which I grappled with yet again as I washed and changed for dinner: What exactly were these people up to, and why had they decided, in Larissa's phrase, that they needed me?

In twenty minutes I was headed back toward the nose of the ship, determined this time to get answers that were more than cryptic.

CHAPTER 13

The conference table in the lowest level of the nose had been draped with a rich cloth and laid with china, silver, and candles, and the color of the panorama outside the ship had turned a rich blue-black, indicating that we had taken an eastern turn into the deeper waters of the Atlantic, away from the waste that had marked the coast. The ship's exterior lights cut lovely shafts through these storied depths, yet even as I admired the beauty there seemed something odd about the sight, something lonely that I couldn't initially explain. I tried to shake the feeling off, attributing it to my own general sense of being on my own in a strange place—and then I realized that it actually stemmed from the surprising but very apparent lack of any signs of life in the water.

Tarbell was already standing by the table, along with the Kupermans; and although I couldn't see who was responsible for the cooking or where it was being done, the aromas filling the area were singularly appetizing. Tarbell handed me a glass of his personal vodka—a Russian brand I did not know—and then Eli Kuperman asked:

"You like lamb, don't you, Dr. Wolfe? Medium rare, I think it was. It'll be ready in just a few minutes."

"None of us has time to eat much during the day," Jonah Kuperman added, heading through a small door that evidently led to some sort of galley, where I could see Julien Fouché laboring in a sweat over a stainless-steel stove. "So we try to make dinners as civilized as we can."

I picked up a few pieces of the china and silver: very elegant and very old. "I guess you do" was all I could say, taking a sip of Tarbell's vodka and trying yet again to orient myself: after all, moments earlier I'd been standing in this same area watching a battle take place outside. "I don't suppose," I went on, "that anybody would like to tell me what it is that keeps you all so busy during the day? I mean, when you're not busting people out of jail."

Fouché raised his voice to call from the galley, "*That* should never have happened! A pet project of *les frères Kuperman* that grew completely out of hand!"

"Oh, come on, Julien!" Eli shot back. "It had just as much validity as anything else we've done. You've seen the statistics: gambling's become an epidemic since the crash, and there's no way I'm going to let a lot of anthropologically nonsensical folklore rationalize it. If we'd been able to plant that evidence—"

" 'Plant?' " I interrupted, surprised. "You mean you weren't stealing anything?"

Jonah Kuperman threw me a friendly glance. "There's really nothing in that particular burial site worth stealing, Dr. Wolfe."

"Gideon," I said.

"All right—Gideon. Well, as you probably know, it's been apparent for years that the various peoples who call themselves 'Native

Americans' were not, in fact, the first inhabitants of this continent. But many of the tribes have attempted to suppress or destroy evidence that might support this conclusion. They're afraid, and with reason, that if they're suddenly revealed as simple conquerors of their predecessors, they'll lose emotional and historical justification for a lot of questionable activities—including the creation of a generation of gambling addicts in their casinos."

"That burial ground in Florida," Eli said, "is currently being explored by a team from Harvard, and Jonah and I were trying to slip several artifacts *in* to demonstrate—"

Eli cut his words short at the sound of Malcolm Tressalian's wheelchair moving about on the control level above us. From the looks on the faces of the men on the lower level with me, I could see that they were all concerned as to what shape their leader was in. They relaxed again, however, when we all heard Tressalian call out:

"It simply would not be dinner without one of our rousing professional differences of opinion! Though you'll find, Dr. Wolfe, that these discussions can become quite personal as the evening wears on."

Slow, heavy steps on the metal staircase indicated that Tressalian was making his way down with the aid of his crutches, and soon he appeared, his light blue eyes bearing no trace of the agony that had filled them earlier. Behind him I could see Colonel Slayton, ever on the alert for any sign of trouble, as well as Larissa, who looked only more beautiful for having brought us through a hard-fought engagement with law enforcement.

"Well, gentlemen, whom are we beating up on tonight?" Tressalian went on. It occurred to me that once they saw that he had recovered from his bout of illness, none of the others thought to ask the man how he felt, even though the attack that had seized first his head and then his entire body had been savage. I took my cue from their example, remembering Tarbell's statement that these episodes were something of a regular occurrence and assuming, as I had when I'd first seen him struggle out of his wheelchair, that help and sympathy were not things Tressalian desired.

"Oh, Malcolm, it's absurd!" bellowed Fouché, who appeared from the galley. "Eli and Jonah continue to maintain that their Florida escapade was worth the trouble it brought!"

As a general though still good-natured uproar ensued, Larissa moved up close to me. "I'm sorry I wasn't there to settle you in," she said quietly, her dark eyes gleaming in the soft light even more than her silver hair. "Was everything all right?"

"Yes, perfectly," I answered, again feeling very self-conscious in her presence. "Dr. Tarbell did his best to help me get my bearings, though it was a tall order. But your brother—is he—?"

"Fine, now," she said, even more quietly. "But we can talk about that later."

The argument around the table continued, eventually prompting Tressalian to hold up his hands: "Decorum, gentlemen, please. Jonah, Eli—I think that for the foreseeable future we'll have to ask you to confine your activities concerning the gambling issue to *informational* pursuits. No one faults your zeal—we all know the extent of the problem and the false assumptions that underlie it. But there are far larger matters at hand just now. Not to mention that we are being unspeakably rude to our guest, who, unless I'm mistaken, understands only a fraction of what we're talking about."

I shook my head once with a smile. "You are certainly *not* mistaken."

"Then let's be seated while Julien serves." Tressalian moved to the head of the table, directing me to sit beside him. "We shall try to clarify the situation, Doctor, after which you can see our ideas at work in Afghanistan." He leaned toward me, the blue eyes alight. "And then you can decide if a life of brewing global chaos holds any appeal . . ."

CHAPTER 14

Fouché soon emerged from the galley bearing great platters of simply but delicately prepared food: the kind of diet, I immediately realized as I glanced at Tressalian, that would appeal to a man with a severe neurological condition. This impression was confirmed when I observed that he drank no alcohol.

"Excuse me," I said as I studied the man, "but did you say 'global chaos'?"

"Oh, all in a good cause," he rushed to reply. "Well—generally, at any rate. But to understand that cause I'm afraid you'll first have to wrap your mind around the philosophy we've all chosen to share."

"I'm listening."

Tressalian nodded. "Well, then, where to start? Perhaps simple observation would be best. Did you enjoy the sights along the coast?"

I looked up suddenly: Was *that* why the ship had spent so long in those filthy waters? To make an impression on *me,* just as Larissa had done when she'd so expertly manned the ship's big rail gun during the battle with our pursuers? "It was fairly depressing," I said carefully.

"And the sea around us now," Tressalian went on. "Does anything appear to be missing?"

"Just the fish," I joked; but the tableful of straight faces that looked back at me indicated how terribly serious my words had actually been. "Jesus," I fumbled. "Have things really gotten that bad?"

"The sights speak for themselves, Doctor," Colonel Slayton said gravely, running a finger along the scar on the side of his face. "The Atlantic seaboard is almost literally a hog sty, and the last of the important fish species, thanks to government lies about enforcing fishing regulations around the world, have been chased into the furthest recesses of the ocean, where they'll be found and, soon enough, slaughtered." He kept gently rubbing that scar, reminding me of how much "government lies" had contributed to his own disastrous experiences during the Taiwan campaign.

"Yes," Tressalian agreed gloomily. "I only wish I could say that such developments were outside the norm of modern human behavior. And yet, according to a generation of rhetoric, our own age should have separated itself from that norm, shouldn't it, Doctor?"

"How do you mean?"

"Well, after all, the dawn of this century *did* present humanity with an enormous opportunity to improve both its own lot and the condition of the planet. The necessary tools were all at hand." His voice became distinctly ironic. "The *age of information* had been born."

I was puzzled by his tone. "Yes—thanks in large part to *your* father."

Tressalian's irony quickly took on a hard edge. "True. Thanks in large part to *my father* . . ."

I pushed my plate aside and leaned forward. "You referred to his work earlier as a 'sin'—why?"

"Come now, Doctor," Tressalian answered, toying with a slender silver knife. "I think you know exactly why. And what's more, I suspect that you agree with the assessment."

"I may share some of your opinions," I said, weighing the statement. "But I also may have arrived at them through entirely different reasoning."

He smiled again. "Oh, I doubt that. But let's investigate, shall we?" He struggled to his feet, having eaten only half his food, and began to slowly circle the table. "Yes, Doctor, my father and his colleagues made certain that most of the world was given access to the modern Internet. To what was marketed—quite seductively and, of course, successfully—as 'unrestricted information.' And in an era when capitalism and global free trade had triumphed and were running rampant, such men had little trouble further promoting the belief that by logging on to that Internet, one was tapping in to a vast system of freedom, truth—and power. The mass of mankind withdrew to its terminals and clicked away, and those afflicted with philosophical scruples allowed themselves to be cajoled into believing that they were promoting the democratic cause of a free exchange not only of goods and information but of ideas as well. Convinced, in other words, that they were changing the world, and for the better."

His face turned toward the ocean again, and his manner softened once more. "Yet in the meantime, inexplicably but undeniably, the water and the air grew dirtier than they had ever been. New pandemics appeared, with no medicines to treat them. Poverty, anarchy, and conflict ravaged more and more parts of the world." He sighed once, his brow arching. "And the fish—disappeared . . ." When he turned to me again, his face radiated a paradoxical and disquieting calm. "How did it happen, Dr. Wolfe? How, in an age when the free flow of information and trade was supposedly creating a benevolent global order, did all this happen?"

Just then the shipwide address system issued another gently

throbbing alarm, at which Colonel Slayton announced that there was to be another "system transfer" in two minutes. "We're heading into the stratosphere for a few hours, Dr. Wolfe," Tressalian said. "How would you feel about coffee and dessert at seventy thousand feet?"

I hadn't noticed, but during dinner the ship had inclined its angle of progress, and in just a few seconds the rippling image of the nearly full moon became visible through the surface of the ocean. Maintaining its speed, the vessel rushed up out of the water and into the open air, its superconductive electromagnetic generators propelling it into the heavens at a fantastic rate that did not even rattle the china on the table.

Colonel Slayton moved quietly toward the stairs and headed up to the control level with calm purpose. "There's no need to contact the island, Colonel," Tressalian called after him. "I've already double-checked the apparatus. We're set for dawn."

"Sorry, Malcolm," Slayton answered, continuing his climb. "The military penchant for redundancy dies hard."

Tressalian laughed quietly in my direction. "The Islamic terrorists in Afghanistan," he explained, "have refused to heed our warnings about the American strike, so we'll have to force them to leave. They've got their women and children down in those tunnels with them, and that's not blood I particularly want on my hands."

"But how can you *force* them to go?" I asked.

"Well—I *could* tell you, Doctor," Tressalian said as he began to drag his body away from the transparent hull. "But I think it'll be far more effective if you observe."

CHAPTER 15

Once we'd leveled off in the thin, cold stratospheric air, Tressalian led a slow procession up to the observation dome atop the nose of the ship. As we stopped by the guidance center on the middle level to pick up his wheelchair, I saw and heard the consoles of monitors blinking and humming under Colonel Slayton's direction, and noted that my earlier amazement at the fantastic advances embodied in the ship was beginning to fade. I found myself marveling at how quickly the human mind can accept and become adjusted to technological leaps—although of course, Tarbell's vodka and Larissa's continued and ever-more-pointed physical overtures were going a long way, on this particular night, toward assisting my own acclimation. But ultimately it was a testament to the seductive power of technology, a power that my host—who refused to explain any further about the Afghanistan business until we got there—expounded on as he sat in his wheelchair in the observation dome:

"While the average citizen, Doctor, was engaged in this mass love affair with information technology—and while the companies that produced that technology happily painted themselves as the democratizing agents of a new order—real economic and informational power, far from being decentralized, became concentrated in an ever-decreasing number of megacorporations, companies that determined not only what information was purveyed but which technologies were developed to receive and monitor it. And while in your own country there was at least a struggle early on for control over this mightiest and most pervasive public influence in history, the crash of '07 put an end to the fight. In a collapsing world, Washington had no one to turn to for help except my father and his ilk. And they offered it, to be sure—but only for a price."

"To put it simply," Colonel Slayton said as he rejoined us from the control level, "they *purchased* the government."

Tressalian smiled at him, then turned back to me. "The colonel has a gift for brevity that is sometimes mistaken for detachment. But remember that no one experienced the practical effects of what we're talking about more than the soldiers of the Taiwan campaign, who—as you yourself have pointed out, Doctor—unknowingly sacrificed themselves for a bigger share of the Chinese market. Yes, the information technocrats, my father among them, purchased the government, and after that all legislative initiatives and material resources were diverted from regulatory programs, from environmental and medical research, from education and foreign aid, even from weapons development—diverted from *everything,* that is, save the opening of new markets and the expansion of old ones."

"All right," I agreed, Larissa's ever-closer presence making me feel steadily more at ease. "I'll admit I agree with you, but so what? You've said yourself that this sort of thing has happened before in human history."

"*Non,* Gideon," Julien Fouché said as he wrapped one meaty

hand around a small espresso cup. "That is most distinctly *not* what Malcolm has said. The beginning of the story may have precedents, but this last chapter? There has never been anything like it. The floodgates were thrown open, and human society, already saturated with information, began to *drown* in it. Tell me—you are familiar, I suppose, with the concept of the 'threshold moment'? When a process increases so drastically in rate and severity—"

"That a quantitative change actually becomes a qualitative one," I finished for him. "Yes, Professor, I know."

"Well, then," Fouché went on, "let us put it to you that world civilization has itself reached just such a moment."

I sat back for a moment. Extreme as his words might have sounded, they could not be dismissed, given their source. "You're saying," I eventually answered, "that the growth of these latest technologies has been so quantitatively different from other informational developments—from, say, the invention of the printing press—that the effect has been a qualitative shift in the nature of society itself?"

"Précisément," Fouché answered with a nod. "But don't look so amazed, Doctor. The people behind these technologies have themselves been claiming for years that they were bringing about enormous changes. It is simply that we who are assembled here view those changes as"—he took a sip of espresso as he struggled to find a word—*"ominous."*

Then it was Leon Tarbell's turn: "The 'information age' has not created any free exchange of knowledge, Gideon. All we have is a free exchange of whatever the sexless custodians of information technology consider acceptable."

"And the very nature of that technology means that there *is* no real knowledge anymore," Eli Kuperman piled on, "because what those custodians *do* allow to slip through their delivery systems is utterly unregulated and unverifiable. Mistaken facts—or, worse yet, deceptions on a simple or a grand scale, supported by doctored evidence and digitally manipulated images—become commonly accepted wisdom before there's even been a chance to determine the validity of their bases."

"And remember," Jonah Kuperman added, "that we've now raised not one but *several* generations of children who have been exposed *only* to that kind of questionable data—"

"Whoa, whoa, slow down!" I finally called out, holding up my hands. During the brief respite that followed, I let out a deep, troubled breath. "This is starting to sound like some kind of runaway conspiracy theory—technoparanoia of the worst kind. What in the world makes you think that people can pull off deceptions on a level that will change the fundamental underpinnings of entire societies, for God's sake?"

Everyone around me suddenly grew strangely silent; then, one by one, they turned to Tressalian, who was staring at his fingertips as he slowly bounced them together. After a few seconds he looked up at me, the smile on his face more charming and yet more devious than it had been at any point in the evening. "We know, Doctor," he said quietly, "because we've done it."

"You?"

Tressalian nodded. "Quite a few times, actually. And the best, I dare say, is yet to come—if you'll help us."

"But—" I tried to grasp it. "But I mean—I thought you were *against* all that."

"Oh, make no mistake, we are." Tressalian struggled to turn his chair and then rolled to the forwardmost area of the dome, real disgust and even anger coming into his voice. "Human society is diseased, Doctor—this fatuous, trivial, information-plagued society. And our work?" He stared at the eerie, half-lit sky outside, growing calmer. "With luck, our work will be the antibiotic that spurs society to fight the infection." A nagging doubt seemed to tighten his features. "Assuming, of course, that we don't kill the patient . . ."

I was about to ask for clarification of this apparently unbalanced statement when the ship's alert system suddenly sounded again. Slayton informed us that we were descending to "cruising altitude," an innocuous expression that I soon learned had to do not with any kind of pleasure traveling but with flying some hundred feet above the landscape as we had done when I'd first boarded the ship in Florida. Everyone stood, the general level of excitement growing, and gathered around Tressalian; and while I tried to follow as best I could, my movements were slowed by the mental need to wrestle with everything I'd just heard. Could they be serious, these people? Could they really mean that they believed it was possible to manipulate the dissemination of important information to the public as a way of alerting that same public to just how easy—and therefore dangerous—such manipulation had, in our time, become? It was absurd, impossible—

And then, with a shudder that had nothing to do with Larissa's close presence, I remembered the scenes of President Forrester's assassination on the disc that Max and I had been given. For a year the world had accepted as true a version of those momentous events that was not even remotely factual. And now the strongest power in the world was about to engage in a military strike that was based on that same misapprehension—a misapprehension manufactured by Tressalian and his team, who were currently on their way to the scene of that strike to—what? Observe? Participate, with their amazing ship? Or manipulate the proceedings with still more manufactured information? Almost afraid to know the answers, I silently turned to watch the darkness ahead of us with the others.

Even through my renewed bewilderment, I realized that the ship had once more shifted altitude dramatically without so much as a bump or a perceptible change in cabin pressure. We were flying low over the ocean again, although I was shocked to learn that *this* ocean was the Arabian Sea, which meant that our high-altitude speed had been considerably in excess of anything achieved by the most advanced supersonic airplanes currently in use. As I watched the moonlit waters speed by under us, Larissa turned to murmur into my ear:

"Not that I don't agree with everything the others have been saying, Doctor—I assure you I do—but try to put it aside for a moment and experience this ride. Can any philosophical discussion really make your blood race like this ship? I doubt it. So when you think about joining us, think about this, too—" I turned to face her. "You and I could travel to literally every corner of the world, just the way we are now—with no restrictions and no laws but our own. Are you game?"

I looked back outside. "Jesus—I'd like to say that I am," I told her uncertainly. "But it's all so—" I tried to get a grip. "Impulsiveness has never been the most comfortable mode of behavior for me."

She let me have the coy smile. "I know."

"That doesn't bother you?"

She made a judicious little humming sound. "Not *entirely.* It's part of the reason we wanted you, after all." She put a hand lightly to my cheek. "*Part* of the reason . . ."

Without turning toward us Tressalian called out, "Oh, Sister—if I may interrupt, perhaps you'd care to explain what avenue of approach you've chosen. Toward our *geographical* objective, that is."

Larissa gave me one more searching look before answering him. "*Very* droll, Brother. We'll make landfall south of Karachi, then follow the Indus Valley north. We're safe from any radar, of course, and because the river's been a nuclear dead zone since the start of the Kashmir war, we shouldn't be risking any visual contact. We'll move west along the thirty-fifth parallel into the Hindu Kush, then north to the valley of the Amu Darya. The camp is strung out along the Afghan side of the border with Tajikistan. We'll arrive just past dawn, right on schedule. The apparatus will already have engaged."

"Good." Tressalian turned away from the transparent hull just as a black strip of coastline became faintly visible in the dark distance and fixed his gaze on me. "Then there's time, yet, for the doctor to ask the rest of his questions."

"Questions," I said, trying to focus. "Yes, I've got questions. But there's one thing I've got to know right now." I moved over to stare down at him intently. "How many other lies like the Forrester assassination story am I believing without even knowing it?"

"You mean," Tressalian answered, "how much of the *information* that makes up your reality is utterly unreliable?" I nodded and he opened his eyes wide, raising his brows as if to prepare me for what was coming: "Certainly more than you'd suspect, Doctor. And, quite probably, more than you'll believe . . ."

CHAPTER 16

How can I describe the hours that followed? How do I explain my transformation from skeptical (if fascinated) observer of Malcolm Tressalian's outlandish, even mad, schemes to full-fledged participant in them? There were so many factors involved, not least the lingering trauma of having seen my oldest friend murdered before my eyes, along with the lack of any meaningful sleep in the days since that event. Yet mere emotional and physical exhaustion would be inadequate hooks upon which to hang my swift spiritual metamorphosis. No, the cascade of intellectual, visual, and physical stimuli that continued to rain down on me in those predawn and morning hours would, I think, have converted the strongest and most doubting of souls, and I say that not simply to excuse my reaction; rather, it is a testament to all that I heard, saw, and felt as we passed over the Pakistani coast and penetrated to the interior of the subcontinent.

As Larissa had said, the valley of the once-proud Indus River, mother of one of the mightiest and most mysterious of ancient civilizations, had been turned into a nuclear wasteland during the still-raging war between India and Pakistan over Kashmir. But my beautiful companion's further statement that the valley was uninhabited was not, strictly speaking, correct. As we sped along above the surface of the water, past riverbanks strewn with rotting bodies and bleached skeletons, we occasionally saw groups of what were perhaps the most desperate people on earth: farmers and villagers whose bodies and ways of life—whose very chances *for* life—had been terribly damaged as a result of the vicious nationalism and religious zealotry of both their enemies and their countrymen. They were moving down the hillsides in limping, shuffling lines, those weakened wraiths, moving down by the light of the moon to fill buckets with the river's poisoned waters, which they would later boil in a futile attempt at purification so that they might try to go on for a few more days or weeks in the only way that, given the decimated condition of their nation and the unwillingness of the rest of its citizens to accept such nuclear lepers, was possible for them.

The sight hit all of us hard, suspending even my urgent curiosity about my companions; but it seemed to take the greatest toll on Malcolm. It was well-known that the development of India's rabidly bellicose new breed of nationalism in the years since the turn of the century had coincided with the rise to economic and social primacy of information technologies and networks in that country; and Larissa would later tell me that Malcolm had always held their father and his ilk personally responsible for the fact that the systems they had designed could be and were used to disseminate lies and hatred among such peoples in as unregulated a manner as characterized the purveyance of consumer goods. The extent of Malcolm's anger, despair, and what I took at the time to be guilt over this matter was certainly evident as I watched him that night; indeed, it soon propelled him into something of a relapse. He once again began to hiss and clutch at his head—more covertly now, given the size of his audience—and these telltale signs quickly brought Larissa to his aid. She took his right hand in her two, whispered a few calming words in his ear, and then, reaching into the pocket of his jacket, withdrew a small transdermal injector and held it for an instant to a vein in his left hand. In moments he seemed to be dozing, though fitfully, at which point Larissa spread a small comforter over his legs.

Only when they were sure that Malcolm was asleep did the rest of the ship's company feel comfortable attending to other duties. Colonel Slayton descended to the control level of the nose to man the ship's helm, while Fouché and Tarbell went off to make sure that the vessel's engines had come through the various "system transfers" smoothly. As for the Kupermans, Larissa asked if they wouldn't mind prepping me for our visit to Afghanistan while she continued to look after her brother. Jonah replied that he thought it imperative that everyone on board get some rest before we reached our destination, but both he and his brother did agree to take me down to the armory first to show me how to operate the basic gear with which I would need to equip myself when we arrived. On our way out Eli added that the session would offer me a chance to ask at least a few questions about the group's past activities, and it was therefore in a mood of no little anticipation that I descended into the deepest recesses of the vessel.

As we approached and then entered the armory—a compartment filled with racks of weapons unlike anything I'd ever seen—Eli and Jonah told me that the first members of the team to find their way to one another had been themselves and Malcolm, who had all been in the same class at Yale. Apparently the Kupermans—who since childhood had been idealistic opponents of the dominance of information technology over every field of human endeavor, including scholarship—had originally sought the young Tressalian out to confront him: Malcolm had recently assumed control of his father's empire following the latter's death under seemingly tragic circumstances, and Eli and Jonah wanted to know if he intended to end the Tressalian Corporation's reliance on Third World hardware sweatshops, as well as conduct the company's other operations in a more ethical and responsible manner. On finding that Malcolm's philosophy was in fact far closer to their own than to his father's, Eli and Jonah took to spending long hours in the company of the silver-haired young man in the wheelchair, hacking into corporate and government databases and generally raising informational hell. Malcolm eventually proposed that the three take their activities to a new and more daring level, and the twins quickly signed on for what turned out to be the first in a long string of attempts to hold a mirror up to the global information society and point out its very serious flaws and dangers. The result of this endeavor was to become infamous, in the years that followed, as the "Fools' Congress" of 2010.

Utilizing the Tressalian Corporation's resources but working in strict secrecy, Malcolm and the Kupermans created an imaginary, digitally generated candidate for the U.S. Congress. The fact that they were able to convince the good people of southern Connecticut that their almost absurdly virtuous creature actually existed was remarkable enough, but when they went on to get the imaginary character elected to office through clever manufacture and manipulation of bogus background information and news footage on the Internet and in other information media—and when genuine news cameras failed to find any trace of the up-and-coming leader on the day he was supposed to report for duty in the Capitol—a national frenzy was touched off. So great was the reaction, in fact, and so dire the threats of punishment from federal authorities, that Malcolm, Eli, and Jonah did not again return to the business of disseminating false information until they'd finished graduate school and had begun to make names for themselves in their respective fields. When they finally did indulge their passion for zealous mischief again, however, the effects were even more astounding—and dangerous.

Joined now by Larissa, who had earned several degrees of her own in physics, chemistry, and engineering (as well as gaining some darker experience to which I shall shortly turn), the young men selected for their next target nothing less than the whole of the European continent, over which the clouds of internecine conflict had by 2017 once again gathered. Economic pressures brought on by the '07 financial crash had finally forced the United States to withdraw the last of its peacekeeping troops from the Balkans, and the hatreds endemic to that region had once more become glaringly obvious. The European Union, as pusillanimous as ever when it came to matters that involved not money but lives, had refused to fill the expensive gap left by the Americans and indeed prevented the only member state willing to undertake the task, Great Britain, from doing so. Thus it came about that, for a decade after the crash, the Balkans endured massacres and reprisals on a scale not seen for generations.

In concocting a hoax designed to show how little the development of information technology had done or could do to defuse such ancient animosities, Malcolm brought onto his team both Fouché, under whom he and the Kupermans had studied at Yale, and Tarbell, an accomplished scientist and scholar but expert in nothing so much as highly advanced forgery. It may be difficult to believe that the great divisions that still mark Europe were set in motion by a few sheets of paper created by the burly, congenial Fouché and the frenetic, gleeful little Tarbell; yet I can now report that such was indeed the case. Julien used his skills to molecularly manipulate samples of ink and paper so that they duplicated examples from a century earlier, while Tarbell, using a text dictated by Malcolm, turned these materials into a series of notes supposedly written by the British statesman Winston Churchill to none other than Gavrilo Princip, the

Serbian nationalist who shot the Austrian archduke Franz Ferdinand and set in motion the chain of events that led to the outbreak of the First World War in 1914. In the notes, Princip was "revealed" to have been a British agent and the assassination to have been a plot engineered by the ever-devious Churchill and several other British leaders to ignite a war that, they believed, would end in the triumph and expansion of their empire.

The idea was far more outlandish than the Fools' Congress business had been, but once again—and this was the very crucial point—Malcolm's speedy and thorough manipulation of all materials relating to the "discovery" of the notes, on the Internet and in all ancillary information systems, led to their being accepted as genuine long before careful observers could offer more skeptical or scholarly opinions. The Germans rose to the bait laid out by Tressalian's team, declaring that they would not sit in the halls of European power with the British until London had disavowed Churchill and accepted full responsibility for the war. France, too, seized the opportunity to wax indignant, as did every other country that had been involved in the conflict. The British, for their part, were not about to accept the demonization of their greatest twentieth-century hero; and so the first of what became many tumultuous cracks went singing through the Union, causing riotous demonstrations and several threats of war.

Even Malcolm had not anticipated either the violence of the reaction that his European work sparked or the danger to which he'd exposed himself and his team. Investigations were launched not merely by police forces and academics but by the various European security services, especially the British; and none of the band wanted to end up with an SAS bullet in his or her head. Realizing that they were now playing on a new and much more deadly field, Malcolm decided to enlist the aid of someone who could help him organize his efforts along the lines of what they appeared to have become: a campaign.

He examined the dossiers of disaffected military officers from around the world, although it was Larissa who eventually brought Colonel Justus Slayton to her brother's attention. And in learning why she'd been in a position to make that introduction, I discovered something that caused me to recoil in shock:

Apparently, after completing her university studies, this impressive, beautiful girl with whom I'd been so taken since the moment of our first meeting had become an international assassin.

CHAPTER 17

The revelation hit me like a proverbial brick. I stood there for long, dazed minutes, attempting to regain my composure as Eli fitted me first for a pair of highly insulated but lightweight boots and then for a seemingly ordinary suit of coveralls that was in fact highly advanced body armor. Jonah, meanwhile, removed some kind of handgun from one of the many racks around me and, slapping the thing into my palm, said, "There—that seems like a good fit. How does the balance feel, Gideon?"

"How—" I mumbled. "How does the—*what*?"

"It's a long-range neural interrupter," Jonah answered, pulling my limp arm up and squeezing my hand around the weapon. "In other words, a stun gun, though an extremely sophisticated one. Painless, with absolutely no aftereffects. I'm assuming that since you're in the medical profession, you don't want to carry anything lethal. But you *will* need protection—"

"Excuse me, " I said slowly, "but would you repeat that last bit?"

Eli's tongue began to click as he stared at the legs of my coveralls. "You're really a very in-between size, Gideon. We had a hell of a time finding clothes for you, and I'm afraid this body armor's strictly off the rack."

"The targeting and firing mechanisms," Jonah continued, still focused on the gun, "are very easy to operate—Malcolm was able to simplify the design sketches that Colonel Slayton brought with him when he left the Pentagon. You can choose either manual or voice-operated—"

"Jonah?" I said, trying to be calm. "I really will pay attention to the gun in a minute. But just that last bit again. Please."

"Uh-oh." Eli smiled, rolling down the cuffs of the coverall legs so that they touched the boots. "Didn't I warn you not to go blurting it out, Jonah?"

"What?" Jonah let my arm fall. "You mean about Larissa?" I nodded once slowly, and he said, "I don't know why you'd be shocked. Did you think a woman like that wasn't going to have a past?"

"A *past*?" I echoed. "What—how—I mean, how did she—"

"Well," Jonah went on, "so far as I know, she's always had a kind of fascination with personal violence—especially politico-corporate killers. I think she got actively involved through a contact in Germany, and pretty soon she found out that she was very good at it. In her first year she knocked off three chief execs of multinationals, along with two heads of state. I'll let her tell you which ones."

"Okay," Eli said, standing up. "Listen, Gideon, the suit will monitor your body's vital signs and make most microclimate and physiological adjustments automatically. But in Afghanistan there may be—"

I held a quick hand up. "Just—one second, Eli. Just one damned minute, okay?" I turned back to Jonah. "But—I mean, *why*? She couldn't have needed the *money*."

"Of course not," Jonah replied, opening a shoulder pouch on the coveralls to reveal a flexible, highly miniaturized control board. "Hydrocarbon in the microturbine, check, operating at one hundred watts. Armor integrity uncompromised—"

I put a hand over the pouch, blocking his view of the board. "Then *why?*" I repeated.

Jonah shrugged. "You've talked to her. She's got a highly developed, albeit highly idiosyncratic, moral code. She and Malcolm both do. Take the case that Colonel Slayton tracked her down on—"

"The case that she *let* Colonel Slayton track her down on," Eli added, helping me back out of the coveralls.

"True," Jonah agreed. "You see, Gideon, she was trying to lure him into a private meeting so she could convince him to join our effort. It worked, too—and why not? I mean, there was Slayton, stewing in the Pentagon about the way he and his men had been betrayed in Taiwan, and then he hears about the murder of an American software magnate in Taipei. The man had been killed, according to an anonymous tip, because he'd made an immoral fortune by exploiting the horrendous prison-labor laws that the Chinese instituted on Taiwan after reunification. Given Slayton's experience, the story interested him. But he hit a blank wall, I mean, there were *no* leads. And for the Chinese police to turn up no leads on that kind of case, well—that's a lot of torturing for no result. But as Eli says, Larissa eventually let Slayton find her so she could make the offer." Shifting gears again, Jonah indicated the racks of weapons. "Now, most of this stuff you're probably never going to use—advanced antiarmor and antiaircraft ordnance, the rail weapons that you've already seen, highly miniaturized nuclear devices—"

"Jonah," I said, "can you please just stay on this subje—*what?*" I moved closer to a rack of what looked like small compressed-air canisters. "*Nuclear* devices? What the hell are those doing here?"

"Slayton again," Eli answered. "When Larissa and Malcolm

talked him into defecting, the man took everything out of the Pentagon that wasn't nailed down. He had the highest possible security clearance, you see, as he was—"

"One of their top men in weapons R and D," I finished for him, remembering what Malcolm had said. "But why did he agree to come over?"

"Well, the rest of us have speculated on that quite a bit," Eli answered. Then he smiled as I cautiously edged just my face closer to the nuclear devices. "Oh, go on, Gideon," he said, picking one up and tossing it to me. Screaming as I caught it, I glanced up, only to see his grin getting bigger. "They're not armed," he said with a laugh. "How crazy do you think we are?" I looked at him dubiously, and he nodded. "Point taken. But they *are* safe."

"All right, then, *you* play with them," I answered, tossing the canister back. "And go on about what Slayton's doing here."

Eli laughed again as Jonah took up the story: "He'd been working on one of the highest-priority projects in American military history—ever heard of 'influence technology'?"

"No," I answered. "Doesn't sound particularly deadly, though."

"Maybe not in the conventional sense," Jonah said. "It's basically the development of advanced population control techniques—figuring out ways to give the military the power to make whole communities believe whatever the Pentagon wants them to believe. You know how every few years most of the population of Phoenix claims it's being invaded by UFOs? That's Slayton's department—they use air force squadrons flying in highly synchronized formations, equipped with new kinds of running lights."

"So you think he got fed up with the government after Taiwan," I said, "then got interested in pulling off hoaxes when he was doing this influence technology, and *that's* why he decided to join you?"

"Close as we can tell," Jonah answered. "He's never been the most forthcoming person, the colonel. At any rate, he brought along the designs for most of these weapons—and for some that you'll see later. Most were abandoned by the Americans because of prototype failures and cost overruns, neither of which presented Malcolm with much of a problem."

I took in a very deep breath, still studying all the hardware around me. "So what happened then?" I said. "With your work, I mean."

"Then things *really* got busy," Jonah said, checking a nearby clock. "We don't have time to tell you all the stories, but I suppose you'd better hear the big ones, if we expect you to believe us."

"Yes," I said. "I suppose I had."

The pair of them exchanged one of those quick looks of unspoken communication and understanding that are so often characteristic of twins; then they both nodded, and Eli said to his brother, "You take the gospel. I'll take the bones."

"Excuse me?" I mumbled.

Jonah turned my way. "Right. Basically, Malcolm thought it was time we addressed the general subject of religion, since people had decided to start killing each other over it again in ways that hadn't really been seen since the Crusades. And thinking of the Crusades, along with other things, he decided to make Christianity the specific target." To my immense shock and irritation, Jonah proceeded to pick up three of the nuclear canisters and begin juggling them. "It was another document job for Leon and Julien. You must've heard of it—the Fifth Gospel?"

Coming on top of the juggling bombs, this news was enough to send me reeling into a corner. The "Fifth Gospel," as not only I but most of the world by then knew, was a text discovered several years earlier in a remote part of Syria. Purportedly written by the apostle Paul in the mid–first century, the document described the need to lie about the life and supposed miracles of Jesus Christ in order to spread the faith and gave instructions on how to do so to various sect leaders throughout the area. The results of this "revelation" I hardly need record—for while the Fools' Congress and Churchill controversies had been focused, at least initially, on political and historical circles, most of the world was immediately swept up in and polarized by the battle over the Fifth Gospel, which inspired the creation of an unprecedented number of Web sites and on-line journalistic organs devoted entirely to the debate.

"That was *you* people?" I said, stunned. "But it's the most scientifically examined document in history!"

"Yes, those boys really did their work well," Eli answered.

"Jesus," I whispered without realizing what I was saying and getting a laugh out of the other two for it.

"For the next big job," Eli said, "we did a complete one-eighty." As he spoke he stepped out and started to receive and return the flipping bombs from his brother. "I'm sure you know that one, too, Gideon—'*Homo inexpectatus*'?"

My shock instantly became blatant disbelief. "Now you're pushing it," I said, pointing at him. "You couldn't have done that, that's been scientifically proved *absolutely* genuine!"

"Of course," Eli said, almost dropping one of the bombs. "Scientifically proved genuine because scientists designed it. Which is to say, us. And Julien, of course. See, Malcolm thought it was only fair to give science a dose, since we'd taken a shot at religion. So Jonah and I got hold of a group of anatomically convincing contemporary skeletons—comparatively small ones, but adults—and Julien did a little molecular manipulation. Then Jonah and I snuck them into a remote dig in—"

"In South Africa," I said, and all of a sudden I was back in limbo: for the remains they were talking about, when they'd been found, had ignited an international firestorm, as even the most skeptical scientists could find no way to dispute the assertion that they were at least five million years old. In other words, the supposed existence of any "missing link" between man and ape, along with the entire theory of evolution, had seemingly been discredited, inasmuch as humans very much like us had apparently existed alongside more primitive types of man. What the Fifth Gospel had done to religion, the aptly dubbed *Homo inexpectatus* did to science; in less than three years two of the most powerful faiths in the world had been thrown into disarray.

"This is unbelievable," I muttered. What I did *not* say, though I felt it strangely and strongly, was that there was something intriguing about it all, as well.

"And you've only heard *stories,*" Eli said. "Wait until you see the—" He stopped when he again caught sight of the clock. "Whoops, look at the time. Sorry, Gideon, but we should really try to get a couple of hours' rest."

Jonah nodded. "Believe me, you're going to need it. Things in Afghanistan may get hot in more ways than one."

"What's *that* supposed to mean?" I asked, a little perturbed.

"Nothing," Eli answered evasively, gathering up the bombs and restacking them on the rack. "You'll see. Come on, we can talk more while we're walking—about the other jobs, if you like."

"Other jobs?" I echoed, further astounded; but they were already hustling me outside the room and then on through the corridors and up to my quarters.

I discovered as we went that the "other jobs" they'd mentioned were much smaller undertakings, really just amusements to keep the group's collective hand in, as the Kupermans' Florida escapade had been. But this didn't mitigate the central conclusion to which such revelations inescapably led: that Malcolm's earlier claim about it being nearly impossible to guess at or believe the extent to which contemporary conventional wisdom and popular debate had been choreographed by his group was entirely justified. Like those individuals who had been manipulated by "recovered memory" therapists during the late twentieth century, human society had begun to view itself, as a result of these people's hoaxes, in an entirely new experiential context. Our utter reliance on information technology had caused us all—even those who, like me, vainly fancied ourselves to be skeptical by nature—to accept the shocking new "facts" that those systems were delivering and to argue their details rather than their provenances; and in doing so, we validated all of Malcolm's profound indictments.

Weary though I was, these realizations made it difficult to drift off straight away when I finally did slip into the small but plush bed in my quarters. However, once I achieved sleep it was a deep and disorienting one, a treatment that turned out to be very nearly worse than the ailment of exhaustion—for I was awakened far too soon by the ship's pulsing alarm.

Apparently we had arrived in Afghanistan.

CHAPTER 18

I managed to ignore the vessel's Klaxon for several minutes, but then it was joined by the sound of firm knocking on my compartment door. I dragged myself to my feet and soon found myself looking into Julien Fouché's broad, bearded features. He was wearing his body armor and had a sidearm strapped to his waist.

"It's time, Doctor," he said, handing me my own coveralls and boots, as well as the same stun pistol that Jonah had shown me in the arsenal. "The Americans will launch their raid soon, and apparently our Muslim friends are not entirely cooperating. The situation is delicate—Malcolm feels your assistance on the ground will be of great value."

"Mine?" I said, trying to get into the coveralls. "But why?"

"Their leader is a particularly neurotic and unpredictable fellow who seems genuinely prepared to make a martyr of himself, which would be perfectly acceptable to all of us, if only he had not convinced his wives and children to remain with him by offering assurances of favored places in Paradise. Malcolm seems to think that you may be able to persuade him to change his mind." Watching me struggle half-wittedly with the coveralls, Fouché began to help me into them impatiently. "*Tonnerre,* Gideon, one would think you had never dressed yourself!"

I made a more concerted effort to focus, and as I did, a question occurred to me: "Say, Julien, there's one thing I don't understand. It was the Chinese, not the Afghans, who killed President Forrester, right? And that's why we're here. But what made the Chinese do it?"

"Your Madame President had something resembling scruples," Fouché answered, "though they were well hidden. When shown pictures of the final massacre of the Falun Gong cult in 2018, she told her cabinet that she intended to bring Beijing's trade status up for congressional review."

"Her cabinet? So how'd the Chinese security forces find out?"

"Gideon," Fouché scolded, hustling me down the corridor, "are you really so naïve? Since the turn of the century the Chinese have made a point of having at least one American cabinet minister in their pockets—further proof, of course, that increased trade with the outside world has done nothing to change the way the Chinese do *real* business. No amount of money, however, would have prevented a crisis if the truth about the assassination had become known. And war between America and China would have been—"

"Catastrophic," I said with a nod. "So that's why Malcolm doctored the footage."

Fouché smiled. "Righteous mischief *is* irresistible to him."

We arrived amidships, and Fouché reached up next to one of the golden-framed paintings that hung on the corridor wall to touch a concealed control panel. "The others have gone on ahead to clear a path, and Larissa will cover us all from the turret." Suddenly a section of the deck below me began to rise, revealing a hatchway that contained a retractable flight of steps extending down to a few feet above the ground. Echoing up through the hatchway, I could hear voices shouting and the sounds of helicopter and diesel automotive engines.

But what I noticed most was the fantastic heat that was radiating up from the ground: it was far in excess of anything I'd expected or could explain.

"Yes," Fouché said, catching my consternation. "The apparatus has engaged. We have less than an hour."

"Until what?" I queried nervously as he started down the steps.

"Until any human foolish enough to remain in this area burns up like so much paper," Fouché answered, jumping to the ground and then waving me down. "Come! Time presses!"

The landscape surrounding the ship was not unlike that of many other countries in the "analog archipelago," that patchwork of countries that had fallen so far behind in the digital technology race that they'd given up the struggle. But the chaos that was enveloping this stretch of the valley of the Amu Darya was alarming even for one of the most backward of nations. Emerging from large tunnel entrances supported by enormous timbers and fortified with sandbags was a host of people, some dressed in military fatigues and some in traditional Islamic garb, all rushing toward a great collection of buses, helicopters, and jeeps. Many of the women bore small children who were, for the most part, screaming, and small wonder: the noise and the heat, combined with the looming silhouette of Tressalian's ship, would have been enough to terrify much older and more comprehending souls. Me, for instance.

Looking ahead and through the dust whipped up by the chopper blades, I could see Slayton, Tarbell, and the Kupermans fanned out with weapons drawn. They were moving toward one tunnel entrance in particular, using their own stun guns to incapacitate the occasional confused man who, apparently mistaking our team for members of the approaching American task force, stepped forward to try to stop us. As Fouché and I followed the others to the tunnel, I called out:

"Julien! Just what *is* this 'apparatus,' anyway?"

"A euphemistic label, eh?" Fouché answered with a laugh. "It is a weapon that your country's air force began to research in the late twentieth century—but they were never able to build a successful prototype. Colonel Slayton brought us the plans, Malcolm and Larissa refined them, and observe—a small glimpse of Hell!"

"But what does it do?" I asked, realizing that although the sun had only just come over the eastern horizon, the temperature was climbing fantastically from one minute to the next.

"Destruction of the ozone layer over a confined area!" Fouché shouted back. "The Americans were never able to keep the hole stable or to close it when they wished!"

"And you can," I said, astonished. "But where *is* the damned thing?"

"The projecting unit is on Malcolm's island in the North Sea! It operates through a series of satellites—Tressalian satellites!"

Suddenly and from all too close came the sharp report of small-arms fire. With a speed that shocked me, Fouché almost flew in my direction, enveloping me in his big arms and then gracefully rolling with me behind some nearby rocks. When we looked up, we saw that the shots had been fired by a man who was trying to keep any more people from boarding his already overloaded helicopter, which in a few seconds took off and began a flight toward the southeast.

"Do not stand," Fouché said, "until we have received the all clear from the colonel."

Breathing hard and shaking my head, I studied my companion for a moment. "Julien," I gasped, "what the *hell* are you doing here, anyway?"

He smiled again. "Saving your skin, just at the moment, Gideon."

"You know what I mean," I said. "What are you doing out here with this bunch? You were one of the most renowned and respected scholars in your field."

"Yes," he said with a nod. "And one of the unhappiest." Then, catching sight of a signal from Colonel Slayton, he pulled me up. His voice softened somewhat as we continued to move forward through the dust and the heat toward the target tunnel's entrance. "You see, Gideon, my wife was one of the first victims of the staphylococcus epidemic." I tried to express my sympathy, but he quickly waved me off. "There were many millions who shared my tragedy. But what troubled me most was that she had predicted the manner of her own death years earlier. She was a surgeon, you see. And she had repeatedly told me that economic pressures were causing her colleagues and their nursing staffs to attend to so many patients that they had begun to ignore fundamental practices that took up precious minutes—such as washing their hands. Did you know, Gideon, that the breakdown of hospital hygiene was the single greatest cause of the '06 plague? And why? Why should people like doctors and nurses, people with lives dependent on them, feel such pressure?"

He spat at the ground, anger mixing with his sorrow. "Because our world had sanctified the goal not of success but of wealth. Not of sufficiency but of excess. And nothing has embodied and propagated that philosophy more than the Internet and all that has followed in its wake. All that mindless, endless marketing of useless goods to those who do not need them, who cannot afford them—until one day compassion is utterly destroyed by avarice gone mad. Politicians, insurance companies, and, yes, even doctors and nurses become so madly bound up in the desire for profit and acquisition that they forget that their first duty is to serve and to heal. They neglect every fundamental principle and practice—even something so simple as *washing their hands* . . ."

So there it was. Of all the people on the ship, Fouché was the one whose reasons for participation I hadn't yet been able to fathom, simply because molecular biology didn't seem to have any obvious connection to the business of revising history and combating the information society. And, as it turned out, it was less a professional imperative than a personal one that had driven him into this active exile.

"At any rate," he went on, "when I was a teacher to Malcolm and *les frères Kuperman,* I at first thought them simply an amusing collection of university pranksters. But when I later learned how deep their convictions ran, I decided I would cast my lot with them. And perhaps if we succeed—perhaps if Malcolm is right and the great body of the world's people can be shown the dangers of this age—then perhaps also the deaths of the millions in such nightmares as the epidemic will mean *something.*"

His eyes went narrow as he continued to watch the others, and then his voice picked up strength: "Ah! We are cleared to enter the tunnel, I see. Time for you to make your first appearance on the grand stage, Gideon!"

The events of the next hour or so were a strange but exhilarating combination of a visit to a hospital for the criminally insane and some boyhood adventure tale brought to life. Leaving the Kupermans to stand guard at the tunnel's entrance, Slayton, Tarbell, Fouché, and I made our way down through the Islamic terrorists' labyrinthine underground lair to an enormous chamber that was hung with silk banners. Against the walls of the chamber sat a collection of young women who appeared, through their veils, to be extremely beautiful, along with a dozen children. And atop some cushions placed on a plush carpet in the center of the space reclined its sole male occupant, that internationally infamous character who went by the rather ambitious name Suleyman ibn Muhammed. From the look of things in the chamber I guessed that ibn Muhammed was a firm believer in polygamy; and from the look in his eyes, I could see that he was also quite a disciple of opium, the sickly sweet smell of which mingled with the strong scent of earth to produce an oppressive atmosphere around us.

It was obvious that ibn Muhammed was in a deranged state, so I focused my attention on his women. Speaking through Tarbell—who turned out to be a master linguist, in keeping with his work as a consummate forger—I described what was about to happen to the countryside around them, using what imagery concerning divine fire I could remember from a college reading of the Koran. As I was speaking, the temperature, even that far underground, continued to rise at an alarming rate, and I pointed out that this had nothing to do with the Americans, which meant that if the women and children died, they would not enter Paradise as martyrs. Ibn Muhammed tried to voice protests but could make no sense; and so eventually the women took their children and followed us out, boarding one of the last vehicles to depart the area and leaving their leader behind to bake in what would shortly become an underground oven.

Our team got quickly and safely back aboard our vessel, to be greeted by Malcolm, whose condition was much improved. As the ship began to withdraw to the north, he asked a flood of questions about the mission, but I for one was utterly spent and told him that I couldn't possibly talk without getting some more substantial rest than I'd had that morning. Stumbling back through the corridors and into my quarters, I found them darkened, save for the glow of a lone candle that was sitting on an antique night table—

And by the light of that singularly low-tech implement, I could see Larissa waiting in my bed, naked under a comforter and smiling her most charming smile. Ordinarily this would hardly have been an unwelcome sight; but given all I'd heard that morning, there was nothing ordinary about the situation.

Larissa instantly read the trepidation in my face. "Oh, dear," she sighed, the silver hair wafting around her face and the dark eyes glittering. "The boys have been talking, I see."

"Yes," I said.

She studied me carefully, and behind the coyness I thought I could see genuine disappointment. "Scared you off, did they?"

I shook my head. "Not necessarily. But I'm curious, Larissa. You see, they ***didn't*** tell me the only story I really need to hear."

"Oh?" She dipped a finger in the candle's pooling wax. "And which one might that be?"

I took a tentative step inside the doorway. "What drove you and your brother to do all these things? Originally, I mean. I'm sorry, but I am a psychiatrist—you must've known that I'd ask. Surely Malcolm knew."

Larissa just kept smiling. "Yes. We both did. Well . . ." She lifted the comforter that covered her. "You'd better come to bed, Doctor, and let me explain."

I stepped fully inside and closed the door to my quarters just as, in the distance behind us, the first of the pilotless American fighter-bombers began to release their payloads, raining cataclysmic destruction down on the now-burning Afghan plain.

CHAPTER 19

That man's brutality conceals itself behind a respectable face more often than an evil one should come as news to no one, though I've never found it any less sad or infuriating for being so apparent. Having passed my own childhood among socially admired but covertly violent adults, I've always felt a particular kinship with those who have not only suffered abuse but suffered it at the hands of people who are deemed in some way estimable by society at large. Which is why, I'm sure, my comradeship with Larissa and Malcolm Tressalian was cemented so firmly during our journey north that morning. Among the many cases of childhood horror that I've investigated, theirs remains the only one I can call truly unique; and if ever there were a story guaranteed to rouse the familiar pangs of sorrow and outrage in my heart, the one that I listened to Larissa tell in the candlelit stillness of my quarters was it.

As I've mentioned, Malcolm and Larissa's father, Stephen Tressalian, was one of the first and most powerful leaders of the information revolution. A celebrated prodigy as a child, the elder Tressalian went on in early adulthood to design the hardware and software for an Internet routing system that became standard international equipment and the cornerstone of his empire. The achievement brought him fame, wealth, and a wife, a beautiful film actress possessed of that polished but no less pedestrian form of mental facility that so often passes for intelligence in Hollywood; and further dramatic innovations in the field of information delivery added even more stature to what had already become a household name.

From the beginning Stephen Tressalian was portrayed in the media as somchow nobler than the average information baron. He spoke about the social and political advances that information technology was supposedly bringing to the world often, publicly, and well—well enough to have legions of admirers among not only international business and political leaders but rank-and-file Internet users, as well. There was much tabloid interest, therefore, when the technocrat and his bride announced the birth of their first child, a boy, in 1991. As a toddler Malcolm displayed a precocious brilliance that equaled his sire's; yet that ambitious man was not to be satisfied with a son who could merely match his own achievements. Unlike most fathers, Stephen Tressalian longed for an heir who could outstrip him, believing that such would only add luster to his own legacy. And so he began to cast about for ways to artificially augment Malcolm's nascent genius.

By sinister coincidence, during the mid-1990s scientists at various universities and institutes were tampering with the genetic structure of intelligence in mice and other small animals by altering the biochemical mechanisms that controlled learning and memory. Responsible researchers shielded both their work and its as-yet-inconclusive findings from the general public, reminding the curious of the eternal biological verity that mice are not men. But rumors about the studies began to circulate, and before long there was irresponsible speculation about the possibility of genetically treating human children—whether in the womb or after birth—to enhance their ability to comprehend and store information.

For the right price, then as always, scientists could be found who were eager for a chance to experiment, even if illegally; and thus it was that Malcolm, at the age of only three, found himself entering a small private hospital in his family's home city of Seattle. The official explanation, formulated with almost incredible cunning by Stephen Tressalian and the gene therapist he had selected, was an attack of the new strain of antibiotic-resistant bacterial encephalitis that had been popping up in various parts of the world. In well-rehearsed, utterly convincing statements that prompted widespread public sympathy, Tressalian and his equally ambitious wife tearfully announced that Malcolm's case was so severe that he might emerge from his hospital stay with permanent neurological damage: an actual and distinct possibility, of course, given the experiments that were about to be performed on his mind.

I still shudder to think what those weeks must have been like. At first the treatments seemed to go well, and Malcolm exhibited a radically expanded mental capacity: a disorienting enough experience for a three-year-old. But then, midway into the course of the injections, his body seemed to rebel. Primitive functions—breathing, digestion, balance—became impaired, and there were unexplained bouts of terrible systemic pain and headache. The gene therapist had his own theory as to why—the human brain was not possessed of infinite resources, he told Stephen Tressalian, and with so much neuronal activity going to higher functions, there was the distinct possibility that the autonomic systems were being starved. But he was no physician, and Tressalian was too committed to his plan (as well as too afraid of being found out) to bring in any specialized medical help. Then too, despite all the terrible side effects, the boy's intellectual powers did continue to grow at an exponential rate, producing results that eventually satisfied even his father. After three months Stephen Tressalian called the project off, telling himself, his wife, and anyone else who knew about the work that it had been a gift for his son as well for genetic research and the future of mankind.

Small matter that when Malcolm emerged from the hospital—his arms gripping a pair of pathetic little crutches that had to do the work of his suddenly disobedient legs, and his hair mysteriously turned almost silver—he was faced by a crowd of reporters whose expressions of horror he was now entirely wise enough to comprehend. What was important was that the boy would be brilliant—no, *was* brilliant—and that the next time Stephen Tressalian engaged in such an experiment he would be armed with enough data to do a far better job.

For there *would* be a next time. Soon after Malcolm's release his mother became pregnant again, and this time it was she who entered the private hospital, as Stephen Tressalian's gene expert had determined that Malcolm's comparatively advanced stage of physical development had had something to do with his adverse reaction to the therapy. The fetus that would become Larissa received a refined course of injections *in utero,* and the change seemed to do the trick: when she was born her body exhibited none of her brother's physical disabilities, while the power of her mind was quickly revealed to be astounding. In addition, her beauty from the first looked to exceed even her mother's. In every way, Larissa seemed the living vindication of all the risks her parents had taken.

Of course, there was the strange matter of that silver hair, with which Larissa too had been born; but Stephen Tressalian refused to see this as anything other than a coincidence and emphasized the differences between his two children rather than their similarities.

"He never even *suspected* the most important thing that Malcolm and I had in common," Larissa said, as we lay on my bed together.

Yes, together: for her story had quickly transformed my uneasiness about her work as an assassin into an emotion that ran much deeper than the infatuation I'd felt to that point.

"Which was?" I murmured, touching her silvery locks and looking deep into her ebony eyes.

She looked at the ceiling rather blithely. "We were both a little mad. At least, I can't think of any other way to describe it."

It didn't seem an entirely serious statement. "I'm sure you were," I said in a tone to match hers. "And your parents never suspected?"

"Oh, Mother did," Larissa answered. "The entire time we were poisoning her she kept screaming to Father that she knew we were killing her and that we were both insane."

I propped myself up on my elbows and dropped the bit of her hair I'd been toying with. " 'Poisoning'?"

But Larissa didn't seem to hear me. "Father never would believe it, though," she went on. "That is, not until we pushed him out of the airplane. Then—just *then*—I think he realized that there might have been something to it . . ."

CHAPTER 20

I sat up on the bed. "How old were you?" was all I could think to say.

Larissa's face screwed up in a childlike fashion. "I was eleven when we took care of Mother. The business with Father happened about a year later."

Utterly at a loss, I found myself reverting to the role of psychiatrist. "And did they—was it—premeditated?"

She glanced at me a bit dubiously. "Gideon, *everything* Malcolm and I do is premeditated. It's what we were bred for. But if what you're really asking is whether or not there was provocation, then the answer is yes, there was." She looked at the ceiling again. "Rather a lot, actually."

I kept watching her, retreating further into professional objectivity yet somehow angry with myself for the reaction. "Such as what?" I asked.

She suddenly gave me a small, genuinely happy smile and pulled me back down against her warm body. "I like sleeping with you," she said. "I wasn't sure I would."

I returned the smile as best I could. "A gift for flattery was not, apparently, the primary goal of your genetic engineering."

"I'm sorry," she laughed. "It's just that—"

"Larissa," I said, touching her mouth. "If you don't want to tell me about it, you don't have to."

She took my hand. "No, I will," she said simply. "It's really not very complicated." She turned to the ceiling again. "Father'd bred me to be smarter and prettier than Mother—so I suppose it shouldn't have been much of a surprise when he decided that he'd rather have sex with me than with her." I winced in shock, but Larissa proceeded with a detachment not uncommon to victims of such trauma. "She thought it was my fault—he'd have sex with me, and then she'd beat me for it. Malcolm always tried to stop both of them. But he's never had any real physical strength." Her eyes glistened with profound love and admiration. "You should have seen him, though—swinging those crutches at them, calling them every evil name imaginable."

"Which they deserved," I said. "You know that, don't you?"

She nodded. "Cognitively, as they say. Emotionally—it's a bit trickier. So—eventually we decided we'd just have to get rid of them. Mother first, because she was not only vicious but completely useless. Father—well, we had to wait, to let him finish building the satellites."

"You went on enduring *that,*" I said, once again stunned, "because you wanted him to finish the *four-gigabyte satellite system?*"

"Well, I knew how much it would be worth to Malcolm and me once he was dead," Larissa replied. "The reinvention of the Internet? Yes, I could endure his touch a few more times if it meant that my brother and I would get those profits. Then, once the system was in place and working smoothly, Father was called in on the '07 economic summit. So we waited until after that. Right after. We went to

Washington with him—even got to meet the president. On the jet back to Seattle it was just the three of us. He was very pleased with himself—why shouldn't he have been? He and his friends had just become the most powerful people in the country. He got drunk. Fell against the emergency hatch and released it during descent. Apparently." Letting out a brief sigh, Larissa held up one finger. "Fortunately, his loving children were smart enough to be wearing their seat belts and to keep their heads while the copilot got things back under control." She shook her head. "I never will forget the look on his face . . ."

As she said all this, the objective detachment I'd been feeling began, without my quite realizing it, to deteriorate, overcome by a set of powerful empathetic reactions that were remnants of my own troubled past. And so, at that crucial moment, I simply put my hand to her face and said, "I suppose it made the assassinations easier—having already done, well, *that*."

She shrugged. "I suppose it must have. But more than making it easier, I think it inspired me. It was quite a feeling, destroying people who so thoroughly deserved it. I got to have quite a taste for the experience. I remember that when I shot Rajiv Karamchand—"

"*You* shot him?" Karamchand, of course, was the Indian president who had authorized the use of the first atomic weapons in the Kashmir war. Despite the best efforts of many intelligence agencies, his murder had remained a mystery.

Larissa smiled and nodded. "And when I did it, I felt just the way that I had watching Father fall out of that plane. A man who takes responsibility for the lives and well-being of others and then betrays that trust so completely—I really can't think of anything quite as vile. Plus"—she turned over onto her stomach, her words coming faster—"think about this: Why has there always been such a taboo against assassination? It's ludicrous. A political leader can order people to their deaths or to kill others, and corporate executives can commit any kind of crime in the name of trade—yet they're all considered untouchable. Why? Why should Karamchand have felt any safer when he went to bed at night than one of his own soldiers or than the Pakistanis he slaughtered? Why should an executive who profits from slave labor be immune to the terror his workers feel? The odd assassination is the only way to make people like that start to think a little more seriously about what they do. As for making the *rest* of the world think a little harder about whose orders they decide to follow and what they choose to believe—well, that's the whole point of what we're doing now, isn't it?"

I weighed the statement. "Yes, I can see that," I answered slowly. "Though I still don't get what part *I'm* supposed to play in it all."

Larissa threw her arms around my neck, again looking very pleased. "Keeping me happy—isn't that enough?" Seeing the continued look of inquiry in my face, she feigned a frown. "No? All right—the truth is, Malcolm wanted a psychological profiler. We made up a list, and your background in history put you at the top of it. Then"—she moved in to kiss me—"when I saw that picture of you . . ."

As she pulled her lips away again, I asked, "But why a profiler?"

"Our various opponents," she whispered. "They've been responding in fairly inscrutable ways. The Americans, for instance, with that ridiculous raid on Afghanistan. They had suspicions that the Khaldun footage was doctored. We even gave them hints. But they went ahead anyway. Malcolm wants you to try to predict things like that. And, of course, perform the odd little job like the one in the tunnel back there—"

Larissa was cut off when the entire ship suddenly shook more violently than it had at any time since I'd been aboard. I spun toward the tinted transparent panel in the hull near the bed and saw dim, eerie light outside: apparently, we'd once again climbed to a very high altitude. Against the mists of the stratosphere and the darkness of space beyond I could see dozens of glowing objects streaking toward us. Most of them were fairly small, I saw as they passed; but some, as they approached, grew to a considerable and disturbing size.

A second explosion lit up the sky around us and rocked the ship again, knocking me off the bed. When I righted myself I saw that Larissa was already halfway into her bodysuit and had one hand to her throat, activating the surgically implanted communicator that linked her to Malcolm. "Yes, Brother dear," she said, looking more annoyed than concerned at the peril into which we'd suddenly been thrown. "I can see them—it would be a little difficult not to. I'm on my way to the turret now with Gideon. Tell Julien to divert whatever power he can to the external fields—you know how damned unpredictable these things are."

I started to hurry into my own clothes. "What's happening?" I said, trying to match her calm.

"Our admirers in the Defense Department," she muttered, looking outside. "One of their pilots must've caught sight of our ship in Afghanistan. Looks like they've deployed their whole collection of toys: EKVs, LEAPs, ERIs—there's even an SBL out there."

"Larissa," I said, doing up my coveralls, "arcane acronyms really aren't going to reassure me right now."

Even in the midst of such an attack—or perhaps because of it—Larissa became playful and coy: "No, but you'll need to memorize these things, Doctor," she said, giving me a quick kiss. "Believe me, there *will* be a test." She began to point around the sky at the streaking objects. "Lightweight exoatmospheric projectiles, or LEAPs—they're the smaller ones. Then there are the extended range interceptors, or ERIs, and the exoatmospheric kill vehicles—"

"EKVs," I said, watching the wild display outside.

"And the really troublesome bastard," she finished, pointing to some sort of satellite or platform in the distance. "An SBL—space-based laser. All part of THAAD, the 'theater high-altitude area defense' against ballistic missiles. You know, the Star Wars nonsense." She grabbed my hand, and we rushed out into the corridor.

"How accurate are they?" I said.

"It's not their accuracy we have to worry about," Larissa answered, moving toward the ladder that led up to the ship's turret and the big rail gun inside it. "The THAAD boys have never managed to hit *anything* intentionally. But that doesn't keep them from throwing all that firepower around the atmosphere like they're in some kind of high-tech spitball fight—and an accidental hit could do real damage."

We reached the ladder and started up. "It's a little like skeet shooting," Larissa said with a laugh as we entered the turret to find Eli Kuperman waiting for us. "And don't worry, they're all unmanned vehicles, so you won't actually be killing anybody." She climbed into the seat of the rail gun and smiled at me in a devious way that hours earlier would have seemed very disconcerting.

Now, however, I found myself smiling back.

CHAPTER 21

As Larissa began to direct the rail cannon's fire in every direction, pounding away with glowing bursts at the midsize and larger interceptors that were being sent against us (the ship's magnetic fields deflected the smaller ones), the stratosphere was lit up by dozens of explosions, as well as by the indiscriminate but no less dangerous fire of the space-based laser. My job during the encounter was to help Eli try to determine just which long-range radar station was giving our position away to the American THAAD command. Apparently there were only a few monitoring sites sophisticated enough to be able to thwart our ship's stealth technology by doggedly fixing on the confusing combination of wave reflections and absorptions that the vessel was orchestrating (and that the Americans had presumably tagged as ours after they'd made visual contact in Afghanistan). Using the banks of equipment in the turret, Eli—operating in that cool but no less energized and sometimes even jovial manner that I now accepted as normal for everyone on board the ship—finally determined that a remote English base was the most likely culprit. His hypothesis was confirmed by Leon Tarbell, who, working on a lower deck, managed to intercept and descramble a series of communications between the English and American air forces.

We needed to know all this, Eli explained, because now that our ship was definitely being tracked, once we dropped back down out of the stratosphere, we could expect to be greeted by more conventional but no less deadly air ordnance than was currently being thrown against us. If we could determine what and whose planes they were going to be, Colonel Slayton could program our ship's computers to fly in an appropriately evasive pattern at a requisite speed. Eli seemed quite confident that this represented no overwhelming challenge, and as we talked over the prospect of going up against warplanes—be they human- or computer-piloted—I found myself being infected by his eager, slightly piratical enthusiasm.

This surprising reaction was only heightened when the ship's alert system went off, letting us know that we were beginning to descend and needed to get ready for a new and perhaps deadlier kind of action. Our enemy now would be not some antiballistic missile system that since its deluded inception had been destined for failure, but attack craft fully intent on shooting us down. Apparently there had been other such encounters; indeed, according to various radio transmissions intercepted by Tarbell in months past, Malcolm's ship had assumed a sort of mythical status among the world's air forces and navies. And given the very powerful ordnance that the warplanes of such countries as England and the United States were now routinely carrying, along with the skill of the pilots who both flew them personally and—as in the case of the American raid on Afghanistan—guided them from the remote safety of theirs ships and bases, escape had sometimes been a near thing.

So it would be on this occasion. As we dropped into the cloudy skies over the North Sea near the fifty-ninth parallel, we were almost immediately intercepted by Royal Air Force fighters. The planes struck dark, angular silhouettes against the setting sun, giving them a very intimidating appearance. When I turned to Larissa, I saw her sizing them up with a nod and a defiant smile; but concern was evident in her look, as well.

"Gideon," she called to me, "see if you can find out what's happening forward, will you?" She clutched the control handles of the cannon tightly but did not fire. "My brother doesn't like to use lethal force in situations like this, but if those things don't actually have pilots I'm going to indulge myself . . ."

Rushing down the ladder and through the corridor, I entered the nose of the ship to find Malcolm and Colonel Slayton at the control panels, Slayton calmly but quickly tapping information into one of the guidance terminals. "They're the new Joint Strike Force ultra-stealth models," he said. "First-day-of-war, highly survivable aircraft, armed with AIM-10 Predator missiles that can carry biological, nuclear, or conventional warheads."

"Manned?" Malcolm asked.

"I'm afraid so. They haven't worked the kinks out of the remote guidance system on this model, yet." Slayton turned to give Tressalian a very serious look. "We may not be able to get out of this without returning fire."

Malcolm—who, I now noticed, looked somewhat feverish—seemed deeply troubled by this statement; before he could answer it, however, Tarbell's voice came over the shipwide address system. "They're hailing us," he said. Then he patched the voice of one of the pilots through: "Unidentified aircraft: you are in violation of British airspace. Accompany our escort to the nearest field or be fired upon."

Touching a keypad on the console in front of him, Malcolm replied pointedly, "*English* aircraft: as far as we're concerned this is

Scottish Republican airspace. You therefore have no authority to challenge us." He turned to Slayton. "Can we outrun them?"

Slayton shrugged. "We haven't come up against this model yet. We *should* be able to, but they've got a signature lock now—wherever we go they'll be able to track us, and if we head for the island they'll come after us with a lot more than just a squadron. We could dive, but we'll have to slow down—not much, but it would be enough to let one of the Predators catch up to us. And over the open sea I don't think they'd hesitate to go nuclear. The only choice I can see is going back up, but—"

There was a moment's silence, leaving it to me to step in: "But what?"

Malcolm, whose face was definitely growing paler by the minute, tapped a finger impatiently. "Colonel Slayton is attempting to be tactful, Gideon. The truth is that we've been away for an unusually long stretch, this trip, and it's becoming somewhat urgent, as I'm sure you've noticed, that I get back to our medical facilities on the island." Beads of sweat began to form on his brow, as had happened before: clearly another attack was coming. Knowing the origins of his mysterious illness and the circumstances of his past as I now did, I was filled with even greater sympathy than I had been on the first occasion. I also felt heightened respect for his stoicism: "This really is irritating," was his summation of the situation. "All right, then, Colonel, if we must—" He stopped suddenly, listening; then he held a hand to his collar. "You're sure?" he said over the link to his sister. He began to crane his neck, looking all around the transparent sheathing of the hull. "How far? I can't see—wait, there they are!"

Slayton and I turned with him to catch sight of another squadron of planes descending from behind and above us. Their silhouettes were more conventional than those of the British planes, and they weren't as fast—clearly, these were much older models. But they nonetheless swept in to engage the superior craft of our pursuers courageously. As they passed close by, I could see that they had large crosses of Saint Andrew painted on their fuselages.

To my puzzled look Slayton said, "Some of our friends in the Scottish Republican Air Force, Dr. Wolfe."

One of the results of England's international redefinition following the controversy over the Churchill-Princip letters that had "revealed" British leaders to have been responsible for the First World War had been a decision by the Scottish Parliament to formally declare its nation's independence. What was unknown to the world was that Malcolm's team, having forged those letters, had been indirectly responsible for that momentous vote. In addition, when Malcolm had sold his controlling interest in the Tressalian Corporation so that he could devote himself fully to his disinformation campaign, he'd used some of the fantastic proceeds to secretly purchase a group of small Hebridean islands from the Scots. The price had been substantial enough to allow Edinburgh to launch an effective armed resistance to England's efforts to resubjugate its northern neighbor, and in the years since, Malcolm had continued to contribute generously to what London insisted on calling "the Scottish rebellion" but the rest of the world had dubbed "the Scottish war of independence." Some of the practical results of his generosity were apparently now on display in the air around us.

"But will they really attack the English planes?" I asked. "They don't look like they'd stand a chance."

"They wouldn't," Slayton said. "They're flying old Harriers, armed with Sparrows—too slow, and not enough punch. But that's not the point. All they have to do is keep the English planes occupied long enough to give us a chance to dive."

So they, and we, did: within moments our ship was once again under the waves. We cruised quickly through the Pentland Firth and westward into the Atlantic, then southwest, at a shallow enough depth to be able to tell that the ocean surface above us was extremely agitated. I was nevertheless unprepared for just how rough the waves were when we shot back up into the air: it was fortunate that we didn't have to ride them but could cruise along at an altitude of some fifty feet.

In a matter of minutes our destination became visible: seven small bits of land dotted the water ahead. As we approached, I could see that they were marked by high, dramatic rock formations, hidden coves, and windswept green fields.

"Well, Gideon," Malcolm said, his discomfort alleviated at least somewhat by the prospect of an end to our journey, "welcome. Welcome to the Islands at the Edge of the World . . ."

CHAPTER 22

Such, apparently, was the sobriquet long ago given to the little archipelago that was collectively known as St. Kilda. Protected most of the year by waters so rough that ships did not even attempt to approach it, St. Kilda seemed the perfect haven for Malcolm and his team. It had been uninhabited by humans since 1930 and was now home primarily to a fantastic assortment of seabirds—gannets, kittiwakes, puffins, and the like—which flocked so densely at various points that they changed the very color of the landscape. But what was most striking about the islands was their air of almost palpable mystery: the sea-sculpted rocks, remnants of an ancient volcano, bespoke a shielded past full of dark secrets and perilous adventures. A romantic assessment, perhaps; but then, by the time we landed I had become possessed by every kind of romance.

On the main island of Hirta, Malcolm had constructed the base of his operations near the decaying remains of a small village that was centuries old. The buildings that made up his facility were cleverly designed to match those older stone ruins, though the technology that the newer structures housed could not have belonged any less to the past. All maintenance and operative systems were so fully automated that there was no need for any human presence at all; the island could be left deserted for weeks or even months at a time. As to style, the interior of the compound echoed the marked contrast aboard ship: functional minimalism in the laboratories and control rooms, inviting antiques in the living and lounging areas. Housed in one mock church was the projection unit for the ozone weapon, which apparently could also be used to adjust conditions on the island temporarily when the climate of the North Atlantic became too severe.

As Larissa and Colonel Slayton got Malcolm settled into his regimen of rest, self-treatment, and self-medication (he had an understandable aversion to doctors), the others showed me to a room that had a truly striking view of an eerie cove and the sea beyond. During the next two weeks or so, as Malcolm privately regained his strength and then went to work in a lab that he reserved as his sanctum, I passed the time with the rest of the team, investigating the islands, learning more about the technologies the group had developed, and pondering the effects of our recent escapades. It was an energizing time, and as it passed I became aware that I was speaking and acting not like Dr. Gideon Wolfe of Manhattan, professor at John Jay University and respected member of American society, but rather as someone who, like the others, had renounced his native citizenship and become a man without a country. When I'd boarded Malcolm's ship in the Belle Isle prison, I'd become an outlaw—in the finest sense of the word, I told myself, but such distinctions would matter very little if I crossed paths with the authorities. And so I dived headlong into my new role, discussing potential new hoaxes and learning about new weapons and technologies during the day and becoming ever more passionately fascinated by Larissa at night.

It seems a dream now, a dream to which I would gladly return if only I could forget the horror that woke me from it.

That horror was not without its warnings, though in those early days I was far too swept up by emotional and intellectual excitement to recognize them. The first still stands out vividly: one evening, with the sun bouncing off the cove outside the leaded bay window in my room (at that time of the year it became truly dark on St. Kilda for only about three hours each night), I happened to be going through the jacket I'd been wearing during the jailbreak just days earlier and found the original computer disc that Mrs. Price had given me. Staring at it, my first thoughts were of Max: not as I'd last seen him, with much of his head removed by a CIA sniper's bullet, but alive and as full of banter and laughter as he'd always been. Then, slowly, I recalled the information that was on the disc—*all* the information. I'd been so focused on matters surrounding the Forrester assassination that I'd completely forgotten that Max had managed to crack the encryption of a second set of images: the old footage of a Nazi death camp, through which wandered the digitally inserted silhouette of an unidentifiable figure.

Popping the disc into a computer terminal that sat at a rustic desk by the bay window, I called up those images and reviewed them once again.

"Anything good?"

I started a little at the sound of Larissa's voice and turned to see her striding quickly through my open door. I let out a small, pleased groan as she threw herself into my lap, kissed me quickly, and then turned her dark eyes to the monitor. "What in the world is that? Trying your hand at a little revisionism, are you?"

"You mean you don't recognize it?" I said, surprised.

Larissa shook her head. "Doesn't quite look finished, whatever it is."

"No," I said, replaying the images. "Max found it on the disc that

Price's wife gave us. I'd forgotten about it—and when I saw it again I assumed it must have been another job Price did for your brother."

"If it is, I've never heard anything about it." Larissa leapt up and went to a glowing keypad by my bed. "Maybe Leon knows something." She touched a few of the keys. "Leon, come over to Gideon's room, will you? He's found something odd."

In a few minutes Leon Tarbell came shooting in, a cigarette hanging out of his mouth. "Well, what is your mystery, Gideon?" he said. "I was rather busy when you—" He stopped suddenly when he saw the images on the screen. "What the devil is *that*?" As I explained the origins of the disc once again, Tarbell's gaze focused ever more intently on the gray figure on the monitor.

"I know who that is," he said, fascinated yet frustrated. "Yes, I'm *certain* I know who that is, but I can't seem to—there, you see? When he turns in profile. I *know* I've seen that silhouette somewhere before."

"That's exactly how I felt the first time I watched it," I answered with a nod. "But I couldn't place—"

"Wait!" A look of sudden recognition came into Tarbell's satanic features, and then he rushed around to the computer's keyboard. "I believe I may be able to . . ." His words trailed off as he went to work on the keyboard. Then a new succession of images began to rapidly appear and disappear on the screen.

"What is it, Leon?" Larissa asked. "*Was* Price doing something other than the Forrester job for Malcolm?"

Tarbell shrugged. "If he didn't tell *you,* Larissa darling, he certainly wouldn't tell the rest of us. But as for *this* mysterious fellow—" He pointed to the screen, where the footage of the concentration camp reappeared, frozen on one frame. Tarbell tapped at the keyboard a few more times with a bit of a flourish. "Here . . . he . . . *is*!"

The mysterious silhouette was suddenly filled in perfectly by a photograph of a man whose name we all knew well:

"Stalin," I said, more confused than ever.

"Yes, it's Stalin, all right," Larissa agreed, looking as perplexed as I felt. "But what interest could Price have had in placing *him* at a Nazi death camp?"

Tarbell only shrugged again, while I asked, "Do you think it's important? I mean, maybe we should ask Malcolm—"

"No, Gideon," Larissa said definitively. "Not now. I've just come from him. He worked all night and drove himself straight into another attack."

My attention diverted to Malcolm's condition, I wondered aloud, "What does he *do* in that lab, anyway?"

Larissa shrugged in frustration. "He won't say, but he's been at it for months. Whatever it is, I wish he'd drop it—he needs rest desperately. As for this business—" She reached over to shut off the terminal screen, then removed the disc and tossed it to Tarbell. "I'd say it was just some movie that Price was working on. Forget it, Dr. Wolfe." She turned my face toward hers and moved in to kiss me. "Right now I require your full attention."

Tarbell cleared his throat. "My cue," he said, pocketing the disc and leaving as quickly as he'd come. "I told you once, Gideon—you're a lucky man . . ."

Perhaps I was. But luck is, of course, transitory; and had I known how close mine was to changing at that moment or how much the disc I'd rediscovered would have to do with that change, I would never have let myself be distracted, even by Larissa. For a completed version of the images we'd been watching would all too soon trigger a crime so incomprehensible that it would bring even our senselessly hyperactive world to an astonished, bewildered halt. It would also propel me into this, my jungle exile in Africa, where I await the arrival of my former comrades with the most profound confusion and dread I have ever known.

CHAPTER 23

As the rest of us continued to wait for Malcolm to emerge from his laboratory and announce that it was time to move on to some new deceptive enterprise, patience at times became difficult to sustain—though I'll admit that it was, as Leon Tarbell repeatedly pointed out, easier for Larissa and me than for the others. In fact, so agitated did Tarbell become over the mere thought that members of our group other than himself were engaged in a physical relationship that he first almost fatally electrocuted himself in a supposed "virtual reality sex suit" (really nothing more than thin rubber long johns embedded with powerful electrodes) and then, a few days later, took a small jetcopter that was stored in one of the mock barns of the compound and headed off for Edinburgh. As he prepared to lift off, I pointed out that Glasgow was closer, but this only brought a look of supreme disdain to his mercurial features.

"Drunken laborers and heroin addicts!" he bellowed. "No,

Gideon, the prostitutes of Edinburgh service sex-starved lawyers and deviant politicians—they have immense sexuality, they are for me!"

And with a roar of the aircraft's engines he was gone.

So began a most remarkable evening. I was, unusually, alone, because Larissa had decided to keep watch through the night by her still ailing brother's bedside, to make sure that he spent the time resting rather than working in his laboratory. Again I found myself speculating about what could possibly be consuming the man so ravenously; and it occurred to me that while Larissa had said she didn't know, the ever-secretive and reticent Colonel Slayton might. On asking around I discovered that Slayton had ensconced himself in the compound's communications monitoring room. So I set off to see whether or not, with my supposed psychological guile, I could maneuver him into revealing something about Malcolm's activities.

The monitoring room was located in a mock tavern opposite the church that housed the projection unit of Malcolm's ozone weapon. Beneath the tavern was an underground chamber some hundred yards square, which housed the equipment that did the actual work of listening in on the world's electronic communications, both official and private. The governments of the United States and its English-speaking allies had for decades operated a similar system called Echelon that required several such monitoring installations, each made up of acres of equipment: once again, Malcolm had achieved the next level of technological development.

I knocked on the simulated wood exterior of the room's door several times without receiving any answer. But as I could hear unintelligible chattering noises within, it seemed safe to assume that the colonel was indeed at work. So I quietly entered—only to be faced with one of the stranger tableaux that I had come across since my arrival.

The overhead lights in the room were out, but the darkness in the windowless chamber was cut by the light of some twenty monitors, most not particularly large but a few taking up the better part of a wall. The flashing shapes on these screens at first appeared nonsensical, but as my eyes adjusted to the gently stroboscopic light I realized that they were rapidly changing bodies of text, both encrypted and decoded, as well as an occasional blueprint or diagram. Each screen's contents varied from the next, and the cacophony that I'd heard outside, which became quite deafening once I entered, was being produced by dozens of audio signals—again, some intelligible and some encoded—that were playing at the same time.

Slayton sat at a console in the midst of all this, facing the largest pair of monitors and staring at them, even though the information that was flashing across their screens was clearly moving too fast for him to comprehend fully. Wanting to ask what in the world he was doing and unable to gain his attention even through the loudest and most absurdly theatrical of throat clearings, I took one or two steps further into the room. But then I froze:

As I came around his side, I could see that the long scar on his face had been moistened by a thin stream of tears. His expression, however, was as dispassionate as ever: only the slightest quiver of his grimly set jaw indicated any emotion at all. In such a man, however, even so tiny a movement bespoke volumes.

It was a moment of profound embarrassment for me, and I tried to end it by slowly retracing my steps to the door. But before I'd gotten halfway there I saw the colonel's hand reach slowly for a keypad, and touch one of its glowing keys with a finger. The volume in the room came quickly down to a level that only intensified my embarrassment. Then, without turning, Slayton said quietly:

"What you're hearing and seeing, Doctor, are the transmissions of various defense and intelligence agencies around the world."

"Ah" was all I could think to answer.

"Tell me," Slayton went on. "Is it true that the human ear is not sensitive enough to detect dishonesty?"

There seemed to be nothing to do but continue the conversation. "Most of the time, yes," I said. "Those kinds of interpretations are usually emotional judgment calls, not perceptive certainties."

The colonel grunted. "Perhaps. Perhaps my ear has simply become finely turned over the years. But I can tell you with absolute certainty, Doctor, that this"—he raised the volume in the room again—"*this* is the sound of *lying* . . ."

I don't know how long I stood there, watching Slayton's rigid form as he continued to stare at the enormous monitors. Eventually he reached out to knock the volume back down, and then, after quite openly dabbing at his scar as well as his opposite cheek with a handkerchief, he turned his chair to face me. "Something I can do for you, Dr. Wolfe?" he asked, scrutinizing me with curiosity.

"I—I was wondering—" As I fumbled for words, it occurred to me that Slayton might be taking pleasure from my discomfort; but further inspection of his features revealed nothing to support such a suspicion. "I was wondering about Malcolm, actually. If I could be of any medical assistance."

"You think he needs psychiatric help?" Oddly enough, the question seemed entirely sincere.

"That wasn't what I meant," I answered. "But I *am* a doctor, I can recognize chronic pain when I see it. And Larissa's told me his—story."

"Has she?" Slayton's eyes narrowed. "Well, if she's told you that, Doctor, then you must already have concluded that there's nothing you or anyone else can do. Pain medication and rest—that's all there is for him. That's all there ever has been."

"And clearly he has no trouble taking medication," I said, detecting an opening. "But why isn't he getting enough rest?"

Something vaguely approximating a smile seemed to creep into one corner of the colonel's mouth. "Clever, Doctor," he said. "But I can't answer that. None of us can. For the simple reason that none of us, not even Larissa, knows what work is keeping him from sleeping."

"I see." Glancing around the room I asked, "And you?"

The phantom smile seemed to gain some substance. "Jonah and I have been assembling and installing a holographic projection mechanism for the ship. It should allow us to move about unseen and avoid messes like the business in Florida."

"That's possible?"

Slayton inclined his head judiciously. "We were close at the Pentagon. Malcolm believes he's worked out the details."

"Ah." I stood my ground, shuffling a bit. "But that—that really doesn't explain all this, does it?" I indicated the screens.

I don't know what kind of a reaction I expected to such a direct question, but it certainly wasn't the one I got. Slayton chuckled good-naturedly, then held one hand out to an empty chair that was next to his. "Sit down, Doctor, and I'll explain," he said. "Since the entire idea depends on *you* . . ."

CHAPTER 24

As I took my place by the colonel, he said, "In some priestly and monastic orders the custom of self-flagellation is still practiced. Do you find such behavior aberrant, Doctor?"

"Extreme," I replied, looking up with him at the monitors. "But not aberrant. Is that what this is for you—self-flagellation? With painful light and sound taking the place of the whip?"

"In some way, I'm sure it is," Slayton answered with a frankness that was, like everything else about the man, very impressive. "For most of my life, Doctor, this world"—he indicated the screens—"was the wilderness into which I traveled, battling to bring the faith of democracy to the heathens. Until . . ." His attention began to wander, but he soon caught himself. "It's one thing to discover that your god has feet of clay. It's quite another to find that those feet are soaked in blood. Not only the blood of your enemies but of your comrades, as well. And to realize that you yourself were complicitous in their deaths. Complicitous—by omission . . ."

I watched as tears welled up in his eyes again, then said, "Colonel, you're thinking of the Taiwan campaign. But you can't—"

"Bosnia, Serbia, Iraq, Colombia, and yes, Taiwan," he interjected quickly. "Or any of the half-dozen other places where I killed and let my troops be killed in the name of freedom. Can you imagine what it was like to discover that the only freedom my superiors were ever really interested in was the freedom of their moneyed masters to do business in those places? I'm not a fool, Dr. Wolfe. At least, I don't like to think of myself as one. Why, then, didn't I see it? Any of it? The international trade organizations and security alliances whose authority we guaranteed—did they ever stamp out tyranny, exploitation, or inequality in any of the places we were told they would? Did they ever bring real freedom to a single country that didn't already have it?"

Slayton shook a tightly clutched fist. "And yet we continued to obey. To shed our enemies' blood for them and let our own soldiers die. Then in Taiwan, it became obvious that we were there only *to* die—that Washington had no intention of stopping Beijing's takeover, that they were actually *in league* with the commu-capitalists. I held no brief for the government of Taiwan then, Doctor, and I still don't. But why should my troops have died for that kind of cynicism? And above all"—Slayton's chest heaved mightily—"*why* didn't I *see* it?"

I shrugged—there was no point pulling punches with such a person: *"Mundus vult decipi,"* I said quietly.

His fleeting smile returned. "Thank you, Doctor."

"I'm sorry—"

"No, I'm perfectly serious. Thank you for not patronizing me with false rationalizations. Yes, everyone wants to be deceived, and so did I. I wanted to believe the lessons I'd learned as a boy. When my father came home from the Persian Gulf in a bag and we buried him at Arlington, I wanted to believe that his war hadn't been one of blood for oil. Somewhere deep inside me the genes that had been passed along from an African slave told me I was being a fool, but I didn't listen. I fought every attempt to expose the deception. And then, in Taiwan . . . it all fell apart. By the time I went to work in the Pentagon I was a ghost, one who, having *been* deceived, learned *to* deceive. And I would have stayed a ghost if I'd never met Malcolm. Yet even during my time with this team, something's been missing." He turned to me, his face full of purpose. "Something that *you,* Doctor, are going to help me put right."

Somewhat taken aback, I asked, "Why me?"

In reply Slayton stood and moved around the room. "Psychology and American history, Doctor—I require your expertise." He folded his hands together once and wrung them hard. "It would surprise you, I think, to learn that I lobbied very hard to get you on this team."

I almost laughed in amazement. "I'll admit that it would."

"Not that it was a tough sell, once they read your book." Slayton picked a copy of that same *Psychological History of the United States* up off the console and began leafing through it. "*And* saw your picture," he went on, sounding for a moment like a knowing, mildly disapproving father. "Your selection at that point was guaranteed. But I was the one who brought you to their attention." He stopped his leafing and focused on one page of the volume, then gave me a bemused look. "Do you *really* think that the death of Jefferson's mother had something to do with his writing the Declaration of Independence?"

I chose my words more carefully than I had in the book: "The timing of the two events always struck me as too close to be a coincidence. They had a difficult relationship, by all accounts."

Slayton nodded. "There was a time when such an idea would have disgusted me, Doctor. When this entire book would have disgusted me. You force the American nation onto the couch and find it laced with neuroses."

"A good deal more than neuroses," I ventured.

"Yes," Slayton said. "And as I say, once I would have cursed you for it. But now . . ." His voice trailed off again as his eyes fixed on the dancing light on the floor.

"Colonel," I said, "please don't take this as any diminution of your own feelings, but—surely you realize that what you're going through is nothing new in the American experience? The 'deception' you're describing is only the need to believe in the inherent philosophical and ethical superiority of the United States—what's generally called our moral exceptionalism. And it's been with us since the beginning. Any country commits great crimes to reach a position of unchallengeable power; ours was no exception. A method of rationalizing those crimes has to be devised for people to be able to live with themselves."

"All true," Slayton said, still looking at the floor. "But you and I are going to shake the foundations of that exceptionalism."

My comforting little sermon suddenly went out the window. "We are?" I said.

Slayton nodded slowly, then snapped out of his reverie, turned his chair to face mine, and sat down. "I spoke with Malcolm an hour ago. He was deeply angered by the Afghanistan raid, even though we got the people out. He's agreed to my suggestion—the same hypocrisy that has rationalized everything from the enslavement of my ancestors to that same Afghan raid will be the target of our next job. He's leaving it to you and me to work out the details."

"Oh." I took it in as best I could: I'd expected to be *part* of the next effort, but to *design* it . . . "Well—did you have any specific thoughts?"

"Not yet," Slayton answered. "I've been sitting here with your book trying to come up with something, but every time I start to consider it my mind gets so swept up in—"

He stopped suddenly, his head cocking as he listened to the

noises coming from the monitoring equipment. "There it is again," he murmured. "That's three times tonight."

"What's three times tonight?"

Slayton shook his head, still listening; and it dawned on me that what he'd called his "finely tuned" ear was actually capable of picking individual messages out of the confusing din. "It's the Mossad," he said. "Israeli intelligence. Three times tonight I've caught pieces of wireless calls from or to several of their European operatives. They keep talking about some kind of terrorist activity that's focused around a German concentration camp."

I considered it. "Might be the militant wing of New Germany," I offered. "Ever since the Freedom Party took over in Austria, their friends across the border have been getting mighty obstreperous."

"It's possible," Slayton said, clearly unconvinced. "But the Israelis seem much too worked up for it to be just European head butting. Well"—he reached over and shut off the room's audio and visual monitors altogether—"we have our own work to attend to, Doctor."

And thus did another clue to the staggering tragedy that was shortly to engulf us appear and fade very nearly unnoticed. Even now I cannot speculate on how many lives might have been spared had Slayton and I chosen at that juncture to listen more closely to the mysterious messages that were speeding through our monitoring systems—for contemplating such lost opportunities would surely lead to madness.

CHAPTER 25

How ingenious, how *vital* did the scheme that Colonel Slayton and I concocted over the ensuing days seem at the time—and how proud was I to be working alongside a man whose deeds had inspired young boys and shamed grown men! Though there was never any question of actual *equality* in our partnership, Slayton was a more-than-indulgent (if occasionally cutting) tutor, and we quickly established an effective working rhythm that allowed us to outline a plan of attack within the first twenty-four hours. The next forty-eight fairly flew by, and by the end of the third day we were certain that we had contrived a plan that would more than serve our purpose—although the only way to be certain was to test it on our colleagues.

We waited a day longer to do so, until Tarbell returned from his excursion. Grinning in deep satisfaction and walking with an exhausted, limping gait, Leon entered the room in which the rest of us (save Malcolm) had gathered for dinner to announce that he was ready for a decent meal—"How can the Scots *exist* on such food?"—and a productive conversation (apparently it was only after he'd spent a few days with women of "immense sexuality" that he was possessed of truly sound judgment). With that assurance, Slayton nodded my way: he'd earlier decided that I should be the one to actually propose the plan, saying that he lived in the world of action, not words, and would only wind up making a hash of it. In view of its source I allowed the implied slight to roll directly off my back and began to outline what we'd come up with.

By way of introduction, I noted that the team's successes to that point seemed to me to have rested on one element above all: plausibility. Each hoax had been accepted by the public because it had made some kind of fundamental sense. American politicians, for example, really were little more than televised ciphers to most people; whereas anyone who was aware of Winston Churchill's remarkable cunning and willingness to sacrifice human life in pursuit of his political goals would have had no trouble accepting the Princip letters. As for Jesus, little about his life had ever been verifiable; and even the thousands of fossils that archaeologists and anthropologists had unearthed over the years had not provided any absolutely indisputable proof of the evolution of man. Finally, of course, with respect to the Forrester footage, people had always been willing to blame just about anything on Islamic terrorists. Therefore, our first goal was to put our plan on a sound historical footing, in order to maintain that same power of plausibility.

The others accepted all this without much comment, at which point things got a bit trickier. I announced that Colonel Slayton and I proposed to use, as our jumping-off point, the murder of George Washington, a statement that was greeted by a host of blank expressions that clearly said that either our colleagues didn't know Washington had been murdered or that they had forgotten the story. I explained that their lack of awareness was understandable, since the murder was an ugly chapter of American history that was usually swept under some collective psychological carpet. But yes, I continued, he had indeed been murdered: he'd come down with a throat infection, for which several doctors had prescribed bleeding. Those doctors had, however, been secretly bribed by a group of businessmen and politicians—including several of the other Founders—who wanted the Father of His Country shut up for good. During the last months of his life Washington had come to realize the extent to which the fledgling United States had been sold to the moneyed and merchant classes, and he intended to say something about it—publicly. But the powers that were, being remarkably similar to the powers that currently be, were having none of it. The result: assassination by bleeding knife.

Fouché reacted to this tale by saying that it seemed to present an excellent core event for a hoax, speaking, as it did, to the originating moment of the United States while at the same time containing immense potential for controversy. But what, he asked, was the hoax we intended to build around the story? At that point we had to come clean: the story *was* the hoax. Slayton and I had determined that while Washington's being murdered by corrupt politicians in the pay of big money certainly represented an apt parallel to the current condition of the United States, it had no basis in historical fact. A moment of silence ensued; and then the table erupted with howls of laughter and mock indignation, followed by a healthy round of applause. Larissa, never one to be nonplussed, declared that she'd known I was lying all along; but she didn't maintain the act for long, and when everyone had calmed down we began to discuss just why the idea held such potential.

First of all, if our goal was to strike a blow at American moral exceptionalism there was no point in mounting a hoax that would concern modern American leaders. The citizens of the United States had long since recognized their national and local representatives for what Slayton had called them, the paid servants of the corporate class, and any attempt to foster a widespread philosophical crisis by ascribing vicious or corrupt motives and actions to such people was doomed to fail. Nor could we reference facts and personalities that were excessively obscure, given the low regard in which history was held by the general public. But while most people might not be able to say just when or how the United States had been born, the vast majority of them still nurtured the vague yet essential idea that its birth had been a good thing, openly and honestly achieved—with George Washington leading the way. Toy with those notions in an unabashedly tabloid manner, and the resulting scandal might well stand a chance of grabbing the national spotlight and making Americans rethink some of their fundamental moral preconceptions about their country.

A murder plot seemed much the best way to go about this, better even than a good sex scandal. After all, the words "president" and "sex scandal" had long since become inextricably associated in the popular consciousness, while assassination conspiracies—as evidenced by what Malcolm and the others had been able to do with the footage of Emily Forrester's death—still moved the public to extremes of fascination and emotion. And while the fact that Washington, like so many of his day (or, for that matter, our own), had been killed by incompetent doctors was fairly well-known, the further "revelation" that this act had been the result of a plot would likely raise as little skepticism in the country and the world as it had around our dinner table. In short, plausibility would once again sow controversy.

By the end of the evening there was general agreement that the plan was sound enough to be taken to Malcolm. Slayton volunteered for this duty, which he undertook the next day. I spent the hours he was closeted with our ailing chief pacing the floor of my room, with Larissa lying on the bed assuring me that things would go off without a hitch. And so they seemed to: Slayton emerged from the meeting quite pleased, telling me that Malcolm had approved the idea and wanted the others to start preparing the false documents we would need to pull the business off.

Yet it seemed strange to me that Malcolm should not have come out of seclusion long enough to give his approval personally. I asked Slayton if he had been entirely satisfied with our chief's reaction, and he claimed that he had; but I could see that he too was at least mildly disappointed at the reception our work had received. And while I tried, during the busy days that followed, to attribute such feelings to Malcolm's ongoing physical battles and the emotional as well as intellectual volatility that accompanied them, doubt would not be expelled from my mind altogether: during random idle moments I found myself wanting to ask the man just what was behind his attitude.

The chance to do so would not come, however, until we had once more boarded the ship and headed out over the Atlantic to actively pursue our goal of altering the world's perception of the birth and national character of the United States. During that voyage I would discover that Malcolm's seeming lack of enthusiasm had nothing to do with Slayton's and my plan in particular; rather, it sprang from worries of a much more comprehensive nature, worries that would soon be validated by, of all things, that same little computer disc that I'd found in my jacket pocket.

CHAPTER 26

The main thrust of what we took to calling the Washington hoax was embodied in two sets of forged documents. The first was a group of deathbed confessions from three guilt-racked conspirators involved in the murder: Thomas Jefferson (his personal peccadillos and hypocrisy concerning slavery having long since laid him open to almost any indictment in the public's mind), John Adams (whose passionate, at times irrational, Federalism had established him as a perennial target of populist wrath), and finally one of Washington's knife-wielding physicians. The second batch of bogus documents consisted of several letters to intimate friends from Washington himself, in which he announced his intention of making a warning address to the nation concerning the rising power of those who controlled the country's wealth.

By the time Slayton and I finished composing the texts, Leon and Julien had already altered the necessary ink and paper; the completed documents were soon ready. And so we boarded the ship and headed off for New York and Washington, to secrete our creations in various archives. The Kupermans were already hard at work planting manufactured documents and journal articles on various Web sites, all of which would support our fabrications once they were found. Soon after our departure it was decided that since the skies might still be full of patrols searching for the mysterious aircraft that had eluded them over the North Sea, we would do well to cross the Atlantic beneath the waves: we reentered those lonely waters soon after our departure, moving southwest just above the ocean floor until we hit the continental shelf, at which point the world itself seemed to drop away beneath us.

Descending further, we crossed over the hump of the great undersea ridge called the Porcupine Bank, heading on toward Porcupine Plain at a depth of nearly three thousand feet: an unheard-of accomplishment for most conventional submarines but apparently just another remarkable feat for our vessel. The landscape of the ocean floor was spectacular (much more so than when we'd crossed the first time because of our greatly increased depth), yet the continued and dispiriting absence of any appreciable signs of life was only pointed up all the more by the heightened beauty. The same odd mixture of rapture and sadness that I'd experienced during the eastbound crossing quickly returned, and when Malcolm's voice came over the ship's address system, asking me to join him in the observation dome, his melancholy tone seemed to match the plaintiveness of my own inner voice.

He was alone when I entered the dome, sitting in his wheelchair and watching the powerful exterior lights of the ship play off the dramatic seascape. I approached him quietly, and he indicated a nearby chair. "Sit down, Gideon," he said. "Please." He was massaging his forehead in what seemed deep discouragement, but then he started suddenly, touched my arm, and pointed through the hull at a magnificent sight: a lone fish about twenty-five feet long, a strange creature that appeared to be some sort of shark. But its movements seemed too slow and sluggish for that family, while its eyes, far from being the dead black one generally associated with sharks, were brightly luminescent.

"It's a sleeper shark," Malcolm explained, his face gladdened by the sight of it. "A deepwater fish." Suddenly his features darkened again. "It's being driven up by the sonic herding emitters that fishing fleets drop on the ocean floor. There must be a trawler up above—this creature will probably be dead before the day's out. The meat doesn't fetch much, but the eyes, like so many things, are believed to enhance virility in various parts of Asia." He sighed in exasperation. "I never *have* understood why people who can't stop breeding are always so worried about virility."

I was about to reply, but Malcolm held up a hand to ask for silence as he went on watching the sleeper shark execute its graceful but fatal swim up toward the surface and death. When he spoke again it was in a murmur: "To view the wonders of our world clearly, Gideon, without the effects of medication, is so remarkable." In a few seconds I noticed that his teeth had begun to grind and his brow was arching in discouragement. "And yet so *painful*," he whispered. The whole of his body began to quiver noticeably. "How pain *telescopes* time . . . minutes, hours, days—obliterated." He leaned forward toward the glass and gasped, "How long have I been watching you, my poor, doomed friend?" It seemed to me impossible that he could endure his agony with such control for very much longer; but it wasn't until the shark had disappeared from view that he finally gave up the struggle and pulled his transdermal injector from one of his pockets. "I trust you'll excuse me, Gideon," he said, placing the thing to a vein in his left hand and releasing its contents into his bloodstream. He leaned back and closed his eyes for a moment.

"Malcolm," I said carefully. "If you don't mind my asking, have you found the rate or severity of these attacks to be increasing?"

He nodded. "If I could get more rest," he said, opening his eyes.

"But there's no time. Not now." He took a deep breath and finally turned to me. "You did very good work on the island, Gideon. The others, too, of course, but given that it was your first attempt I wanted to tell you personally—an excellent job."

I smiled with relief. "Colonel Slayton and I were worried that maybe you didn't really think so."

"Because I didn't participate? Yes, I'm sorry about that. But I only have so many hours of work I can do now, and I must—*budget* them. But that's no reflection on your efforts, which were exceptional. In fact, my main concern about the project is that it may be *too* good."

I paused in confusion for a moment. "I didn't think a hoax could *be* 'too good.' "

"A hoax that's designed to be exposed can," Malcolm replied. "Has that thought occurred to you yet, Gideon?"

"Which?"

"That our work has yet to be refuted."

My confusion deepened. "I thought that was the whole point."

"Hardly the *whole* point." Malcolm sounded deeply disappointed, an impression that was increased when he spun his chair around in frustration. "Scarcely *half* the point!" he went on, the medication reviving both his strength and his passion. "Eventual discovery was part of the overall plan—we've disseminated these fabrications as a method of exposing the dangers of this age, not to fill people's heads with more meaningless information!"

I shrugged and tried to calm him down: "It's an inherent dilemma, Malcolm. Only sound hoaxes will demonstrate your point—yet sound hoaxes will, at the same time, prevent that point from being recognized. In the end, I suppose, you yourself will have to reveal what you've done."

"I've tried!" he shot back. "Surely Larissa's told you—we as good as revealed to the Americans that the Forrester images had been doctored. And what happened? They still unleashed those damned pilotless monstrosities on Afghanistan! And just last week I sent messages to the English and the German governments about the Churchill letters, but what was their response? Dismissal from the Germans, who have no interest in exposing the hoax—and the English say they are not prepared to present the public with refutations that are bizarre, self-serving, and therefore utterly without credibility!" He attempted to get a grip on himself. "I have not voiced these thoughts to the others, Gideon, and I would ask you not to repeat them—but there are times when I have doubts about this entire scheme. Something else, something far more drastic, may be called for."

Remembering his passion for secrecy, I tried not to sound as curious as I felt. "Is that what you've been working on?"

"No." The hardness of his tone was startling, as was the way in which his features became utterly still; then he shook his head several times, looking very uncomfortable. "That is—perhaps." He banged a hand on the arm of his chair. "I don't want to discuss it! The point is, I want you and the colonel to build some kind of guarantee into this one. I want to be sure—" He spun his chair to face me and held up a finger. "I want to be very, very sure that this thing will eventually be exposed. This goes much deeper than the Forrester job—we're tampering with the very psyche of the most powerful nation on Earth, a country that no longer has to even risk the lives of its young people to enforce its political morality. We must get this one *right.*"

It was a little difficult to absorb this idea after so many days of trying to ensure that our hoax would be more plausible than anything the group had yet done; and with my thinking warped by those days of work, I think I might actually have tried to argue the point with Malcolm, had Tarbell's voice not suddenly come over the address system:

"Gideon—where are you, in the turret?"

Giving Malcolm another bewildered glance, I touched a nearby keypad. "In the observation dome, Leon. Do you need me?"

"No, stay, I will come up," he answered. "I have something that may interest you."

For almost a full and very awkward minute neither Malcolm nor I spoke; then he said, very quietly and a bit contritely, "I know all this must sound odd, Gideon. And I know how you must feel, given the effort you've put in. But there's a great danger in this work of becoming overly enchanted by the ability to deceive people en masse. I've been as guilty of it as anyone. That's why—"

"Ah, there you are!" It was Tarbell, bounding up the stairs from the control level. "And Malcolm, as well—you may also find this of some interest, as it concerns our old friend Mr. Price."

The blackness that had seized Malcolm's features moments before returned, even more quickly this time. "What are you talking about, Leon?" he said apprehensively.

"Gideon here—or rather his friend Mr. Jenkins—happened on the results of some other project for which Price had been engaged. We assumed it was a film, but now, Gideon, I'm not so sure." Shooting over to a terminal, Tarbell sat before it and called something up on the screen, while I followed behind quickly; not as quickly, though, as Malcolm. "Here," Leon eventually said. "Transcripts. After that evening, Gideon, I programmed the global monitoring system to pick out any messages involving combinations of the keywords 'Dachau' and 'Stalin.'" Malcolm took in a sudden breath, which, though not loud enough for Tarbell to hear, caused me to turn to him.

He was pressing his body against the back of his chair, looking worse than I'd ever seen him; but it was very apparent that this time his trouble was not physical.

"I had no luck until today," Leon continued. "And then, in a cluster, several hits came up. All from Israeli intelligence." With a sickening droop of my own insides that I didn't really understand, I suddenly thought of the night when Colonel Slayton had sat listening to Mossad agents feverishly talking about terrorists and a German concentration camp. "Apparently they know about the images," Tarbell went on, very amused. "Though the odd thing is that they seem to think that they are entirely genuine! They've got dozens of operatives out now, looking for one of their men who was the first to get hold of a finished version of the sequence." His amusement subsiding, Tarbell's eyes narrowed. "And that's the puzzling part. Why would they be looking for one of their own people—"

"His name." It was Malcolm, who'd finally conquered his shock long enough to speak.

Tarbell turned. "I beg your pardon, Malcolm?"

"His name, damn it!" Malcolm cried, his knuckles going white as he clutched his chair.

Tarbell recoiled a bit. "I—don't know. They make no mention of his name. Deliberately so, I would say."

With one quick move of his arms Malcolm propelled his chair to the screen. He examined its contents for a moment, then grabbed Leon's shoulder hard. "Gather everyone downstairs, Leon," he said, trying to control the inner tempest that was obviously tossing his emotions about. "Right away, please."

Tarbell knew enough to comply quickly, and after he withdrew, Malcolm, eyes wide and empty, turned his chair away from the screen and rolled slowly back over to the transparent hull.

"Malcolm?" I eventually said. "What is it?"

"You were able to break the encryption of those images?" he asked, in the same low voice.

"Max was, yes," I answered.

Nodding for a moment, Malcolm murmured, "He was very good at his job, your friend Mr. Jenkins . . ."

"Would you like Leon to bring the disc up?"

Malcolm held up a hand. "Unnecessary. I have a complete version."

As the situation began to clarify, I felt my gut ripple again. "Then Price *did* create them for you."

"Yes," Malcolm whispered with another nod. He paused for what seemed a long time, then went on, "Well, Gideon, I'm afraid your Washington project will have to wait. If I'm right—" He lowered his head and placed his hands on either side of it. "But I must not be right. In fact, we must pray, Gideon, that I am as mad as I sometimes seem . . ."

CHAPTER 27

Whether or not Malcolm was mad, he was certainly justified in his fearful suspicions about the mysterious Israeli communications concerning the Stalin images. When we'd all gathered at the table that did double duty for dining and conferring on the lower level of the nose of the ship, Malcolm showed us the completed version of those images and explained how they had come to be; and though just a few months earlier it might have been difficult for me to appreciate the dangers posed by such a seemingly random bit of visual documentation, I was now well versed enough in the power of cleverly packaged disinformation to know that we were faced with a potentially disastrous situation.

The images themselves were simple enough: they showed several separate shots of Josef Stalin touring various parts of the Dachau concentration camp sometime in the late 1930s (Dachau having been the first of the really large-scale, factory-modeled German extermination centers). The Soviet strongman was seen watching the laboring prisoners, their abusive guards, and the executions and corpse disposals with an approving eye, occasionally even chuckling as he pulled on his pipe and exchanged information and jokes with several high-ranking SS tour guides—including, in one shot, Heinrich Himmler. The implications were obvious: the Soviet government had been involved not only in its own domestic genocidal policies but, during the years prior to Hitler's invasion of Russia, in the Nazi Holocaust, as well.

"But what was the purpose of creating such an impression, Malcolm?" Jonah asked, deeply troubled by what he'd seen—as, indeed, were we all.

"The Russian government has degenerated from merely unstable to dangerous, even grotesque," Malcolm declared, fists still tight atop the arms of his chair. "Since taking power, the right wing has employed the same tactics that leveled Chechnya in four other rebellious regions. Nuclear weapons and technology, though admittedly crude, are being sold to whoever has the hard currency to pay for them. Virtual slavery is being practiced in factories and fields, and toxic and nuclear wastes are being dumped into shallow repositories in Siberia, which is why that region's separatist movement has become so violent. Each new problem only brings more vicious solutions from the central government, until it now looks as though Russia will be the black hole of the modern world, taking all of civilization with it when it collapses. Yet the rest of that modern world does nothing. Foreign investment in Russia is running at absurdly high levels, and no one can afford to tell the truth or to have it told—information and communications companies are, after all, among the most severely overextended in the Russian market. The argument that loans and investment will bring reform continues to stand as self-serving nonsense of a variety to match the Chinese model. Putting money into such a situation is simply throwing gasoline on a fire." He caught his breath and sat back, his anger slowly giving way to regret. "It seemed to me, in other words, that some kind of popular redefinition of Russia's place, in the world and in history, might be called for."

"You could hardly have picked a more . . . *provocative* event of which to make use, Malcolm," Tarbell said; and there was no note of irony or amusement in his voice now.

Malcolm nodded grimly. "Or a worse person, as it turned out, to do the work. I hired John Price because none of us had his visual manipulation skills—but I always had reservations about him. It wasn't just that he was a freelance operator, though that did trouble me. But a freelance operator from a place where betrayal is the unspoken stuff of amiable meals in pleasant restaurants . . . It was my mother's world; that in itself should have kept me away. But I thought we could control him."

"I thought we *had*," Larissa said, in a tone that clearly indicated she had no regrets about having been Price's executioner.

"Sometimes, Larissa," Malcolm said, "death doesn't put an end to the dangers a person can pose."

"And what do you think those dangers are?" I asked, looking around the table.

"I've studied the communications Leon intercepted," Colonel Slayton replied. "And putting them together with what *I* heard, I'd say the situation is very bad. Worse yet, it's fairly advanced. The Israelis are clearly worried about some specific terrorist response to this new revelation about the Holocaust, a response that's apparently going to come from one of their own operatives. Probably the same man who discovered the images."

"A fanatic?" Eli asked.

Malcolm nodded, self-recrimination all over his face. "It's why I canceled the project in the first place, before even telling any of you about it. There are certain historical events, I've come to realize, that even we must never toy with—the violence of the emotions they unleash is simply too great. We're talking, now, about what is quite probably the blackest moment in all of human experience. Even the tortures and brutalities of the Dark Ages had nothing like the scale, the systematic insanity . . ." Malcolm shook his head. "This man may have lost family in the Holocaust. Or he may simply have grown unbalanced contemplating it." I felt a quick pang of dread at this thought: not only did it seem entirely plausible, even likely, but I'd dealt with similar characters before and knew what they were capable of. "Whatever the explanation," Malcolm continued, "he has now joined the ranks of those whom the world should always fear most, those who were responsible for the Holocaust in the first place: *fanatics.*"

"The Mossad is full of them," Colonel Slayton said, "unlike most intelligence agencies. But they're being very careful not to use this character's name in communications that are not absolutely secure—they're determined to handle this internally."

"That is understandable," Fouché judged. "Ever since they entered the Turkish civil war on the side of the Kurds, there has been enormous tension between America and Israel. It may be that the Israelis had no choice, now that they are dependent on water that flows from Kurdish territory, but this does not change the fact that Turkey remains an American ally."

"I have checked CIA communications," Tarbell said. "To no one's great surprise, I am sure, they know less than we do. They are aware that the Israelis have a problem with one of their people but have no idea why. Still, they are interested. And when the CIA staggers blindly in the dark, well . . . unfortunate things have a way of occurring."

"Not to our people," Larissa said firmly. "The real thing to worry about is this Israeli. Who is he? How the hell did he get hold of the images in the first place?"

"And what is he intending to do about it?" Malcolm added. "These are all questions that *we* must answer. Not the Israelis, not the Americans, not anyone else. I want *us* to find this man, secure his copy of the images, and finish him."

The ruthless finality of this statement caught me off guard. "But—surely we can just hand him over to his people after we have the images," I said.

"No," Malcolm replied with the same chilling determination. "If he gets back to Israel, he'll spread rumors and stories that will be worse than the images themselves. If he vanishes—or better yet, if we can force him to tell his superiors that the images are actually fabrications *before* he vanishes—then and only then will it all blow over."

I glanced quickly from face to face. I knew that what Malcolm had said made sense, but I nonetheless found myself hoping that someone else would raise an objection.

None came. "Where do we begin?" Fouché asked solemnly.

"Unfortunately," Malcolm said, "if there were any more information in Price's New York residence, his wife would, I suspect, have turned it over to Gideon. Which leaves . . ." His face filled with deep reluctance.

"Los Angeles," Jonah said with a nod.

Slayton tapped the table. "It won't be easy—the city's in chaos, along with the rest of southern California."

"Water again," Eli agreed.

"Yes," Malcolm said, "but we have no choice. Set a course to approach Los Angeles from the sea, Colonel—I don't want to get tangled up with any of the National Guard or militia units. People who've been without adequate water for long enough can be worse than ethnic fanatics."

"Understood," Slayton replied, rising.

"Let's hope this will be simple," Malcolm said as the rest of us moved to follow Slayton. The last to go, I was almost out the door when I heard him mutter quietly, "By all means, let's hope once more for the impossible . . ."

CHAPTER 28

The developments which led to the "water wars" that have consumed the American Southwest for the last five years have been so well scrutinized that it seems unlikely anyone today could be unfamiliar with their details. True, such an assumption is belied by the fact that the same drastic suburban overdevelopment that originally brought violent chaos into the sunniest corner of the United States is today going on in other similarly warm but arid parts of the world; so perhaps in this instance—as in, I now believe, so many others—it's wrong to think that awareness of history is anything other than intellectual vanity. Whatever the case, my principal concern in these few pages is not to summarize the origins of those vicious conflicts but to tell what came of our efforts to find in water-hungry Los Angeles a connection between John Price and the unknown Mossad operative who had taken possession of the Stalin images and then become a fugitive from his own people.

Following Malcolm's directive, we avoided the skies above southern California, not because we were aware of any specific danger posed by such a route but precisely because the situation was so unpredictable. Throughout the region National Guard units—and on a few occasions even federal troops—were desperately trying to preserve order among battling gangs and militias, each of which believed that their particular town, city, or county held the most legitimate claim to the water they had all once shared. Such engagements might involve sticks and knives, but they were just as likely to involve tanks and handheld missiles captured by the militias during run-ins with state and federal troops; and while it was unlikely that any of these weapons could score a chance hit on our ship (particularly now that we could travel under a holographic cloak), it was best to indulge the better part of valor and approach from the sea. So we climbed back into the stratosphere for half an hour or so, then waited for dark before descending to cruising altitude above the Pacific near the island of Catalina.

During that descent we received a series of satellite images which told us that although the California National Guard was still very much in evidence on the streets of Los Angeles, the city itself was relatively calm south of the Santa Monica mountains. North of that line, however, our aerial reconnaissance revealed a patchwork of hot zones, indicating that the residents of the San Fernando Valley—one of the first places to feel the full effects of the region's water depletion—were rioting and engaging the authorities with the same crazed determination that had consumed them for years. Fortunately, our particular business lay in the fashionable west side of Los Angeles: John Price's appallingly tasteless home was situated in that equally tasteless city-within-a-city, Beverly Hills.

Engaging the holographic projector, we were able to blend the silhouette of our ship seamlessly into its surroundings and thus enter the environs of the wealthy little city and deposit a search party made up of the colonel, Larissa, Tarbell, and myself in a public park. From there we made our way through palm-lined streets and entered Price's house—which was still under scrutiny as part of the investigation into his death—with comparative ease. Several hours of searching produced but one lead, although it seemed at least a hopeful one: Tarbell, digging in a group of seemingly innocuous documents, managed to find a note from one Ari Machen, a well-known film producer of Israeli origin who, Colonel Slayton informed us, had ties to various departments in the Israeli government—and to the Mossad in particular. We took the note, which made tantalizing reference to "the Russian business," and then fled the premises, very narrowly avoiding an encounter with a group of heavily armed policemen and women who were on patrol with attack dogs that had been specially trained to sniff out water: pilfering and hoarding were a booming southwestern industry, even in Beverly Hills.

Back aboard the ship we withdrew to the safety of a high altitude in order to try to piece together a plausible scenario for the several days that John Price had spent in Los Angeles before flying to New York and his fate. This task was made exponentially easier when Tarbell managed to recover the man's e-mail records and discovered a carefully worded correspondence between the special effects genius and Ari Machen. If read by someone who hadn't seen the Stalin images, these communications might have passed for the ordinary dealings of a producer with one of his department heads; but knowing what we did about Machen's ties to Israel and about the Stalin material, we had little trouble determining that Price had shown Machen those images without revealing that they were forged. Machen, horrified, had then contacted his friends in the Mossad, several of whom actually held positions as executives at the studio where Machen currently had a production deal: given the manner in which the entertainment industry's influence on American politics and politicians had skyrocketed during the last thirty years, the

Israelis—and, according to Slayton, several other foreign governments—had found it necessary to have ears in the corridors of Hollywood power.

In his dealings with Machen, Price had, as always, been motivated by money: Machen had promised him a respectable fortune for his copy of the images on the strict understanding that Price would not copy them before turning them over. Should he ever be found to have deceived Machen on this point, Price was informed, he could expect to receive certain visitors who would be happy to end his life. Indeed, from the overall tone of the communications it became clear that Machen liked playing the role of suave yet hard-boiled Zionist agent, an impression that was confirmed when Slayton said that he and Machen had crossed paths many years earlier at a Washington cocktail party. There Machen had bragged of having once been a Mossad agent himself, of having killed several Palestinian leaders, and of having arranged the disappearance from the Los Alamos, New Mexico, lab of several computer discs that contained vital American nuclear secrets. In recent years, it seemed, Machen had grown increasingly angry over the rift between Israel and the United States that had followed Israel's backing of the Turkish Kurds (another dangerous situation created by a need for water) and had used his prominent position in one of America's most crucial international industries to both promote the Israeli cause and perform intelligence services for the Israeli government.

Price had agreed to Machen's rather ominous terms concerning the Stalin images, given the amount of money involved; but that same seemingly insatiable avarice had very soon cost Price his life, when his argument with Jonah and Larissa over the Forrester business had turned violent. (Ironically, had he kept his temper and then gone through with his threat to reveal that those images had been doctored, and had the American government believed him, it would only have served Malcolm's larger purpose.) Up to this point the facts as we were able to piece them together were fairly clear; but we were still left with the rather pointed question of where the chain of revelation started by Price and Machen had broken down. Did Machen himself know the agent who was now on the loose and hiding from the Mossad? Or had there been another intermediary involved in getting the Stalin images to Israel? Such questions, unfortunately, could be answered only by Machen himself, so I made ready to accompany Colonel Slayton and Larissa back to the surface and into the fortress-community of Bel Air, behind whose high electronic fences the very wealthiest of Los Angeles's citizens had withdrawn over the past decade to enjoy their success (and copious amounts of airlifted water) under the protection of a private security force that resembled nothing so much as a secular Swiss Guard.

How, one might legitimately ask, could I have displayed or indeed felt so little reluctance about participating in an endeavor that had as its ultimate object the killing of a man? As a doctor, I had once taken an oath to do no harm, and even as we made ready to visit Ari Machen's expansive Bel Air villa I rationalized to myself that I would certainly not be the one to actually execute our unknown Israeli agent, should we discover his name and whereabouts. But there is no denying that I had gone past the point of questioning whether or not he *needed* to be executed, a fact for which, even now, I find that I cannot apologize. A man originally trained but now considered dangerous by such lethal shadow creatures as the Mossad was surely just that; and from the moment I'd come aboard Malcolm's ship I had learned and relearned that the seeming game he and the rest of the team were playing with the world had a lethal dimension, revealing as it did that modern economic, political, and social hierarchies were as brutal as any of their historical antecedents. I therefore accepted the kiss and the passionate embrace that Larissa tendered just before we left the ship as readily as I'd accepted her past as an assassin; and I returned them in kind without further question or doubt, prepared to do whatever was required of me. Perhaps I could have chosen differently; perhaps I should have; but I'll wager that those who think so have not faced the hard reality of a constellation of powerful enemies bent on their imprisonment or, worse yet, their destruction.

Would that I too never had.

CHAPTER 29

In the United States of the information age there are many grand houses that were once inhabited by people who brought life into their rooms but that have now fallen into the hands of wealthy international transients who do not so much live in this world as move through it, grabbing at whatever power and pleasure they can. Ari Machen was such a person, and his villa in Bel Air was such a place. Built in the mid–twentieth century by that rarest of Angelenos, a person with genuine style, the house as we approached it that misty night after again being deposited in an out-of-the-way spot by our ship seemed to cry out for habitation by someone who would make it a home, who would plant foliage and install furniture that were expressions of personality rather than of the ability to hire what I'm certain Leon Tarbell would have called "sexless" designers and decorators. Melancholy prevailed over obvious signs of money in every chamber of the place; although, given what we had come to do, such an atmosphere was only too fitting.

Disabling first the heavyset security guards who prowled about the estate and then the place's electronic surveillance system did not even amuse Larissa enough to bring out her predatory smile; or perhaps the importance of the work at hand was too great for even her to view it as sport. With weapons at the ready we swept silently through the house, finally detecting signs of life in the master bedroom upstairs. It is unnecessary to detail herein what exactly was going on in that room; suffice it to say that Machen was afflicted by all of the usual sexual neuroses that so often characterize men whose craving for power and excitement betrays even to the layman an almost fantastic insecurity. The sight of strangely dressed and armed intruders was enough to send Machen's several male and female prostitutes (he likely never would have conceded them to be such, but they had all the earmarks) screaming toward another room, into which Larissa promptly locked them after delivering a stern warning to be silent. Machen, meanwhile, attempted to grab an old Colt .45 automatic from a wall full of vintage weapons but was thwarted by Colonel Slayton, who, it seemed to me, handled the producer in a particularly rough and humiliating manner. When Larissa returned, she and I took up positions by the door and window, keeping watch over the house and grounds as Slayton's interrogation began.

"You don't remember me, do you, Mr. Machen?" Slayton asked after trussing our host up in his bed with some drapery cord.

Machen—a small but athletically built man of about fifty, with deeply tanned skin, thinning hair, and piggish eyes—shook his head nervously while using his feet to try to cover his naked body with a sheet. "Are you CIA?" he managed to get out. "Do you work for the Palestinians?"

"The two most logical choices, given your past exploits," Slayton answered, pulling up a chair and straddling it. "But let's ignore the question of our identity for the time being." Glancing around, the colonel looked both disgusted and amused by the situation. "I admire your collection," he said, indicating the wall of weapons. "You find they're useful in your current line of work? Or are they trophies of your heroic service to your homeland?"

"I—I am an American citizen," Machen said.

"Yes," Slayton answered slowly. "The generosity of this country never ceases to amaze me." He stood up and went to the wall, taking down an old revolver and opening its cylinder. "Well," he said appreciatively. "Hollow-point bullets." He began to point the gun around the room, finally bringing its barrel to rest in Machen's direction.

Shying away a bit but desperate to preserve some semblance of what he apparently believed was manliness, Machen said, "I've been tortured before—by the Syrians!"

"Excellent," Slayton answered. "Then you know what to expect." Machen's tan face paled a little at that, and Slayton moved closer to him. "Recently you purchased some materials from a mutual acquaintance—John Price."

Giving courage another shot, Machen said, "Of course. He worked for me many times."

That brought the muzzle of the revolver to his temple and an involuntary whimper from his throat. "Since you own these weapons, I'm going to assume that you know what they do," Slayton said quietly. "If I pull this trigger, there won't be enough left of your brain to feed a cat. Mr. Price is now dead. We know you weren't responsible for that, because we were. So take this situation very seriously. Now—you maintain links to the Mossad, and you passed the materials you bought on to them. But somewhere along the line they got lost." Slayton cocked the revolver. "*Where* along the line?"

"I—" Machen was by now filled with such fear that his legs, instead of trying to cover him for dignity's sake, were throwing the bedsheet away from him as if he were an infant. Still he managed to declare, "I would die for Israel!"

"You *will* die for Israel," Slayton assured him, "unless you talk to me." Machen's whimpering became more pronounced, prompting Slayton to give him a click of the tongue. "You've never killed an armed man in your life, have you, Ari? Those Palestinians you murdered—they were tied up just like you are now. And that's why you're so afraid."

"No!" Machen cried out, clamping his eyes closed. The mere possibility of having more of the lies he'd evidently generated about himself exposed was enough to reduce the man to submission. "One of my contacts—Dov Eshkol—I gave what you're talking about to him. But he—" Recovering a bit, Machen suddenly stopped; too late, however.

"But he's gone missing, hasn't he?" Slayton said. No confirmation on this point from Machen was necessary; there remained only the final questions: "How much do you know about Dov Eshkol? And where is he now, would you guess?"

"I can't—" Machen stammered. "You don't understand—Dov is—"

I studied the man for an instant as Slayton kept the gun at his head and thought I saw something. "Just a moment, Colonel," I said. Then I asked Machen, "It was Eshkol who threatened to kill Price if he kept copies of the disc, wasn't it?"

Relieved not to have been forced to say it himself, Machen nodded. "Eshkol is old-school counterintelligence—he's the first person the Mossad calls on if one of their own people has turned or even gone soft and needs to be taken care of. He'll—if I tell you anything more, he'll come back for me."

"He may or may not come back," Larissa said. "But we're already here. So tell us—where would he be coming back *from*?"

"I don't know," Machen answered, at which Slayton ground the muzzle of the revolver into his scalp with a vigor that made me wince. "I don't!" Machen cried. "Nobody does! He's disappeared!"

"Why?" Slayton demanded.

"He thought that the disc warranted an active response," Machen explained. "But word came down that the government was going to handle it quietly and give the Russians a chance to explain. Eshkol couldn't tolerate that. He exploded and said he'd deal with it himself." Trying very hard to get a grip on himself, Machen went on, "You have to understand, Eshkol isn't—well, he's extreme. And this . . . one set of his great-grandparents were Holocaust survivors. And a lot of other people in his family didn't make it."

The same dread I had felt at Malcolm's earlier mention of this possibility returned with Machen's confirmation of it, and the feeling must have been all over my face, for when I turned to Larissa she gave me a look of concerned confusion. But I just shook my head and tried to stay alert as Slayton kept after our prisoner.

"Has the Mossad been able to track him at all?" the colonel asked.

Machen shook his head. "They were expecting him to go public with the images—give them to a newsgroup or post them on the Net himself. They've been tracking down the correspondents with the most contacts in the Middle East—so far, nothing."

"No sign of where he's gone?" Slayton asked.

"No, and there won't be. If Eshkol goes deep, not even the Mossad will find him. He's that good."

Suddenly a deep rumble resonated through Machen's house, making me think that an earthquake was under way; but then I realized that the thunderous sound and feeling weren't quite seismic and that I'd heard and felt them before. As if to confirm my intuition, Larissa suddenly put her hand to the collar of her bodysuit.

"Yes, Brother?" Her expression never changed as she nodded and said, "Understood." She looked at Slayton and then to me, calling over the low, growing hum, "It's Bel Air Security—Machen's guards were due to report in three minutes ago. A personnel carrier and an infantry squad are on the way." She opened a pair of French doors that led to a balcony.

In seconds the air outside the house began to shimmer and ripple as if it were being exposed to a great heat; then a seeming crack in the very fabric of reality opened up, revealing Julien and, beyond him, the interior of the ship's corridor, all seemingly suspended in midair. The bizarre sight—a product of partially shutting down the vessel's holographic projector—brought screams from the prostitutes in the next room and prompted Machen to squirm with heightened vigor. "Who *are* you people?" he said.

But Slayton only released him in reply, as Fouché began to wave to us vigorously. "Quickly, all of you!" he cried.

We bolted for the balcony just as the ship's humming began to rattle the house hard enough to cause Machen's weapons collection to crash to the floor. A few of the guns went off, prompting more howls from Machen; but our thoughts were now all on escape, and in seconds Larissa, Slayton, and I were back aboard and the ship had gotten under way.

Thus were we able to give a name—and soon, thanks to the continued hacking efforts of Tarbell, a rather hard and frightening face—to the man we were seeking. Further monitoring of official Israeli communications indicated that Machen had not lied when he had said that Dov Eshkol's superiors believed the bitter passions inspired in their wayward operative by the Stalin images would find their vent in some kind of public exposure of the materials. But those of us aboard the ship suspected, only too presciently, that the world would not get off so lightly.

CHAPTER 30

Unaware of whether Dov Eshkol had yet made his way out of California or even the United States, we again sought refuge in the deep Pacific as Tarbell—assisted now by the Kupermans—continued to hack into the databases and monitor the communications of various American and Israeli intelligence agencies in order to assemble a complete picture of the fugitive. The rest of us, meanwhile, gathered once more around the conference table to fuel ourselves with an impromptu meal prepared by Julien and to discuss the few bits of information we'd been able to squeeze out of Ari Machen. This conversation produced few new insights, and those few were deeply discouraging: Machen's claim that if Eshkol went into deep cover even the Mossad wouldn't be able to find him seemed entirely plausible, given his ability to elude detection thus far; and we all agreed that if the Israelis failed in their efforts to find him, the chances of the United States (the only other nation aware that there was some sort of problem) turning anything up were virtually nil. Nor did the confirmation of Malcolm's instinctive feeling about Eshkol's being descended from Holocaust survivors give us any sense of encouragement: clearly the man was considered highly violent and something of a loose cannon by his superiors, and if his murderous tendencies—which had apparently been turned, on occasion, against his own countrymen—stemmed from rage over the fate of his relatives and his race, he would have little trouble thinking in large numbers when it came time to conceive a punishment for any and all previously unexposed accessories to the genocide in Nazi Germany.

But we would need more hard information before we could determine just what form that punishment might take; and after several hours Leon, Eli, and Jonah were able to provide it. They filed bleary-eyed into the nose of the ship, hungry and bearing a raft of notes, as well as several pictures of Eshkol, each of which bore little resemblance to the next. These they began to explain as Julien brought them food; and while the information they'd gleaned offered no reason to doubt that Eshkol was an extremely dangerous man, it also showed why our team might be better equipped to hunt him down than either the Israelis or the Americans.

"He is a murderer, yes—a butcher, really," Tarbell said, cramming food into his mouth, "but he also plays on our field, you might say."

To the rest of our puzzled looks, Jonah, who was eating slightly less ravenously, said, "He's got the usual undercover and covert skills—disguise, languages—but the real secret of his success is that he's an information junkie. He's a brilliant researcher, and he can manufacture any sort of personal documents and records to gain access to just about anything—and then destroy any evidence that he was ever there. He's even fooled the universal DNA database."

"I thought that was impossible," Larissa said.

"Not impossible," Eli answered. "Just very, very difficult. The trick is getting the corroborative samples. If you're going to, say, travel by air using the identity of someone who's actually dead, you're going to need some sample DNA to offer when you check in, and it had better come from someone who bore more than a passing resemblance to you—and, most important, someone whose death was not recorded in the database. Eshkol's apparently got quite a collection of alter egos—and I think you can guess how he got them."

"The other Mossad agents he executed," Colonel Slayton said with a nod.

"Also many of the Arab operatives he's killed," Tarbell confirmed, checking his notes and indicating the pictures, some of which showed Eshkol in traditional Arab dress. "The narcissism of minor differences, eh? Your colleague Dr. Freud would be deeply satisfied, Gideon. At any rate, whichever side they serve, such victims are not given obituaries—and their deaths are, of course, kept from the DNA database. They are ideal, really, as sample donors—nearly untraceable."

"Eshkol was reprimanded several times," Jonah said as Tarbell went back to eating. "The first was in 2011, when he was twenty-six. Mutilating the body of one of his victims, was what the Mossad called it."

"It's not exactly unknown in that game," Larissa said. "That kind of trophy taking."

"True," Eli agreed, flipping through still more scribbled pages, "and so they let it go at a warning. Quite a few times. And that's where we may have him. Neither the Israelis nor the Americans know about Eshkol's modus operandi—we only happened to stumble on it when we cross-referenced the names of his victims, which we got out of the most secure Mossad files, with every travel database we could crack into. A few hits came up, then a few more."

"He's gone on several extracurricular outings over the years,"

Jonah threw in. "And I don't think it was tourism—not the way he was covering his tracks."

"You're saying he's engaged in private vendettas," Malcolm judged, quietly and grimly.

Eli nodded. "Neo-Nazis, skinheads, Arab intellectuals at foreign universities who are ardently opposed to peace with Israel—they've all mysteriously died when Eshkol has been in their respective countries, under cover of his identity-switching scheme. In a few cases we can even put him in the specific town or city where the execution took place."

Malcolm nodded slowly, gazing silently out at the ocean in the way he generally did when things took an ominous turn.

"And you think you can track him?" Slayton asked, recognizing Malcolm's mood and assuming the mantle of leadership for a moment. "Using this method?"

"We've already begun," Jonah answered with an enthusiastic nod.

"And?" Larissa asked.

"And," Eli replied, "it seems that he has in fact left the United States—for Paris. Two days ago."

General murmuring ensued as we all puzzled with the question of why Eshkol should have chosen to flee to such an apparently visible hiding place as the French capital. It was Malcolm who, without turning to us, finally and quietly declared:

"A weapon. He'll want a weapon."

Fouché looked further confused. "But he's moving quickly, Malcolm. He can hardly afford to bring along a tank or even a particularly large gun, which are the usual French exports. Explosives would be easy enough to get anywhere, so why—" His mouth freezing in midsentence, Julien's eyes widened with horrific realization.

Malcolm didn't even need to see the look. "Yes, Julien," he said. "Your countrymen rationalize trading in such technology by saying that it has always been and will always be impossible to get weapons-grade plutonium in France—but the Iraqis were able to get the plutonium elsewhere and the mechanism in Paris. Or, should I say, in a town just southeast of the city."

Instantly we all realized what Malcolm was driving at. In 2006, Iraqi president and longtime Western nemesis Saddam Hussein decided to challenge the economic embargo that had been in place against his country for nearly two decades by declaring that he had attained nuclear capability. This struck many in the West as absurd, since their renewed monitoring of Iraqi weapons facilities had not revealed any sudden advances that would have permitted Saddam to construct such devices. So, to drive his point home, Saddam dispatched a suicide bomber to explode a tactical nuclear device in one of the most prosperous Kurd communities in the Allied-protected north of his country. The man was intercepted, the device was captured, and its miniaturized mechanism was eventually determined to have been purchased in France.

"I suggest that we all man our stations," Malcolm continued. "Set course for France—the quickest course, Colonel, that you can possibly determine. We've no time to worry about interference from any of our usual antagonists."

As the rest of us rose to comply, Eli asked, "What about the Israelis and the Americans? Do we let them know what's happening?"

Malcolm shrugged. "Certainly, though I don't think they'll believe it. Especially as it comes from an anonymous and unconfirmable source. But by all means, tell them." Looking out at the sea again, he added, "Tell them that this marvelous age has produced a monster—a monster who can use their own tools better than they can possibly imagine."

I watched Malcolm for a moment as he glanced down, took out his transdermal injector, and held it to his hand; and I found myself wondering if his last remark had been about Dov Eshkol at all.

CHAPTER 31

Although the need to get to France quickly outweighed that of staying hidden from the warplanes of America and her allies, it nevertheless made sense to take what precautions we could to avoid detection during our voyage east. Malcolm and Eli therefore set about creating a new radar signature for our ship, to ensure that any anomalous readings picked up by long-range stations on the ground would fail to match those that the Americans and English had no doubt put on file following our encounters in Afghanistan and over the North Sea. This undertaking made it necessary for someone else to man Eli's monitoring post in the turret; and since that was a job with which I'd already become at least somewhat acquainted, it seemed logical for Larissa to suggest that I be the one to take over. Yet had logic dictated some other course, she would, I think, have found a way to refute it: the more time I spent with her, the more she seemed to want me around, a situation that was, as I told her, utterly unprecedented in my experience.

"Why?" Larissa asked with a laugh, linking her arm in mine and marching me through the ship's corridors in that inimitably martial yet alluring way of hers. "Have your romantic choices really been that bad? I can't believe it—not the brilliant Dr. Gideon Wolfe!"

"Sarcasm is a genetically inferior form of humor, Larissa," I said, grabbing her around the waist and squeezing hard. "And whatever women may say about *respecting* men who are devoted to their work, that doesn't mean they want them *around*, particularly."

"Nor should they," Larissa answered with a definitive nod. "Every worthwhile woman deserves more than her fair share of attention."

"How fortunate," I mused with a smile, "that returning to my former life is out of the question—what with there being a price on my head and all."

Larissa suddenly stood still and turned to me, looking unhappily surprised. "Gideon—you don't mean to say that you've thought about it."

I shrugged. "Not really. But it's only natural to wonder."

In the time I'd known her I'd seen uncertainty flit into and out of Larissa's features only occasionally; yet now it seemed to linger there. "Oh" was all she said as she looked down at the deck.

"Larissa?" Perplexed, I put a hand to her face. "It's not as though I've planned it—I've just wondered." She nodded and, for the first time I could remember, said absolutely nothing. There was something so unutterably ingenuous and sad in her silence that I couldn't help but wrap my arms around her and pull her in very close. "I'm sorry," I said quietly.

Of all people, I told myself contritely, I should have known better than to make such a stupidly random crack. Someone with a past like Larissa's could not have allowed herself many moments of true emotional vulnerability; and during those exceptional episodes she would have been, would still be, very alive to the possibility of betrayal. In dealing with such personalities no comments about abandonment, however offhand, can be considered anything other than callous. I therefore kept my mouth shut and continued to hold her, hoping that my embrace would be enough to undo the obvious effects of my thoughtlessness but fairly certain that it wouldn't.

As was so often the case during my time with Larissa, however, I was wrong. "It's all right," she finally said, quietly but with real conviction.

"You're sure?" I asked.

"I do sometimes enjoy being childish, Gideon," she replied, "but that doesn't actually make me a child. I know you didn't mean to hurt me." Of course she was right; and as I considered this latest reminder that she was unlike any other woman I'd ever known, I couldn't help but let out a small chuckle, one that she automatically picked up on. "What's so funny, you unimaginable swine?"

"Well, it *does* have a certain ridiculous dimension," I answered quietly. "The idea that *I* would run out on *you*."

"True," she said, her lovely self-possession rebounding. "Now that you mention it, the idea's absurd."

"Okay," I said, shaking her gently. "No need to go to town with it."

She pushed her face harder against my chest, saying, in a voice so low that I wasn't sure that she intended for me to hear it:

"You won't leave me, Gideon."

Had I known that this was to be the last of the uncomplicated moments that Larissa and I were able to steal from our extraordinarily complicated situation, I would have been far more assiduous about prolonging it. I might, to begin with, have tried to ignore the ship's Klaxon, which began with typically poor timing to sound at that very instant. But as we stood there, all danger seemed in my foolish mind to be emanating from, and be directed toward, matters other than my relationship with Larissa; and so I loosened my hold on her, utterly failing to give the moment the terrible importance it deserved. I can now recognize, of course, that this was just one of several bad mistakes that I was then in the process of making; but such understanding does little to dull the pain of the memory.

Several minutes after the alarm began to throb, Larissa and I, once again moving along the corridor, heard footsteps coming toward us from around a corner. We soon found ourselves face-to-face with Colonel Slayton at the bottom of the ladder that led up to the turret.

"We still haven't generated the new signature," he said with something that vaguely—and uncharacteristically—approached dread. "Too late, too *late*—have *you* caught sight of them yet?" His wording seemed to indicate that he'd already asked the rest of the team the same question; yet he neither explained what he was talking about nor waited for Larissa or me to reply before scaling the ladder. "They can't have built the things," he said as he ascended. "Not even they could be so stupid!"

We followed the colonel into the turret, where he immediately went to one side of the structure and, putting his hands against the transparent shell, fixed his eyes on the darkness above and behind our ship. I could see nothing of any note on the arching horizon of the stratosphere; and Larissa, scanning the same area, came up with a similar result.

"Colonel?" she said. "What is it, have you picked up something on the scanners?"

Slayton nodded, a motion that quickly turned into a disgusted shake of his head. "A flock of birds—that's what they read as. I'd love to believe it, but what the hell kind of birds can survive up here?"

I moved around to his side. "Maybe you could back up a little, Colonel. What exactly do you think is out there?"

Slayton kept shaking his head. "Death may be out there, Doctor. And the worst part of it is, it may be a death of my own design."

CHAPTER 32

"We started throwing the idea around at the Pentagon quite a while ago," Slayton explained, never taking his eyes from the dark, mist-banded horizon behind the ship. "For a long time, you see, we'd been trying to work out the problem of modern surveillance. Over the last fifty years every new system of electronic detection has been matched by some new development in stealth technology—and when computers got involved, the race picked up exponentially. All the major powers were looking for some way out, some foolproof new answer, but the technology hadn't yet appeared to make such an advance possible. Or so ran the conventional wisdom. In fact, the seed of the solution had been planted years earlier, during the drug war—the *police action,* as we were trained to call it—in Colombia and Ecuador. And the planting was done by units under *my* command." Fleeting pride seemed to mix with the colonel's gloom for a moment. "We took to using small flying drones equipped with multiple cameras and microphones for recon work, and the tactic was highly successful—although we really had no idea that we'd stumbled onto the answer."

"The answer how?" Larissa asked. "Those devices didn't have any radar or stealth capabilities."

"Exactly," Slayton said, smiling just briefly. "They didn't need them, that was the beauty of it. We'd all gotten so used to working with electronically generated information that we'd forgotten the basic tools that God gave us—our eyes and ears, which the drones effectively became. When the first experiments were successful, we began to miniaturize their flight and audiovisual equipment enough to make them capable not only of enormous range but of penetrating almost any detection field without raising an alarm. After the war word got around the Pentagon, and the drones became standard issue. Then, when major weapons miniaturization reached full speed ten years ago, it became inevitable that someone would eventually put forward the idea of armed drones. They could be guided into remote, even hardened, sites and set off their payloads—conventional or nuclear—with absolute precision. That was the theory. The advantages were obvious"—Slayton's scar glowed hot in the faint light of the turret as his tone became harrowing again—"but so were the dangers. A foreign operative in an American lab could easily walk out with not just the plans but the prototypes. Fortunately, there were tremendous design and system problems that looked insoluble. We abandoned the project while I was still there. Apparently they've revived it."

"Maybe not," I said. "Colonel, for all we know the ship could be detecting a small meteor shower. Or some kind of cosmic dust."

Such were admittedly paltry attempts at an alternative explanation, and Slayton waved them off with appropriate disdain. "Find me meteors that fly in formation and on an intercept course, Doctor, and I'll—" His features suddenly went dead still. *"There,"* he said quietly. I kept staring into the distance and finding no apparent cause for alarm. When I turned to Larissa, however, I could see that she had locked onto whatever the colonel was seeing: her face bore the same expression of apprehension.

"Where?" I asked; but in reply Slayton only turned, approached a keypad on the monitoring console, and activated the shipwide address system. "This is Slayton," he announced. "The drones are now one hundred and fifty yards off our stern. We'll need to go as close to silent running as we can manage—no unnecessary noises, and keep your voices low. Most important are the engines—Julien, we'll need to take them down to minimum output. And Jonah, reset the holographic projection."

The urgency of the colonel's orders caused me to search the stratosphere all the more intently, determined to catch some glimpse of the mysterious inventions that were causing him such evident anxiety. That glimpse, when it came, was as intriguing as it was frightening: the dozens of basketball-sized drones—which looked like something John Price might have dreamed up—had large "eyes" that, I soon learned, were actually housing units for sophisticated optical instruments. Appendages that encased equally complex audio monitors and bodies that contained flight and guidance equipment added to the drones' overall impression of enormous insects, and each of them also bristled with spiny antennae: programmable detonators, Slayton explained briefly, saving further elaboration for another statement to the rest of our crew.

"Remember, please," he said, "assuming I'm right, each one of those things bears a nuclear device capable of vaporizing this ship. We will proceed with the greatest caution."

As if in response to Slayton's words, the drones suddenly shot forward and surrounded us, their many inquisitive eyes now assuming a menacing quality. Pursuant to the colonel's orders, our ship slowed down steadily until it seemed that we were going along at no more than a crawl—a very nerve-racking crawl. Fear made it difficult to keep my voice to a murmur, but I had to ask, "Would anybody really set off a nuclear device at this altitude, Colonel?"

He nodded, matching stares with the drones that were floating around us. "I'm assuming they've armed these with X-ray lasers—they're powered by a nuclear explosion and have enormous destructive potential, but the fallout is minimal."

" 'Minimal'?" Larissa whispered.

"They evidently view the threat we pose as worth the risk," Slayton said. "Even though they obviously don't yet understand the exact nature of that threat. Not unusual thinking for the American national security machine—as you yourself have written, Doctor."

"And will the holographic projector keep us safe for the moment?" I asked.

"It should," the colonel answered. "To the naked eye our ship now appears to be a harmless band of atmospheric mist."

Larissa nodded. "And the projector works as well on these drones as it does on the eye."

"Thus turning the drones' strength back into a weakness," Slayton said. "But as I say, we still haven't started emitting a new radar signature—we can expect them to stay locked onto the old one, waiting for some confirmation of human or mechanical activity. We'll have to continue to be careful about how much noise we make—and how much the ship makes, as well." Seeing that the devices outside were continuing to make no hostile move, the colonel relaxed just a bit. "But for the moment, at least, they appear fooled." He allowed himself one more brief smile. "I wonder what my friends down below would say if they'd known they would be pursuing *me* . . ."

Despite the lessening of tension permitted by the holographic projector, during the initial phase of our journey among the drones we all moved very carefully and, following Colonel Slayton's instruction, spoke in hushed tones. Half an hour of such behavior was enough to loosen our mood a little, but no more than that; and I was still standing motionless by Larissa's side when I heard her start to talk to her brother quietly via their communication implants. She spoke in a soothing, sympathetic tone, and from her words I soon got the impression that the pressure of the general situation and the specific moment might be getting to Malcolm, at least a little. This notion was confirmed when Larissa asked if I would join him in his quarters, where he'd gone after suffering a bout of dizziness. Someone, she said, had to try to talk him through the difficult transit, and she intended to stay at her post, ready to fire on the drones should the holographic system fail for any reason.

Moving in a deliberate manner, I climbed down the turret ladder and crept toward the stern of the ship. On entering Malcolm's quarters—which were styled after the captain's cabin of an old sailing ship, with a wide, mock-leaded window set in the rearmost section of the hull—I initially thought he must still have been in the observation dome; but then I caught sight of his overturned wheelchair behind a rough-hewn wooden table. His body was caught under the thing and sprawled out across the floor.

"Malcolm!" I cried urgently but quietly, for the drones were visible outside the window. I rushed over, carefully moved the wheelchair, and then lifted him up, shocked and appalled by how light his body was. There was a captain's box bed set into one bulkhead, and I put him in it, loosening his collar and checking for a pulse.

But try as I might, I couldn't find one.

CHAPTER 33

Malcolm's return to consciousness had nothing to do with any efforts of mine, for I had not even begun to administer resuscitating measures when his entire body jerked upward as if it had received a strong electric shock. His lungs took in a huge gulp of air and he began to cough hard, though it didn't seem that the noise was loud or distinct enough to attract the attention of our observers. I poured a glass of water from a pewter jug and got him to swallow some of it, and once his breathing had returned to something like normal he whispered:

"How long was I gone?"

"I don't know," I answered. "I found you on the floor." I raised my eyebrows in question. "You had no pulse, Malcolm."

He drank a little more water and nodded. "Yes," he breathed. "It happens—more often these days, actually." Lying back, he tried to calm his body. "One of the more unpredictable symptoms of my condition—spontaneous shutdown of the most basic functions. But it never lasts long." He looked at the wooden ceiling of his bed in seemingly casual frustration. "I wish I could remember whether or not I *dream* while it's happening . . ."

"Have you determined what triggers it?" I asked, slightly amazed by his attitude. "Does exhaustion play a part?"

He shrugged. "Quite probably. However . . ." He rolled over and looked outside, frowning when he saw the drones. "Still there, eh? Well, exhausted or not, I've got to get back to Eli—"

But the man couldn't even sit up straight. "You're not going anywhere just now," I said; and as he reached for his transdermal injector I took it away from him. "And I don't think self-medication following a neuroparalytic crisis of some kind is really called for, either."

Ever since our first encounter I had recognized that Malcolm's pride was more important to him than almost anything: he desperately needed to feel that he wasn't helpless and would go to almost inhuman lengths to avoid that impression. Thus I wasn't at all sure how he would react to the doctorly dictates I was issuing. But surprisingly, he did no more than glance at me with an expression of acceptance, rather like that of a boy who's been told he has to stay home from school. "All right," he said calmly. "But I'll need my chair." He actually seemed somewhat relieved at the prospect of being forced to rest for a bit, though I knew he would never admit it; so I simply nodded and maneuvered the wheelchair over to his bed, letting him get into it himself. "Thank you, Gideon," he said, as if in reply to my not assisting him.

"Just be thankful that your sister worries about you," I said. "God knows how long you might've stayed on that floor if she hadn't asked me to come down. Or what shape you would've been in when we finally did find you."

He acknowledged the statement by holding up a hand. Then,

after a moment's pause, he looked at me with evident curiosity. "You and Larissa—you care for each other very deeply, it seems." Assuming that he was still groggy, I smiled in a cajoling way. "What's it like?" he asked.

I had anticipated Malcolm's eventually asking many questions about my relationship with his sister, but this was not one of them. His disorientation, I determined, must have been greater than I'd originally estimated. "You mean—what's it like to be in love with your sister?" I said.

"To be in love with *any* woman," Malcolm said. "And to have her love you—what's that like?"

As he was speaking, I realized from the clarity of both his gaze and his words that my supposition had been wrong—that, though weakened, he wasn't disoriented at all—and this realization fell like a stone on my spirit. Among the many things of which Stephen Tressalian had robbed his son, this seemed to me the most valuable and shocking. It was unspeakably cruel that Malcolm should not have known the answer to his own question; yet the obviousness of why he did not was crueler still. Desperately searching for an answer that would not betray my own sense of sorrow, I finally said, "Larissa is a far cry from '*any* woman.' "

Malcolm pondered the statement. "Do you *know* that?" he eventually asked. "Empirically, I mean."

"I think so," I answered. "At any rate, I believe it. That's what's important."

"Yes," he said, touching his mouth pensively with his fingers. "That *is* the important thing, isn't it? Belief . . ." We sat there without saying another word for about a minute, as air wheezed noisily into and out of Malcolm's lungs. Then he repeated the word: "Belief . . . I haven't studied it enough, Gideon. I've focused on deception—the deceptions of this age and my own attempts to reveal them *through* deception. But I should have paid more attention to belief—because it's what's put us in this predicament." He seemed to be gaining strength, though I got the impression that it was more the chance to talk about what had been bothering him than any genuine physical improvement that was behind his surge in energy. "What is it, Gideon? What makes a man like Dov Eshkol so committed to his beliefs that he's capable of committing any kind of crime?"

Given the palliative effect that the conversation was having on him, I kept up my end; and there, in the bizarre, threatening quiet of the slow-moving ship, surrounded and constantly scrutinized by the mechanized minions of our enemies below, we began to pick away at the mind of the man we were hunting.

"There are a lot of factors involved in that kind of belief, of course," I said. "But if I had to pick one as paramount, I'd say it was fear."

"Fear?" Malcolm repeated. "Fear of what? God?"

I shook my head. "The kinds of fear I'm talking about strike long before we encounter any concept of God. From the day we're born, there are two basic terrors that consume all people, whatever their background. The first is terror prompted by a sense of our true aloneness, our isolation from one another. The second, of course, is the fear of death. No matter how in particular, these fears touch each of our lives and are at least partly responsible for all crimes—including the types that Eshkol has committed."

I paused and studied Malcolm for a few seconds: he was nodding his head and seemed to be growing calmer by the moment, even though his blue eyes stayed locked on the drones outside. "Go on," he said after a half minute or so. "We've *got* to know how his mind works."

"All right," I replied, "but only if you can stay calm about it." He waved a hand a bit impatiently, a good sign that he was, indeed, feeling better. "Well," I continued, "most people try to submerge the first of these fears—the terror of isolation—in a sense of identification within a group. Religious, political, ethnic, it doesn't really matter—it's even behind most of the mass marketing that's done today and behind popular culture itself. Anything, as long as it seems to break down the wall of alienation and impart a sense of belonging."

"Which creates," Malcolm murmured, his eyes going self-consciously wide, "enormous opportunities for manipulation."

"And manipulators," I agreed. "Otherwise known as leaders. Most of them are simply people who are trying to assuage their own fears by creating a rubric of identity into which the greatest number of souls, differing in everything except their feeling of being disconnected and lost, can fit."

"Are we talking about Eshkol's superiors here?"

"In part, but not primarily. His Israeli commanders do fall into the category we've been discussing so far, the fairly common variety of leaders that includes almost anyone involved in a political, religious, economic, or cultural movement. But Eshkol? There's nothing common about him, and if we want to understand how he works, we have to take the whole business to the next level."

Malcolm sighed. *"Fanaticism,"* he said, with the same loathing he'd displayed earlier.

"Yes. The common leader and his followers work mainly off of the desire to end isolation, but the fanatical leader and his disciples incorporate the second primal fear, the fear of death, into the equation. And by death I mean annihilation—the utter obliteration of any and every bit of a person's earthly existence and legacy. The leader who promises his people that adherence to his laws and teachings will not only relieve the pain of their isolation but also allow them to defy death, to achieve some kind of spiritual immortality through worthy deeds, that type of leader achieves a supreme control that the first type can't match—and creates an entirely different kind of follower in the process. Such a follower is likely to disregard most generally accepted rules of social behavior for the simple reason that to him or her, there is no obscenity save what the leader labels obscene. And such a leader's definition of obscene is likely to be very specific, because he doesn't want to limit the range of possible actions to which he can order his followers."

"All right," Malcolm agreed, his fingers beginning to tap on the arms of his chair. "But who is it, then? Who's the leader who's telling Eshkol what to do?"

"I don't think anyone's telling him, in the way that you mean. But he does have leaders—the worst kind. You said it yourself, Malcolm, when we first found out about him—it's his family, specifically the victims who died almost a century ago."

Malcolm looked momentarily confused. "But—they're dead. And they weren't leaders."

"Not in the obvious way," I said. "And that makes them even more dangerous. They embody all the virtues of Eshkol's ethnic and religious heritage—in fact, being so long dead, they have no flaws of any kind. They demand, in his mind, unquestioning faith—and complete vengeance, to be achieved with the same brutality that caused their deaths. They offer him the promise of welcoming arms, of eternal community, should he die as a result of his efforts. And most of all, the viciousness he embodies, the viciousness that's inherent in all fanaticism, takes on the gentler trappings of love because it serves their memory. Eshkol's the consummate lone wolf, and even the Israelis know it—he answers to only one voice, the collective voice he imagines to be coming from his murdered ancestors."

"And so," Malcolm said, taking up the train of thought, "when he saw the Stalin images he never questioned them."

I nodded. "By now Eshkol is almost certainly paranoid. He's had enough time to obsess over an unequaled cataclysm, to link it to events in his own family and personal life and decide that it's ongoing and requires an active response from him personally. Based on his activities, it's safe to say that he suspects the entire world is involved in a plot to exterminate Jews—indeed, Jews themselves, at least some Jews, are apparently not above suspicion in his mind. Paranoia creates fantastic tension, which can never be relieved through disproof—only through vindication. So when he saw the Stalin images, he saw exactly what he'd always wanted to see—proof that he was right and that all his actions had been justified."

Still staring at the drones, Malcolm began to murmur, "*Mundus vult . . .*" But the statement seemed to give him no satisfaction now, and he finally sat back, letting out a long breath. "Good Lord, Gideon . . ."

"I'm not telling you anything you didn't already know—or suspect. What bothers me now is, how can we possibly hope to catch him? If I'm right—if he in fact answers to no one living and if he can move through modern society like a phantom—then where's our advantage?"

Malcolm balled his hands into fists, but he kept his voice low. "Our advantage is ourselves. It's up to us. No one else can get to him before—"

Malcolm apparently didn't want to finish the thought; but I, wishing to be absolutely sure that we did indeed understand both each other and the situation, looked at him and said, " 'Before . . .'?"

A sudden flurry of movement outside the window distracted us both: in loose formation the drones began to move away from our ship and head back in the direction from which they'd come. Though immensely relieved, I was initially at a loss as to why it was happening. But then I heard Eli's voice coming over the address system:

"It's all right—I've initiated the new signature, they don't have anything to lock onto anymore. We should be safe."

Malcolm turned and touched a keypad by his bed. "Well done, Eli. Julien—let's get back up to speed. I want to be over France within the hour." Putting his hands on the wheels of his chair, Malcolm gave me one more critical look. "I think we both have a very good idea of what we need to get to Eshkol 'before,' Gideon—and I suggest that, however horrifying it seems, we both try to impress that idea on the others." He turned his chair around and headed for the door. "This man's mind may be full of vengeful fantasies, as you say—but they will die with him."

CHAPTER 34

With our ability to move at full speed restored, we were able to reach the English Channel, if not France itself, within the hour's time called for by Malcolm. Our path of descent from the stratosphere ended above the channel just north of Le Havre, and after once again engaging the holographic projector we flew directly over that city at cruising altitude, following the Seine River as it snaked its way through one of the most congested areas of French suburban sprawl. This sprawl, like all things French, had over the years become steadily more American in its details and trappings, yet because it cut through one of the finest and most historic areas of Normandy, it was in some way even more grotesque to look at than its American counterparts.

Most disturbing about the scene was its eerie illumination. In suburban areas of the United States one had long since grown accustomed to the sterile, flickering light that oozed out of homes every night into the dark streets and yards: the emanations of hundreds of thousands of Internet and computer monitors. The French, on the other hand, enjoyed a lower crime rate than the Americans and could therefore afford to be more subtle with their street lighting and more indulgent of their characteristic aversion to window furnishings, all of which made the glow of those same monitors—as ubiquitous in France as in the United States or indeed anywhere else in the digital world—more than simply apparent: it was dominant.

As we got closer to Paris, the residential congestion beneath us thickened and the incandescence of the countless monitors intensified. Malcolm and I, watching it all roll by from the nose of the ship, were soon joined by Julien, who of course had the greatest reason to be disheartened by what he was seeing. Fouché professed to have accepted long ago that his native country, whatever its pretenses and protestations, was as susceptible to the afflictions of the information age as any other; indeed, it was the ongoing denials of this fact by his fellow academics and intellectuals that had, he said, provoked his emigration. But such statements didn't seem to help him face that endless, bright testament to his homeland's secure place in the community of modern technostates.

"One attempts to be philosophical about it," he said, crossing his arms and running one hand through his beard. "And yet philosophy only sharpens the indictment. You have read Camus? 'A single sentence will suffice for modern man: He fornicated and read the papers.' We must now change this sentence a bit, I think: 'He masturbated and logged on to the Internet.' " Fouché's bushy brows arched high. "But perhaps the order of activity in that statement is wrong, eh?" He tried to at least chuckle at what, under other circumstances, might have been an amusing thought; but just then neither he nor I—nor, certainly, Malcolm—could quite muster the enthusiasm.

Several silent minutes later Larissa entered, bearing news that, if not uplifting, was at least somewhat encouraging: Tarbell had been able to identify a man in the general vicinity of Paris who regularly sold stolen technological secrets and advanced weaponry to the Israeli government through the Mossad. It seemed more than likely that, as Eshkol's flying destination had been Paris, he intended to contact this man, who, according to Leon's research, was capable of laying hands on almost any sort of hardware—including miniaturized nuclear devices. The dealer lived in and conducted his business out of an expansive lakefront estate near the medieval city of Troyes, southeast of Paris in the Champagne province. So we maintained our heading and increased our pace, perfectly aware that the likelihood of the dealer surviving any encounter with Eshkol was slim.

Swift as we were, though, we were not swift enough. Our ship had barely reached the rolling landscape around Troyes when Leon began to pick up French police reports concerning a murder at the home of the arms dealer. Given the victim's occupation, the matter was being kept very quiet, though even in their (supposedly) secure communications the police admitted that they had no leads at all: apparently the Israelis were in no rush to acknowledge either that they had done extensive business with the dead man or that one of their own operatives might have been responsible for his death. There was nothing for us to do but program our monitoring system to keep a close watch on all sales of airline tickets for journeys originating in France; by cross-referencing with other databases according to the system already set up by Tarbell and the Kupermans, we could reasonably hope to discover where Eshkol intended to go next.

That revelation, when it came, was more than a little surprising for some of us: *"Kuala Lumpur?"* I repeated after Tarbell broke the news. "*Malaysia?* He's going into the middle of a full-scale war—"

"Ah-ah." Leon wagged a finger. "A *'United Nations intervention,'* please, Gideon. They are very particular about that."

"All right," I said, irritated. "He's going into the middle of a

United Nations intervention that's turned into the biggest regional bloodbath since Vietnam? What the hell for? Is he trying to get himself killed?"

"You are the psychiatrist, Gideon," Fouché said. "That is really a question *we* should be asking *you, non?*"

I took a light but fast swipe at him, but he dodged it with the impressive agility I'd seen him demonstrate in Afghanistan. "This isn't funny," I declared. "I hope nobody's thinking that *we're* going there?"

"Why not?" Larissa asked.

"Into the middle of the *Malaysian war*?"

"Ah-ah," Tarbell said again. "It's not a—"

"Leon, will you *shut up*?" None of them seemed in the least apprehensive, a fact that was wearing on my nerves. "Do I have to remind you that every Western power currently has troops in Malaysia? *Real* troops—not militias, not police, *armies.* And the Malaysians have become so damned crazed from two years of fighting that they're actually giving those armies a run for their money. You don't expect me to waltz into the middle of *that*?"

"Darling?" Larissa cooed with a little laugh, coming up behind me and putting her arms around my neck. "You're not telling me you're *afraid,* are you?"

"Of course I'm afraid!" I cried, which only amused her further. "I'm sorry, but there's only so much you can ask of a person, and this—"

"This is necessary." It was Malcolm, ready with another piece of discouraging but unarguable information: "We have to go, Gideon. There's only one thing that can be drawing Eshkol to Kuala Lumpur. The Malaysians have been financing their war effort in part through one of the most extensive black market systems ever seen—they're laundering Third World drug money, trafficking in everything from rare animals to human beings, and doing a huge business in stolen information technology and databases. None of this, however, will interest Eshkol. He'll want something else, something that will have originated, unless I'm mistaken, in Japan." By now all jocularity had departed the table. "The Japanese economy, of course, never really rebounded from the '07 crash. Like the Malaysians, they've had to use whatever methods have been available to organize even a modest recovery. Certainly, they've had neither the money nor the resources to update their energy infrastructure—they still depend primarily on nuclear power and haven't been able to phase out their breeder reactors."

Eli suddenly clutched his forehead. *"Breeder reactors,"* he said, apparently getting a point that was still very obscure to me.

"What?" I asked quickly. "What the hell's a 'breeder reactor'?"

"A nuclear reactor that makes usable plutonium out of waste uranium," Jonah said. "Seemed a very promising idea at one time."

"An idea that was abandoned by almost every country in the world," Malcolm went on, "because of safety problems—and because of the enormous temptation that copious amounts of plutonium lying around in civilian installations poses for terrorists." Malcolm looked at me pointedly. "As well as for the people who do business with terrorists. Japanese black marketeers—without, supposedly, the connivance of their government—have been regularly selling large quantities of their excess plutonium to such people. In—"

"In Kuala Lumpur," I said, falling into a chair in resignation.

"Actually, no," Jonah said. "The U.N. has control over the capital. Most of the serious black marketeering goes on in the Genting Highlands that overlook the city—the old gambling resort. But Kuala Lumpur's the only place the Allies will permit planes to land, since they control both the city and the airport. Eshkol will head there first, probably masquerading as some kind of humanitarian worker, then make his way through the lines and into the high country."

I took the news as best I could, letting my head fall onto the table and drawing several long, deep breaths. "So what's Malaysian food like?" I mumbled.

"I doubt if you'll have a chance to try it," Tarbell answered. "There is a war going on there, you know . . ."

CHAPTER 35

There was a time when I contemplated the ecological effects of African tribal wars like the ones I have been observing for the last nine months with horrified fascination. I was aware, of course, that this reaction was due largely to the images of those conflicts that were being circulated by the world's news services; yet even as I acknowledged such manipulation, I remained as riveted and moved as was the rest of the world, enough so that I ignored the much more seriously destructive campaigns that were being waged against rain forests in other parts of the world by a constellation of lumber, agricultural, and livestock companies—companies that were vital parts of larger corporations that owned many of the news services that were keeping the public's attention focused on places such as Africa in the first place. The rate of destruction in those other rain forests—which of course were just as vital to the general health of the planet as their African counterparts—was far in excess of anything that such characters as my friend Chief Dugumbe and his enemies could do during even their most bitter engagements; but jobs were jobs and trade was trade, and so the world saw nothing of that more extensive defoliation save for occasional glimpses captured by maverick journalists.

This state of affairs prevailed until it was almost too late; that is, until scientists began to report rather than predict the changes in air quality that accompanied the disappearance of those natural oxygen laboratories. Global atmospheric deterioration, when the general public at last comprehended it, caused widespread panic, and an unprecedented movement to save the forests that were left got under way, one that was belligerent rather than evangelical. Its practical result was the creation of special U.N. "monitoring forces"—multinational armies, really—that inserted themselves into those locations and situations that seemed most salvageable: Brazil, various parts of Central America, and Malaysia.

The Brazilians and Central Americans went along with the policing relatively quiescently. But the Malaysians, drawing on their ancient warlike traditions, rose up against the foreign invaders, determined not to let some of the only sources of income left to them by the '07 crash be taken away without adequate compensation—compensation that no Western nation was in any position or mood to give. Thus was born a new type of resource war, one that made the violent conflicts over oil and water that had already broken out in other parts of the world out seem tame by comparison. True, Eastern Malaysia was subdued fairly easily, thanks to a generous donation to the United Nations by neighboring Brunei, whose sultan was glad for the chance to rehabilitate the image of his scandal-plagued little principality; but Western Malaysia was another matter. After launching an invasion from three directions, the U.N. troops met far stiffer resistance than they'd ever anticipated; and when members of their force were unlucky enough to be captured they were generally tortured to death, mutilated, and sent back to the Allied lines with a small U.N. flag stuffed in their mouths. Eventually the Allied troops did secure most of the cities ringing the peninsula, but several held out; and those several became conduits to and from the jungle highlands, which had already proved a military quagmire for the Allies and were now transformed into a magnet for rogues and mercenaries from all over the world.

Such was the monster into whose maw my shipmates were now dragging me. The journey began in Marseille, for it was from that city that Eshkol had elected to leave France. The same name that was on his airline ticket, "Vincent Gambon," soon appeared on the passenger list of a French bullet train headed south from Troyes, and when it pulled out of the station our ship followed on its shoulder, hugging the French landscape under the protection of our holographic projector so that there would be no possibility of Eshkol's eluding us. The train reached Marseille several hours before Eshkol was due to board his flight, giving him and us enough time to get to the airport: Malcolm was determined that we should stay just as close to his plane as we had to the bullet train, even while it was on the ground. This prospect made not only me but several of the rest of our company uneasy, quite beyond the simple dread that any sane person feels on approaching one of the world's overcrowded and overused international airports. Dangerous as was the elaborate version of Russian roulette known as air travel, flying an unregistered and virtually invisible aircraft into the midst of so deadly a circus seemed the very essence of stupidity. But Larissa, having routed the ship's helm control to the turret, was gleefully anticipating just such an undertaking, and all I could do was trust to her genetically enhanced mental agility and try not to look up too often.

Which proved impossible, for as terrifying as the subsequent exercise was, it was also exhilarating. I could scarcely have guessed that the same ship that had flown so slowly and menacingly over the walls of the Belle Isle prison would be capable of the kind of almost playful aerial agility that it displayed as we darted among the arriving, departing, and taxiing aircraft at Le Pen International Airport in Marseille. Not that there weren't solid grounds for terror: the dozens of commercial planes often veered sharply and unexpectedly simply to avoid hitting one another, so absurdly high was the rate at which they were told to approach and depart the airport; and Larissa did, it seemed to me, derive some perverse pleasure from making her passes at them just a little too close. Yet though I sometimes howled with fright, I never felt myself to be in truly mortal peril, and after several minutes I even began to let laughter punctuate my screams.

All the same, I was not entirely disappointed when Eshkol's gigantic Airbus, its two and a half passenger levels stuffed with nearly a thousand trusting souls, lumbered into the sky and began the flight southeast. The plane's four mammoth engines streamed great trails of exhaust that made it impossible to see out of the turret of our ship while we were flying in its wake, and during those tense minutes we very narrowly avoided a collision with another overcrowded behemoth that was coming in from Africa terribly off course, due to the fact that (as I learned while monitoring air traffic control at the airport) none of the flight crew spoke English or French. Using both computer guidance and her own skills, Larissa soon got us out of that predicament and then to a safe distance just above and alongside Eshkol's plane—although we were still close enough for me to be able to see, through the plane's windows, how dismally cramped the conditions within were and to observe the sudden emergence, from one of the overhead compartments, of several live chickens, which appeared to give the flight crew fits.

There were still more harrowing moments as we plowed along through some of the world's most heavily congested air lanes and across half a dozen time zones. Then, as we moved east and south of India, the traffic mercifully began to thin out; but this respite proved brief. During our approach to Kuala Lumpur the swarms of civilian aircraft were replaced with military models: fighter-bombers, manned and unmanned, as well as transports, radar craft, and refueling tankers were all in evidence. The sun was setting behind us now, throwing a spectacular golden light forward to reveal columns of smoke ascending from the West Malaysian jungle: apparently the U.N. allies, in their zeal to keep the Malaysians from destroying the rain forest, were willing to do the job themselves. Or perhaps their anger over being shown up in battle by a supposedly weak country for what I calculated to be the eleventh or twelfth time in three decades had simply blinded them to logical considerations. Whatever the case, evidence of just how bitter the conflict had become began to mount as we approached the capital's battered Subang Airport alongside Eshkol's plane; and by the time that behemoth set down, we were being forced to dodge not only other aircraft but long-range artillery shells, which were being hurled at the capital from the same Genting Highlands to which we would soon, in all likelihood, be forced to journey.

The sight of the destruction that had been wrought at the airport during the war was not, on a comparative scale, particularly disheartening, for Subang was one of those many twentieth-century terminals designed by architects who had attempted to anticipate the future with results that in that same future looked fairly silly. Nor did one particularly mind seeing that many of Kuala Lumpur's famous but no less ugly skyscrapers—including the Petronas Twin Towers, once the tallest buildings in the world—had been damaged or even leveled. But the havoc wrought in the city's historic district was not so easy to contemplate. During its colonial era Kuala Lumpur had become home to some of the most beautiful late-Victorian architecture ever built, particularly the old Secretariat Building and the famed Moorish train station. Both were gone now and had been little mourned by a world desperate for oxygen. Perhaps this was why, after I was deposited on a field to the west of the airport in the company of Colonel Slayton, Larissa, and Tarbell, my utter lack of sympathy with both sides in the conflict began to take on an angry edge.

I soon discovered that this was easily the most appropriate mood to be in when first laying eyes on Dov Eshkol. We spotted our man right after he got through Subang customs, and although we had all studied pictures of him in various guises and pored carefully over a list of his vital statistics, the bearded, wild-eyed Eshkol gave the impression of being far bigger and more deranged than any of us had expected. Dressed, as Jonah had predicted he would be, in the uniform of a world relief organization (Doctors Without Borders), Eshkol strode through the crowds of weeping Muslims and Hindus who were waiting for other passengers on his plane, as well as the many military personnel in the airport, as if he were untouchable—which he was, of course, proving to be. None of us wondered at his not being stopped for questioning—the watch for him here could not have been vigorous, for what kind of fugitive would seek asylum in a war zone?—and before long we were inside a beat-up, stinking old Lexus taxi, following Eshkol's similar conveyance into the city.

Our destination, it soon became clear, was the battered Islamic-style tower called the Dayabumi Complex, where Eshkol apparently had an appointment. As we drove, our taxi driver began to complain about the questionable ethics of following another cab in a manner that indicated he wanted more money; and listening to him rattle on I found myself once again thinking of Max and laughing quietly as I thought of how summarily he would have dealt with the grousing little man at the wheel. I wondered, too, what he would have made of my recent adventures; but I didn't much care for the answers that I soon gave myself. Although I had no doubt that Max would have greatly appreciated Larissa and abusively condemned Dov Eshkol, the Malaysian situation, and many other things I'd come across and through, I couldn't imagine him actually approving of our current job. I tried to tell myself that such an attitude would have been a product of Max's endless cynicism, of his unwillingness—hardened by years on the New York police force—to believe that anyone actually had a lofty or principled motive for doing anything. Yet this self-serving disparagement of my dead friend's philosophy and motivations only disturbed me further, and by the time we pulled up in front of the Dayabumi Complex I found that it was necessary to force his image from my mind altogether.

We scarcely had time to enter the Dayabumi Complex before we saw Eshkol going back out, now in the company of a man who seemed, from his dress and features, to be a Muslim Malaysian. Most of the country's Hindu and Buddhist minorities, originally of Indian and Chinese origin, had sided with the Allies during the war as retribution for years of mistreatment at the hands of the primarily Muslim government. Eshkol's choice of companion, therefore, was at least a fair indication that he did indeed intend to make a run for the loyalist-controlled mountains. When we returned to the crowded plaza outside the building, we waited until we saw Eshkol and his guide disappear in an old Japanese four-by-four up the Karak Highway toward the mile-high peak beyond the front lines that was the site of the Genting Highlands resort. Larissa then signaled her brother, and we all made quickly for a dark, fairly deserted area beyond the National Mosque to rendezvous with our ship, aboard which Eli was already keeping careful satellite track of Eshkol's vehicle.

We conducted our slow pursuit in a somewhat somber mood. Ahead of us lay what was arguably the greatest center of illegal trade and unbridled hedonism on the planet, a place that could not have had a more fitting title than the "Las Vegas of Malaysia"; but before we reached it still more horror lay in wait for us. We found Eshkol's car and its driver at the start of the eleven-mile, bomb-pitted thoroughfare that led to the resort from the main highway: the unidentified Muslim man, having guided Eshkol through the Allied checkpoints below, had been rewarded with a savage slash to the throat, after which Eshkol had apparently continued his passage on foot. He was evidently determined to leave no witnesses behind, a conclusion from which I actually drew encouragement: it at least indicated that he intended to survive whatever event he was planning, which ruled out a suicide bombing, still the only truly foolproof method of committing a terrorist act.

Had I adequately considered the second possibility inherent in his actions—that he simply enjoyed killing when he could—I would have heeded the voice that I had attributed to poor Max, and urged my comrades to turn back.

CHAPTER 36

Long before the outbreak of the Malaysian war, the group of large white hotels centered around an expansive casino known as the Genting Highlands Resort had established itself as the most luxurious and popular gambling venue in all of Southeast Asia. Over time recreational attractions other than the casino were built at the resort in an attempt to create the illusion of a family vacation spot; but this veil never really achieved opacity, and the gaming tables remained the obvious attraction, as evidenced by the fact that they were mobbed twenty-four hours a day. And though several of the hotels had been damaged during the war and an understandable bite had been taken out of Malaysian tourism, many determined sporting souls continued to make the pilgrimage to the Highlands from abroad. Together with the non-Muslim members of the Malaysian army garrison (Muslims being forbidden to enter the casino), these loyal patrons kept the action at the tables going strong, simultaneously supporting those ancillary industries—prostitution, liquor, drug dealing, and thievery—that generally spring up in places where people exhibit an irrational determination to be separated from their money.

But by 2023 such comparatively ordinary, even quaint pursuits were no longer the biggest businesses in the Genting Highlands, as became clear from the moment Slayton, Larissa, Tarbell, and I were dropped off atop the old Theme Park Hotel, which had been repeatedly bombed during the war and had finally been abandoned. The Highlands' rubble-strewn yet undauntedly merry streets were buzzing with commerce that I can only describe as a kind of doomsday bazaar. Stands of weapons, some of them quite advanced, stood in concrete basins that had once been fountains, their sellers hawking them aggressively to bands of Malaysian soldiers, as well as to visiting dealers and terrorists. Seeing that we were foreigners, tradespeople continually approached our party to find out if we wished to purchase and take home any "servants"—a clear euphemism for what amounted to slaves—while subtler men and women engaged us in quiet conversations concerning any and every imaginable piece of high-tech equipment. Great crowds cheered, drank, smoked, fired off guns as well as fireworks, and had at each other sexually on top of anything that seemed marginally less garbage-strewn than the ground. Through all of these activities the artillery batteries that ringed the resort kept up an incessant fire on Kuala Lumpur, while a giant portable radar dish swept the skies for any sign of Allied planes. It was an utterly stupefying scene, all the more so because of its underlying cause: the rest of the world's simple desire to keep breathing.

The extent of the confusion in the resort did not concern us unduly as we made our way into it, for though we had temporarily lost visual contact with Eshkol, we knew enough about how and why he'd come to the Genting Highlands to be relatively sure that we would be able to relocate him. After making inquiries concerning the purchase of weapons-grade plutonium—inquiries that didn't seem to alarm or surprise the dealers we approached in the slightest—we were told that such transactions were the strict province of General Tunku Said, whose headquarters were in a bowling alley adjacent to the casino, a place that resembled, from the outside, what it had effectively become: a windowless concrete bomb shelter. Said, who had apparently assumed warlord powers over the area since the escalation of the war, also oversaw the casino's business; but it was from the sale of the very rarest types of merchandise that he made his truly serious profits. Larissa had, of course, brought along her handheld rail gun, and after a quick conference we decided among ourselves to demonstrate it for Said in the hope that his desire to acquire such valuable technology would persuade him to share any information he had about Eshkol.

As we approached the guards outside the bowling alley, I noted that my heart rate was remarkably steady; I felt that I now had enough experience of violent situations under my belt—particularly, after Afghanistan, those involving Muslim extremists—to be able to cope with whatever collection of fanatics we might find inside. (Of course, this bravado was fortified by the knowledge that Larissa would be watching my back.) The soldiers standing guard at the entrance to the structure, however, were wholly unlike the terrorists we had encountered during the Afghan episode; indeed, their natty dress and punctilious behavior made them seem singularly out of place amid the madness of the resort. After we identified ourselves in order to establish our credibility, one of the men sent word for a senior officer, a Major Samad, who soon appeared with several more soldiers and, after upbraiding the guards for failing to stand at attention continuously, heard our offer. He pulled out a small communicator and quietly proceeded to have a conversation with someone I could only suppose to have been General Said; and several minutes later we found ourselves walking through a dark corridor alongside the major.

"Please excuse the men outside," he said earnestly and in unbroken English. "In a place such as this, it is difficult to maintain discipline."

"That's understandable," Colonel Slayton replied. "Doesn't it ever occur to your commander to clean up the city?"

"Constantly," Samad sighed, "but our government needs the money, you see. We are down to the last of our F-117s, which, as you know, Colonel, are badly outdated to begin with. The casino has provided us with enough money to buy advanced antiaircraft weapons and artillery from the French, but new aircraft purchases will require more than mere gambling receipts. And so we tolerate that offense to Allah out there"—he pointed back toward the center of town—"and pray that the Prophet—may his name be blessed and his soul enjoy peace—will forgive us, for we fight in his name, and for the triumph of the true faith in Malaysia."

Slayton nodded. "How many sorties a day are they throwing at you?"

"We cannot be sure," Samad answered, "though yesterday we thought we counted at least ninety-seven—" He was interrupted as the sudden sound of crashing bowling pins and very civil applause came echoing down the corridor from somewhere ahead of us. "Ah!" Samad's face brightened noticeably. "The general appears to be doing well!"

The bowling alley that we entered was plushly appointed but nearly deserted. There were two or three groups of guards placed strategically about the large space, and at one pair of lanes another group of very well dressed Malaysian officers stood sipping coffee that evidently came from a large, ornate samovar that stood on the alley's darkened bar. A small man whose uniform was pressed just a bit more crisply than those of the others, and whose gold braid and insignia glowed noticeably brighter than theirs, stood rolling balls down at the pins in one lane. The man was clearly a beginner, but what he lacked in skill he more than made up for in enthusiasm.

This, Major Samad announced, was General Tunku Said, scourge of Kuala Lumpur and bane of the United Nations. The compact commander, told of our arrival, came bounding over, grinning beneath a well-trimmed mustache and extending his hand to each of us—save Larissa—as we were introduced.

"A terribly amusing game, my infidel friends, this bowling!" he said, speaking in English that was even better than Samad's. "I am unclear, however, as to its origins—some says it's a Dutch invention and some that the English devised it. But I suppose it makes no difference, since both were rulers of Malaysia at one time or another!"

An enormous explosion outside suddenly shook the building hard, bringing plaster and concrete dust down from the high ceiling. As more explosions followed, I became possessed by a desire to dive ignominiously under a nearby bench; General Said, however, just stood looking at the ceiling with his hands on his hips. "And now those same Dutch and English bomb us," he said, both amazed and angry. "And bomb the marvelous buildings that they themselves built throughout our country. Can you imagine it, unbelievers? And for what? For the rain forest? For the oxygen? Nonsense! They are destroying the jungle themselves, and their motive is nothing more than pride, which is a sin before Allah!" He caught himself suddenly. "Oh, please excuse me—coffee, infidels? Tea? Perhaps a game?" We began to move slowly toward the lane where he'd been playing, which several of the soldiers were clearing of rubble and dust. "It is said that the Americans are masters of this sport"—he pointed to a large television above the bar—"and indeed it seems so!" On the huge screen several professional American bowlers were hard at work. "We have the Bowling Channel—do you know it? 'All bowling, all the time' is their pledge. Of course, we catch only glimpses, because the Allies are continually jamming—" Just as he said the words, the television screen went snowy. General Said looked for an instant as though he might scream, but he swallowed the outburst and only sighed. "I realize that we are at war, infidels, but I ask you—does this not seem somehow gratuitous?"

Larissa stepped forward. "If you'll permit me, General, I think I can be of some help."

This brought a patronizing chuckle out of the general, and the rest of his officers picked up on the laughter. "You really must excuse us, Lady Infidel," Said managed to say. "It is not your sex that amuses us, although your father or husband or brother must live in a perpetual state of agonizing shame to know that you appear in public as you do. But how can one woman—"

Larissa held a hand up and then turned away, putting the same hand to the collar of her bodysuit and talking too softly to be heard.

General Said gave Colonel Slayton a nod. "Ah. She is favored, then."

"Favored?" Slayton said.

"By Allah," Tarbell explained with a smiling nod of his own. "The general thinks that Larissa is feeble-minded."

General Said shrugged. "She wears the clothes of a man and talks to the air, Dr. Tarbell—can I be wrong?"

"Apparently you can, General," I said, looking to the television above the bar. "If you'll just observe . . ." Suddenly the bowling images returned, bringing delighted shouts and more applause from the officers around us. I'd correctly surmised that Larissa had asked Malcolm to use one of the Tressalian satellites to generate a secure signal and beam the Bowling Channel (and how I would have liked to have seen Malcolm's face when he got *that* request) down to Kuala Lumpur.

"My distinguished infidel guests!" Said gushed. "This is really too kind—too kind! You have won our friendship, doomed unbelievers though you may be! Tell me, what is it we can do for you? Major Samad says you seek plutonium."

"Actually, we seek a man," Tarbell said, pulling out a page of his notes on Eshkol, as well as a photograph of him.

General Said looked confused. "A man? Not plutonium?"

"The man we seek is in the market for plutonium," Colonel Slayton explained. "And that's why we've come to you."

For the first time Said looked slightly displeased, as though he suspected what our business actually was. "And what is this man's name?"

Tarbell handed over the photo and glanced at his notes. "He would be using the name and carrying the identity papers of a man called Vincent Gambon, who once worked for Doctors Without Borders."

As one, General Said and his officers took a quick step back from us, and their formerly friendly expressions grew hostile. Said put a hand to the sidearm at his waist. "This man Gambon—he is a friend of yours?"

"No," I said quickly, sensing that the misunderstanding might easily turn fatal. "He's our enemy. We're looking for him because he's stolen something of great importance from us."

Said's expression lightened just a bit, and his hand moved away from the gun. "Well, then," he said, "you may be interested in what I have to show you."

The general nodded to one of his officers, who led us to a doorway behind the bowling alley's shoe rental counter. As we reached it I thought I made out the sound of muffled screaming; then the officer threw open the door to the shoe storage and repair room, revealing:

Eshkol. He was tightly gagged and strapped into a heavy wooden chair, with his ankles tied firmly to the chair's front legs. A rotating electric brush with wire bristles had been positioned beneath his upturned bare feet and was spinning at high speed, slowly tearing the skin away from his flesh. Saliva was coursing down from the corners of Eshkol's mouth as he continued to scream, and his crazed eyes were opened wide in agony.

When I looked at General Said again, I could no longer see the well-groomed, well-spoken fellow who moments before had so amused me. It was apparent now why he was feared, and all that his continued smiling did was remind me that for centuries Islamic leaders had tortured prisoners in just this manner: by flaying the soles of their feet.

"Here is your enemy!" the general proclaimed proudly. "And it will no doubt please your infidel hearts to know that his death will be a very slow affair!"

CHAPTER 37

I was too stunned to move or speak, and I could see that my three comrades were in roughly the same shape. We'd spent so many hours preparing ourselves for what we had been sure would be a violent confrontation with Eshkol that discovering him in such a condition—and especially in such a place—left us scrambling to determine our next move. Of course, there was the option of closing the door and letting General Said finish the job he had so enthusiastically started; but for all our recent declarations that Eshkol had to be stopped in a permanent way, I don't think any of us had the stomach for playing a part in his slow death by torture. Then too, as Malcolm reminded Larissa when she reported in concerning the latest developments, we couldn't be sure that Eshkol hadn't told anyone else about the Stalin disc: we needed him to declare those images a hoax to his superiors before he died in order to prevent the propagation of rumors that would likely prove even more troublesome than facts. One by one it dawned on each of us that we were going to have to get him out of that room, that building, and that town; but it was the ever-wily Tarbell, not surprisingly, who grasped that fact first and took hold of the situation.

"Tell me, General," he said, nonchalantly watching Eshkol writhe in a successful attempt to impress Said. "What exactly has this man done to you?"

"He is a pig, Dr. Tarbell!" the general declared, spitting on Eshkol. "To begin with, he has stirred trouble for me within my family. He came looking for plutonium and promised a great deal of money for it. Then, on his way here, he murdered the man I had sent to escort him. Why? I cannot say, and he will not."

"He has killed before, and just as unreasonably," Tarbell explained. "It is our belief that he seeks to obscure the trail he leaves behind. He may even have tried to kill you, after your business was done."

"Me?" the general cried, dumbfounded. *"Here?"*

Tarbell let out a flattering sort of laugh. "Absurd, is it not?"

Said began to laugh along with him. "Yes—absurd! He is a madman, then!" Suddenly the general's laughter died down, and he looked at Eshkol in an immensely irritated way. "But the chap he murdered, you see, was my wife's cousin. I had little use for the man, but how does this make me look? Not only to my family, but to that unholy mob outside? Very bad, infidels, very bad. Furthermore"—Said returned to his bowling lane and picked a file up off the scorer's desk—"we are not without our own ways of gathering intelligence. Were you aware that this enemy of yours is actually a CIA agent?"

The general placed a sheet of printout on a lit area of the desk, at which the contents of the page were projected onto a large screen over the bowling lane. It was indeed a copy of a Central Intelligence file, which stated that an agency operative calling himself Vincent Gambon had infiltrated the Doctors Without Borders field office in the Kurdish sector of Turkey, from which, as I have already noted, Israel was currently drawing a good deal of its water, much to the displeasure of the Turks and their American allies. Here, at least, was the probable reason why Eshkol had killed the real and unfortunate Gambon in the first place, although Said apparently knew nothing about such matters, as his next words demonstrated: "No doubt his actual purpose here was to undermine our hold on this mountain—perhaps by way of the nuclear device we found him carrying!" Said held up a small rucksack that bore the same Doctors Without Borders logo we'd seen on Eshkol's clothes. "The very device he intended to arm with the plutonium *we* had agreed to sell him!" With his free hand the general grabbed a metal radioactive materials canister and held it up; then he looked back through the open door of the shoe room. "Oh, this creature's soul is a pit of evil, infidels, and I intend that he shall regret every minute of his loathsome existence before he dies!"

"Quite understandable," Tarbell said, glancing around the bowling alley and, it seemed to me, silently calculating just how many Malaysian soldiers were in it. "*Thoroughly* understandable!" he reaffirmed. Then he looked at Colonel Slayton and Larissa, both of whom shook their heads as if to say that the idea of some sort of breakout was unfeasible. Leon acknowledged their assessment with a reluctant nod. "And yet it seems to me," he went on, turning to Said again, "that you are missing a most excellent opportunity."

"I?" Said asked. "How, Doctor?"

"Well, I can certainly understand your desire to kill this man slowly," Tarbell answered. "But privately? You yourself have said that the people in this ridiculous community are a mindless mob. Why not seize the opportunity to tighten your hold on them?"

General Said pondered the question, then began to smile once more. "Ah! I see your point, Dr. Tarbell—a public execution!"

Tarbell grinned back at him. "Exactly."

Said's face went straight for a moment. "Would it have to be quick?"

"Oh, no, not necessarily," Leon answered.

The general began to pace thoughtfully. "We might do it at the old dinner theater—they love their theater, these degenerates, and we could give them something special." He continued to mull it over. "I might crucify him," he said.

Tarbell cocked his head skeptically. "Well," he said. "It's a bit trite, isn't it? Not to mention the implications—you don't want him to seem the martyr, after all."

"Yes, yes, this is so." Said kept pacing, then finally stopped and turned to Tarbell. "Well, then, Doctor, I open the floor to suggestions."

Tarbell took the general aside conspiratorially. "I'm not sure the length of his death is really the most important consideration. My own idea would be this—have your men escort him to a high public spot after attiring him in one of your own uniforms."

"*My* uniforms?" Said protested. "But why should—"

"I assume," Tarbell interjected soothingly, "that the Americans have you under close satellite surveillance?"

"Oh, by the Prophet, blessings and peace be upon him, they do indeed!" General Said looked momentarily distraught. "Twenty-four hours a day, I can scarcely ever leave this place—" Suddenly he stopped, getting the point. "Ah! Excellent, Dr. Tarbell—truly, for an infidel that is inspired!" He moved toward the shoe room, studying Eshkol. "We shall have to shave his beard, of course, and neaten his mustache, but other than that . . ."

I was utterly in the dark. "Neaten his mustache?" I asked. "Why?"

"So that the Americans will think he's General Said," Slayton explained, smiling as he grasped Leon's idea.

"At which point," Larissa concluded, shaking her head in good-natured wonder at Tarbell, "they'll kill him themselves—a single satellite-guided missile would be enough."

Said turned to Larissa in surprise. "Excellent comprehension! Indeed, given that you are an unbeliever *and* a woman, it is *doubly* excellent!"

Larissa's patience with the general was waning, and Tarbell could see it: he quickly took Said by the elbow and walked him away from her, saying, "His death not only makes a statement to the vermin in the resort but convinces the Americans that you yourself are no longer alive—and so they will suspend their satellite watch."

"Thus allowing *me* to go *outside*! A brilliant plan in all respects!" Said turned to his officers and began barking orders: "We shall use the roof of the Theme Park Hotel—let the fools blow the rest of it up! Inform the manager of the casino that in one hour he will suspend all play. The patrons will be herded outside, at gunpoint if necessary, and everyone in the streets will be forced onto the plaza to watch, as well!"

During the momentary whirl of activity that followed, Slayton quietly told the rest of us to follow him into the shoe room. Once there I adjusted the brushing machine just enough so that it wasn't actually making contact with Eshkol's feet, while Slayton whispered in the captive's ear, "Keep screaming, or we'll all get killed." Eshkol's features had begun to relax with the cessation of the flaying, but he quickly contorted them again, taking Slayton's meaning. "Listen to me, Dov Eshkol," the colonel went on. "We know who and what you actually are, we know why you're here, and we know what your plan is. But if you want to avoid what the general is planning for *you,* do exactly as we say." Eshkol nodded quickly between muffled screams, and then Slayton turned to the rest of us. "We'll need his pack—we certainly can't leave a device like that with these people. We'd better take the plutonium as well. Larissa, tell your brother that we'll want to be picked up off the roof of the casino sometime in the next hour."

"And what happens when the general doesn't get his execution?" I asked.

"Gideon, really," Tarbell scolded. "That question is unworthy of you. By the time the general realizes that he is not to have his precious execution, we will be aboard the ship and far away."

"Oh," I said as we all filed back out of the room. "Yes, of course." I breathed a little easier at the thought and gave Tarbell a gentle pat on the back. "Well done, Leon—you could sell ice to Eskimos, my friend, no doubt about it."

Tarbell laughed, quietly but with his usual fiendish delight. "Yes," he said as he glanced up at me, "it *is* almost frightening, isn't it? But I can't help myself, Gideon. The great throws, the lies told for the highest stakes—so immensely sexual! At such times I really do think that I could talk anyone into anything!"

Even now, as I sit here waiting for dawn to break through the African gloom, I can see my brilliant, strange little friend's grinning face in the flame of the lamp that burns before me; and though the vision makes me smile, I shudder with sorrow as well. For there is one sexless wraith that not even Leon could dissuade from his grim purpose, and he was hovering nearby even as we laughed.

CHAPTER 38

In order for our plan to succeed, it was of course necessary that Eshkol be able to walk. In addition, the torment through which Said had put his prisoner roused some primitive form of empathy in me, despite all the contemptible things I knew about the man. For both of these reasons I did my best to clean, pad, and bind the bleeding soles of Eshkol's feet, forgetting in my disgust with such tortures as he'd endured that someone with his training and temperament could likely have run on bleeding stumps if he'd thought it would serve his fanatical purpose. What I did was not merciful but foolish, and it should have been I and I alone who paid for the mistake. Had it been, the tragedy that ensued might even have made some sort of twisted sense.

Just before the appointed hour of Eshkol's death, we all accompanied Major Sadad to the place of execution: the same abandoned hotel roof where we had first debarked from our ship. Following more of Tarbell's clever suggestions, the Malaysians had created a false command center on the roof, such as General Said might himself have used to direct his forces. Colonel Slayton was relatively sure that we were already under satellite observation—the United States had, after all, gained a great deal of experience with such long-range surveillance operations during its efforts to locate various elusive enemy leaders over the last thirty years—and when we returned to Said, who was staying carefully out of sight in a half-demolished suite on a lower floor of the hotel, the colonel declared that the authenticity of the stage and its props would certainly bring about the desired result. General Said was delighted with this affirmation from a fellow officer, and before long he ordered his men to bring up Eshkol.

The prisoner, in accordance with the plan, had been dressed in a uniform very similar to Said's, and his facial hair had been carefully adjusted. The general expressed some concern about the obvious discrepancy between his own height and that of his döppelgänger; but Slayton told him that this shouldn't matter, since the American satellites would be watching from above. The colonel and Said continued to go over the details of the operation in an increasingly collegial manner, one that succeeded in distracting the general completely; and while he was thus engaged Larissa and Tarbell slipped back to the bowling alley to secure Eshkol's rucksack and the plutonium containment canister. They soon returned with both items, and though at the time this seemed a coup, it, too, soon proved a bad mistake.

At ten o'clock General Said announced that it was time to proceed: Eshkol was to be taken up to the roof, where his men would tether him to a heavy slab of concrete rubble. When we got outside we discovered that, as was apparently often the case on that mountain, a beautiful mist had formed around the resort, though not above it: the starry night sky was still quite visible through the vast white halo. Below the building the enormous crowd ordered by General Said had gathered, and though armed soldiers had surrounded the area, the spectators seemed to need no encouragement to cheer and holler in a bloodthirsty—and bloodcurdling—manner.

Just as five of Said's men were about to secure Eshkol to his Promethean slab of concrete, something that I had hoped and even expected never to see again drifted up from below a nearby edge of the roof: it was one of the American surveillance drones, our companions from the stratosphere, and it was not, of course, alone. Within seconds the entire roof was ringed with the things, and as they appeared General Said asked Colonel Slayton in a very agitated voice what they were, though this inquiry was impeded by the frequent need to tell his severely spooked soldiers to calm down and hold their positions. Slayton did his best to dismiss the drones as mere surveillance instruments, but Larissa, Tarbell, and I knew the grim facts of the situation. To begin with, the drones could at any moment have destroyed the roof or even the entire hotel, depending on their armament; but what was perhaps worse was that those of us from Malcolm's ship had now been recognized by the Americans, and this was likely to lead to a plethora of problems concerning our ship's escape and continued concealment, since any new anomalous radar readings would likely be assigned to us.

Bad as the situation was, it was about to get a great deal worse. The drones did not go on the attack immediately, most likely because of the confusion that their remote operators were experiencing as to just what was happening on the roof; but their appearance gave Eshkol an opportunity, one that he used every ounce of his training to exploit. After breaking free of the five men who'd been detailed to chain him to the concrete, he subdued three of them in a frenzy of savage blows, kicks, and gouges. Having secured a weapon from one of those he'd felled, he used it to blow the other two quickly over the edge of the roof. But Eshkol was far too clever to think that he would make it out of that situation armed with only an ordinary gun. Apparently he had divined, even while he was strapped down and being tortured, that the weapon Larissa wore slung at her side was something very unusual; and, spraying a hail of fire that forced us all to disperse and find cover, he hurled himself at her. Very neatly making it look as though he meant to do her harm, he instead plucked the rail gun out of its holster and rolled with it to the far side of the roof, while Larissa, who had been readying herself for hand-to-hand combat, looked on in stunned amazement.

We were in trouble, though at that point only we four visitors knew how bad the trouble was. Education for the others was, however, on the way. As the drones dashed about the edges of the roof like onlookers at a brawl trying to decide which side, if any, to take, Eshkol began moving among the huge pieces of rubble with an agility that would have been remarkable even had he not just endured long hours of torture. After several minutes of this display, he finally caught one unlucky Malaysian soldier out in the open and fired the rail gun. I had not actually seen the thing used on a man before, and the effect was at once greater and less violent than I had expected. Most of the soldier's body simply disappeared, as John Price's had done; and the pieces that were left, being wholly and cleanly detached from the trunk, had a certain prosthetic quality, as if they had never actually been part of a living human body. General Said lost about half of his men to panic after that, though the few who stayed showed admirable resolve in the face of what seemed certain death. It soon became clear from Eshkol's movements, however, that he wasn't interested in the Malaysians at all.

He began to vociferously demand his rucksack and the plutonium canister, the pair of which he had somehow noticed Larissa and Tarbell bringing up to the roof. Screwing up my courage, I got to Larissa's side with a few leaps and some low running, but she informed me that Leon had the deadly goods. Where Leon might be, however, neither she nor anyone else seemed to know. As General

Said shouted to Eshkol that the rucksack and canister were not on the roof—true, as far as he knew—Slayton, Larissa, and I crawled about as best we could, urgently whispering Tarbell's name. My own attempts to contact him became, out of desperation, rather absurdly noisy; then, from behind the housing of an elevator mechanism, I heard him whisper:

"Gideon! Be quiet, you fool, you'll get us both killed!"

I couldn't yet see him, but I was relieved to know that he was alive. "Are you hurt, Leon?" I called.

"Not yet!" he answered. "Although if you insist on—oh, no." The dread that had suddenly come into his voice indicated that Eshkol was nearby; and when I looked up I saw the huge man lying flat atop the elevator structure, safe from the fire of the Malaysians and pointing the rail gun down over the far side. I heard him demand the rucksack and canister and offer Tarbell his life in exchange.

"You lying eunuch!" Leon said. "We know you too well—"

What came next, though predictable, was nightmarishly unstoppable. Eshkol had demonstrated as pronounced a taste for unnecessary killing as any sociopath I'd ever encountered, and there was no reason to think that Leon—lacking weapons, cover, or bargaining chips—would receive the mercy that so many others had been denied. Still, the quiet discharge of the rail gun when it came brought me out of my hiding place screaming, loud enough for Eshkol to turn in evident alarm. Perhaps he thought that I would be so foolish only if I had some other miraculous weapon; or perhaps he had so squandered any human feelings he still possessed on his dead ancestors that he could not believe that anyone would put himself in danger simply out of brotherhood or grief. Whatever the case, he looked utterly confused, a confusion that probably saved me. Certainly it was a confusion that deepened mightily, as did that of General Said, his men, and, it seemed, the American drones, when the sky above the hotel cracked open to reveal Julien, who was once again standing in the hatchway of our ship.

He was holding a long-range stun weapon, which he aimed at the spot where Eshkol was lying. But again the number of similar situations that Eshkol must have been in during his career became evident: he disappeared off his perch, I think, even before Fouché pulled the trigger of his gun. A sudden outcry from the remaining Malaysians—who had lost the last of their nerve at the sight of the floating, hollering Frenchman—indicated that Eshkol was on his way down to the street from the roof by way of a damaged staircase. None of the soldiers, however, was willing to give chase, at least not until General Said's exhortations turned into open threats. When the troops finally did begin to move, Colonel Slayton rushed toward my position, as did Larissa; but I had already dashed to and around the elevator structure.

There was nothing left of Leon save an arm, probably the arm with which, given the care his murderer had taken not to damage it, he'd held the rucksack and containment canister. Of those items there was no trace, though at the moment that fact meant nothing to me. I fell to my knees and, in a kind of utterly spent mourning, began to chuckle tearfully: for the middle finger of Leon's dead hand was raised, as I was sure it had been when he'd met his end. Larissa soon put her arms around me and attempted to pull me up and toward the descending hatchway of the ship, but in my sorrow I would not be moved from the spot. Fusillades of gunfire began to be directed at us by the troops in the street, while the drones moved toward the hatchway with the clear purpose of inspecting it so that their operators could decide whether or not to attack; yet still I would not go, not until I'd determined what in God's name to do about Tarbell's arm.

It suddenly occurred to me that Leon would have enjoyed nothing more than the terrifying effect that this lone, eerie remnant of his earthly existence would have should it suddenly plummet into the crowd below. Perhaps the jest seems a ghoulish and even grotesque one, removed from its context; but at that moment I was surrounded by so much violence of such bizarre, even absurd, proportions that the idea seemed entirely appropriate. I therefore lifted one foot and sent the remains of the peculiar little man who from the moment of my arrival on Malcolm's ship had proved a genuine friend down to play his final prank on the world.

CHAPTER 39

Of our escape and removal to a safe distance I can say little, for shock had clouded my senses. The closure of the ship's hatchway after we'd gotten back aboard and the reactivation of the complete holographic projection around the vessel apparently threw the drones off long enough for us to reach the coast and dive into the Straits of Malacca; but the fact remained that four of our number had been observed and no doubt identified. That Slayton should have been seen was bad enough, but Larissa's presence would no doubt prompt our antagonists to ask uncomfortable questions about Malcolm and probably about St. Kilda as well, once it was discovered, as seemed inevitable, that he owned the islands. Yet despite both this danger and his own deep sorrow over Tarbell's death, Malcolm was determined that we should remain in the vicinity of Kuala Lumpur until we knew where the now massively armed Eshkol was going. All ship's systems were set to work monitoring air traffic, both civilian and military, along with naval communications, private wireless phone calls, e-mail, secure Internet servers, even the radio transmitters of small commercial fishermen. Eshkol could have been anywhere in Malaysia, but he had to be somewhere, and when he made his inevitable move to depart, Malcolm intended for us to be right behind him.

My initial participation in this endeavor lacked both full concentration and a certain heart. The circumstances surrounding Tarbell's death, like those of Max's, had revealed a side of human behavior that I thought worse, in its way, than anything I had encountered during all my years of studying criminal behavior. But whereas Max's death had filled me with a desire for explanations from and revenge against persons who had grievously abused their positions of power, Leon's fate seemed to confirm what I had already begun to suspect: that participating in such high-stakes games, even for the best of motives, would prove not only disastrous but corrupting. In short, the tragic events we were experiencing were being produced by the collective desires of *all* players, not merely Dov Eshkol, to see their own concept of right prevail.

"What are you saying, Gideon?" Larissa asked me as we lay on the bed in my quarters after some twelve hours of keeping relatively silent vigil in the turret. "That we're as bad as Eshkol?"

"No," I said, bridling a bit at her loaded simplification. "But you can't deny that if we'd just stayed out of the entire thing he would have been quietly killed in General Said's bowling alley. Or what if Malcolm had never ordered the creation of the Stalin images in the first place? Eshkol would have just kept on doing what hundreds of intelligence operatives do every day. There would have *been* no crisis."

Larissa sat up. "I've never had much use for 'what-if's," she said crisply. "In situations like this, in *any* situations that involve questions of force and power, virtue's a relative thing. And speaking relatively, I'd say we're the only ones in this mess even trying to do any good."

I stared at the ceiling. "What's that old saying—about it always being the good men who do the most damage in the world?"

Larissa looked even more irritated; perhaps, I thought, because in her heart she agreed with me. "Old sayings like that tend to depend on who came up with them."

"I think it was Henry Adams," I said. "Who, admittedly, chose to be an observer in the power game throughout his life. Unlike his forebears."

"Exactly." Larissa lay back down, trying very hard to douse the quick spark of misunderstanding that flared between us. "The point isn't that Leon died, Gideon—it's that he died as well as anyone could." She smiled fondly. "Certainly as *characteristically* . . ."

I chuckled once, quietly and sadly, along with her. "He *was* fairly unbelievable. Even when he took pleasure in something he just seemed so—*contemptuous* of it. By the way—" I turned onto my side, my face inches from Larissa's. "Did anybody ever actually find out where he came from? I asked him a couple of times, but he always dodged it."

"He told me a story once," Larissa said. "I have no idea whether it was true. It was just after he'd joined us, and I think he was trying to inspire sympathy as a way of seducing me. God knows sex was the only thing that could ever have made him show that side of himself. He claimed that his mother was a Siberian prostitute in Vladivostok and his father was a visiting English telecom executive. The mother was killed during a Russian bombing raid. After that his grandmother took him to Indonesia to get away from the war and supported his schooling by working in a microchip sweatshop. It killed her eventually. He began stealing and later forging to complete his education."

I considered it. "Well," I breathed, "it would explain at least some of his attitude. And if it's not true, he's the only one who could have made it up."

Although I think she wanted to, Larissa could not let my moment of doubt pass without asking, "So is this going to be a problem for you? What we have to do now?"

I gave it several minutes' hard thought. "I won't deny that I have questions," I finally said. "But I also know that since this situation is at least partly our doing, the solution should be, too. Maybe we shouldn't have walked into it—but things aren't going to get any better if we just walk out."

Larissa pulled me close. "That's true . . ."

I don't think she was entirely reassured by my lofty words; certainly *I* wasn't. But the conversation had nowhere left to go, and it was somewhat merciful, therefore, that Malcolm's voice came over the address system at that moment, telling us to join him forward. Apparently we at last had a lead, one that we were pursuing with evident dispatch; by the time Larissa and I managed to dash through the ship's corridors to the nose, the vessel was already heading up toward the surface at a good clip, and we joined the rest of our team (minus Julien, who was still in one of the labs) just in time to watch as we burst into the sky above the straits. At this point, however, any encouragement that might have been inspired by Malcolm's announcement vanished:

The waters directly below us were full of American naval vessels, which immediately began bombarding our ship. The electromagnetic fields around the vessel succeeded in throwing these missiles off target or detonating them at a safe distance, but that didn't explain how the warships had been able to locate us in the first place.

"They're finally getting smart," Slayton said, anxiously guiding the ship through the hail of fire from the guidance console. "They monitored the wake we left in the water and any air disturbances that originated with our surfacing point. Then they opened a blanket fire."

"But—don't they run the risk of hitting each other?" I asked. "Or other ships that are farther off?"

"Of course," Malcolm said, wheeling his chair into position beside the colonel. "But they seem more willing than ever to take the chance—not surprisingly."

I was confused for an instant, but Eli quickly turned to explain: "We monitored a Malaysian transmission about fifteen minutes ago, which said that somebody'd made off with the one B-2 bomber they had left—it was being kept at a remote airfield because the only Malaysian pilot who could fly it had been killed. Anyway, there was a lot of garbled, panic-stricken screaming that included a reference to a nuclear device."

"Eshkol," Larissa said. "The bastard can *fly*, too?"

"He's the complete covert operative," Jonah answered with a nod. "We're on his tail, but the Malaysians also talked about the four of you and about what they saw of our ship. The Americans, according to *their* transmissions, have concluded that the mystery vessel they've been hearing about and occasionally running into all these months is on the B-2 job, somehow. So things are likely to get very hot on this ride."

"But why?" I asked. "They can't be tracking us."

"No," Jonah went on, "but we've got to follow Eshkol's plane—"

"Which is an old American model," Slayton said, "whose stealth systems the American air force knew how to defeat even when they were still using it. They think our ship's escorting Eshkol, not chasing him. They'll stay fixed on him and look for patterns of air disturbance that match what they monitored when we came out of the sea."

"Do we have to stay so close to Eshkol, in that case?" Larissa asked. "We can track him from the stratosphere, after all—"

"Where we'll be too far away to prevent his doing anything rash," Malcolm cut in.

Larissa considered this with a nod. "Then we shoot him down."

"The Americans may be willing to risk radioactive fallout," Malcolm answered, "but I am not. No, Sister, this time the idiots have us, I'm afraid. For the moment."

"Just for the moment?" I asked, alarmed at the explosions that were surrounding the ship but more unsettled still by Malcolm's concession of even a momentary disadvantage. "What do you mean? What can we do later?"

"It depends on Eshkol's nuclear device," Eli said. "Julien's studying the plans now. If it has electronic components that can safely be disabled—"

"Which we know his plane has," Jonah added.

"Then," Eli went on, "we can hit him with a pulse."

"A pulse?" I asked, at first making the medical connection; then I remembered the kind of ship on which I was traveling. "An *electromagnetic* pulse," I said, breathing easier as I realized that we might indeed have a chance.

This feeling was reinforced when Julien suddenly burst in from the corridor. *"Tonnerre!"* he cried, seeming a little amazed himself. "It will work!"

CHAPTER 40

During the next several hours the hopes engendered by my shipmates' admirable scheme were summarily dashed by Dov Eshkol's seemingly inexhaustible cunning. It quickly became apparent that his admittedly brilliant plan of escape rested on four principal considerations: first, that the U.N. alliance would hardly allow someone to fly out of Malaysia in a B-2 bomber—an obsolete piece of technology, perhaps, but still a deadly one—without giving chase with a view toward capture or, when that proved impracticable, termination. And when aerial combat was joined, Eshkol would have no chance against the squadrons of more advanced aircraft that would be dispatched to intercept him. Therefore the only real weapon at his disposal was the plane itself: if he kept to the skies above populated areas and refrained from forcing an engagement, no nation in the world would risk having its air force be the one to shower the earth's surface with a flaming mass of wreckage that would conservatively claim hundreds—and potentially thousands—of lives. Finally, Eshkol's tactic would be equally effective against our ship, for while we had planned a less cataclysmic way of ending his flight than shooting him down, the chance that a failure of the B-2's electrical systems might result in a crash as devastating as any result of combat was enough to stay our hand.

What made the situation doubly frustrating was that as we followed Eshkol at a comparatively low altitude into Thai airspace, where he made a point of traveling as far north as he could above the crowded outskirts of Bangkok, the American navy apparently relayed the intricate tracking system it had designed to keep tabs on our ship to their own as well as the English air force: the naval guns that had given us such a rude shock when we emerged from the Straits of Malacca were replaced by the cannon fire of fighter jets, which attempted to harass both our ship and Eshkol's B-2 into landing without a struggle (their missiles went unused, presumably out of the same fear of collateral damage that prompted their reluctance to shoot Eshkol down). We initially assumed that this situation would go on only as long as we were within the range of the first squadrons to intercept us; but as we streaked over Bangladesh we saw fresh squadrons appear from carriers in the Bay of Bengal, and it became apparent that the Allies intended to do everything they could to put an end to what they had no doubt decided was some sort of grand terrorist plot.

So on we went into the Indian sunset, with the Allied planes keeping up an almost incessant fire and Eshkol cleverly matching his course to the population density on the ground. His general heading seemed to be west by northwest, though it was impossible to guess at his ultimate destination due to the circuitous nature of his flight path. We of course feared that he was heading for Russia, a fear that was seemingly validated when he made a run for the Caucasus; but then he unexpectedly moved west into Turkey, flying over town after town along the Black Sea toward Istanbul.

"Can it be that he really *does* wish only to escape?" Julien asked as he stood with the Kupermans, Larissa, and myself behind Malcolm and Colonel Slayton at the guidance console.

Jonah shrugged. "It's possible that he wants to wait until he's under less scrutiny before he carries out whatever it is he's planning."

"I wish that were true," Malcolm answered, never taking his eyes from the great black flying wing that was cruising just below and ahead of us. The B-2 was now becoming increasingly difficult to see against the darkened surface of the Earth, a fact that, while not actually significant, still seemed somehow discouraging. "But let's not fool ourselves," Malcolm went on. "At heart Eshkol is a terrorist, with thc same craving for publicity as *any* terrorist. The fact that he's being watched only makes him more dangerous, I'm afraid."

"We need to start thinking about options," Colonel Slayton said in a tone so steady—even for him—that I knew the situation was indeed as bleak as Malcolm was making it sound. "I know we don't want to bring him down over a populated area, but let's remember what he's carrying. Putting an end to this run could be a question of limiting losses, rather than causing them."

"I've considered that, Colonel," Malcolm answered. "And if he'd continued on into Russia we would probably have been forced to exercise that option. But until we have some better idea—"

Malcolm was cut off by an explosion near the ship, one that indicated that the Allied airmen pursuing us had come to the same conclusion as Colonel Slayton: they were using missiles now, and detonating them close enough to both our ship and the B-2 to make what they apparently believed would be a very serious point. Little came of the outburst, of course—our ship's magnetic fields could play havoc with the guidance systems of any air-to-air missiles in service, and there was certainly nothing that would intimidate Eshkol at that point—but the very ineffectiveness of the attempt was unnerving in the way that it seemed to make the Allied pilots recklessly furious. They began to edge ever closer to the B-2, greatly increasing the chances of a catastrophic collision; and as we flew on through the Balkans and north toward Poland the situation only became more violent and more volatile. The job of avoiding both the Allied planes and the B-2 without being distracted by the exploding missiles and continuing cannon fire eventually proved too much even for Colonel Slayton, and Larissa took his seat at the helm. Powerful though my feelings for and trust in her were, however, the switch did not reassure me, for I knew that Slayton would never allow anger to get the best of him, whereas Larissa? As Malcolm had said when he had first explained John Price's death to me, "Well, *Larissa* . . ."

I don't think any of the others felt any more secure at that moment, except of course for Malcolm; and it was therefore Malcolm who first noticed that our course heading had changed dramatically. "East," he said, so quietly that I almost didn't hear him over the din of the planes and explosions. "East," he repeated, much more emphatically. "He's turned east!"

Colonel Slayton leaned over to one of the guidance monitors, his voice becoming, much to my dismay, only more controlled: "If he stays on this course, he's got virtually a straight line of heavy population—Bialystok, Minsk, Smolensk—" He looked up and out at the B-2, unwilling to name the final link in the chain:

"Moscow," Malcolm announced slowly, his face becoming ashen. His next words were tight but emphatic: "Larissa, Gideon—I suggest you both get to the turret." Larissa needed no encouragement but got quickly to her feet and began pulling me toward the door to the corridor. "We'll wait until he's passed Smolensk," Malcolm called after us. "If there's no deviation—"

Larissa turned. "That's cutting it a little close, isn't it, Brother? Given his speed—"

"Given his speed, Sister, your aim had better be true . . ."

There is a terrible simplicity to what remains of this part of my tale, a barren brevity that I would gladly embellish if doing so would alter the outcome. Larissa and I scarcely exchanged a word as we took up our positions in the turret; and during the next three quarters of an hour, as eastern Poland and western Russia shot unrecognizably by beneath us, silence continued to reign in that transparent hemisphere, unbroken, now, even by the continued sounds of cannon fire and missile explosions; for the Allied planes had abandoned their pursuit long before we entered the unpredictable airspace of that very unpredictable ruin of an empire, Russia. I do not know what Larissa was thinking, as in the days to come I did not think to ask her; as for me, I found myself wondering what must have been going through her mind as she prepared to end yet another man's life. It seemed certain that she would be called on to do so: Eshkol's own behavior had offered us no alternative to his execution, really, since the moment we'd first become aware of him. The only thing left to do now, I mused to myself as we waited in the turret, was hope that as few people as possible would be injured or killed on the ground.

It never occurred to me that Eshkol's plane might simply disappear; yet somewhere between Minsk and Smolensk it seemed to do just that. There was no sign of the thing on any of my equipment, nor, as Malcolm soon informed us, on any of the ship's other monitoring systems. I was profoundly confused, until Larissa pointed out the simplest possible explanation: that Eshkol had crashed. My spirits jumped at the thought, but I forced myself to be skeptical: Wouldn't we have seen the flames? Or detected the descent? Wouldn't Eshkol have ejected if he'd found himself in distress? Not necessarily, Larissa answered; planes could and did crash without significant explosions, and so suddenly as to make tracking their loss of altitude problematic. And nighttime flying conditions could sometimes be so disorienting that a doomed pilot never even knew he was in trouble. All the same, a massive set of double-checks of the area and our ship's systems seemed urgent, and Larissa and I returned to the nose of the ship to assist with them. But the whole of our crew could find neither clues on the ground nor equipment malfunctions on board our vessel. It genuinely did seem that Eshkol's plane had been lost, probably in some field or forest where its hulk would not be discovered until daybreak, if then.

How could we have known? What would have caused any of us to once again turn our monitoring ears toward Malaysia, where we would have learned about the theft of more than just the B-2 bomber? And even had we by some chance learned that a pilfered American stealth system—so advanced and secret that only a handful of people in the United States knew that its design had been stolen—had been installed in that same B-2, would we have been able to meet the challenge of defeating it in time? All such questions were horrifically moot. One fact held sway, that night as this, and on all nights in between:

At the very moment that each of us began to believe that our luck with regard to Eshkol might have changed, the horizon to the northeast came alive with a lovely, brilliant light. Given that our perspective was unblocked, the sudden glow was enough to attract the attention of all of us; and, deathly aware of what was happening, none of us said a word during the inevitable denouement as the signature cloud, angry with all the terrible colors of the explosion that had just been unleashed, slowly began to form above what had once been the city of Moscow.

CHAPTER 41

The horrendous, transfixing fireball had begun to fade long before any of us could find words to acknowledge it. When at last someone did speak, it was Eli, giving voice to the same question that was in all our minds: How had Eshkol gotten away from us? No one could provide an answer, of course, and the terrible query was to hang accusingly in the air throughout our journey back to St. Kilda, where Colonel Slayton, after long hours in the monitoring room, would finally discover the explanation. For the moment, however, we all just shook our heads and went on staring silently, bewildered not only as to how the tragedy had been possible but about what we should do next. At length it was, not surprisingly, Malcolm who brought us out of our horrified daze: in a voice that grated like grinding rocks and matched the deathly pallor of his face, he ordered Larissa to pilot the ship into the burning city, a command that brought a collective gasp of disbelief from the rest of us. Seeing the extent of her brother's devastation, Larissa spoke very gently and carefully when she suggested that such a flight might be dangerous; but Malcolm angrily retorted that the ship would keep us safe from radiation, at least for a time, and that he needed to see the devastation—as, he added, did we all. Without further discussion Larissa took the helm, and we made the flight—and in so doing experienced a loss of innocence such as comparatively few people in the world's history have, thankfully, ever known.

There are no words; none that *I* can find, at any rate. Shall I describe how many shades I discovered there to be in what are usually labeled "gray" ashes, as well as the infinite range of colors that characterize what is generally dismissed as "scorched earth"? And what prose can describe the sickening image of those thousands of brutally burned and torn human bodies, both living and dead, that had escaped actual vaporization? Yet I could not turn away. I once heard it said that destruction perversely but consummately intrigues the eye; but I'd never expected to see the assertion borne out by my own fixation on so nightmarish a panorama.

Ground zero of the blast had, predictably, been the Kremlin, behind whose walls the demented Josef Stalin had once drunk peppered vodka and plotted genocide, though not the genocide in which Dov Eshkol had imagined him to be complicit. Nothing remained, of course, of this structure and its surrounding district; nor was there very much left of Red Square or of the Tverskaya commercial district, which Stalin himself had redesigned, or of fashionable Arbatskaya or of the medieval suburb of Zamoskvorechie across the Moscow River. The miniature bomb had been powerful enough to tear the very heart out of the city, and out of Russia itself—all to avenge an imaginary sin that the profoundly unbalanced Eshkol had desperately needed to believe was real so that he might finally have a rationalization for his brutal maintenance of what he thought was faith with his ancestors and prove himself worthy in the imagined eyes of all those who had died so long ago.

Mundus vult decipi.

The grim tour of the devastated city that Malcolm had believed so necessary ultimately proved too much for him: guilt, exhaustion, and shock all combined with his chronic weakness to produce a crisis, one that I don't think came as a shock to any of the rest of us. Indeed, it seems a wonder now that more of our party didn't collapse under the burden of those sights. Colonel Slayton once again slung the terribly stricken Malcolm's left arm around his shoulders and with his own right arm lifted that drastically underweight body fully off the floor and started off toward the stern of the ship. Larissa pressed herself against me once hard, somehow suspecting—quite rightly—that everything had changed as a result of what we had just witnessed; then she went off to tend to her brother, holding his dangling right hand tightly as Slayton carried him. Eli set the ship's helm on a preprogrammed course for St. Kilda, and then at last the rest of us drifted away, each trying to find some solitude in which to come to terms with the incomprehensible.

Even before we reached the Scottish coast I'd decided that I couldn't go on playing a part in Malcolm's grand scheme. The doubts about his work that perhaps I should have heeded ever since we'd first heard reports concerning the man we would come to know as Dov Eshkol—a man pathologically prepared to be consumed by fabricated information, a man willing, in fact, to commit murder on an unprecedented scale because of it—now created a deafening crescendo in my skull. How many more Dov Eshkols were loose in the world? How could we ever court similar disasters by manufacturing more hoaxes? And hadn't Malcolm's own complaints that the world was unwilling to accept that his elaborate lies were just that now been horrifically borne out? Human society was not becoming any less entranced by or besotted with information as a result of what Malcolm and the others were doing, I now realized; and the responsibility for driving a madman over the edge, if not direct, was close enough, in my own mind, to prevent my continuing to play a part in the operation.

Such intellectual and moral conclusions, while difficult to reach, seemed simple when compared to the emotional and practical problems posed by the prospect of departure. First and foremost, of course, there was Larissa. Having years earlier accepted the unlikelihood of finding a woman who would not only tolerate but admire the way in which I lived and worked, it was no easy thing to contemplate giving up the one I'd finally found—particularly when our natural attraction to and ease with each other were augmented by the strong bonds that often grow between people whose childhoods were marred by violence. There was, of course, the possibility that Larissa would abandon her brother for me; and indeed the alternative was so heartbreaking, and my thinking had become so muddled, that I found myself latching onto that idea more and more during the balance of the flight back to St. Kilda.

This badly misguided fantasy, which flew in the face of not only my professional training but all my experience with Malcolm and Larissa, was nonetheless powerful enough to influence the problem of how I would handle my status as an international criminal, as well. Would I throw myself on the mercy of world justice, explain that I personally had played no part in the hoax that had resulted in the deaths of millions of people, and risk imprisonment? I would not; but I might learn to tolerate and even enjoy life as an international fugitive, using the skills I had learned from Malcolm and the others—provided, of course, that Larissa would come with me. As the ship sped over the Isle of Skye, my dream grew steadily more elaborate and romantic: Larissa and I would live on the run, plucking whatever we needed or wanted from a world unable to stop us.

And so, when at last Larissa entered my quarters after making sure that Malcolm was resting quietly and proceeded to fall tearfully into my arms, I elected to view it as a sign that her love for me was beginning to outweigh her dedication to her brother. I said nothing to that effect and nothing about my deluded plans for the future, thinking it only fair to broach the subject with Malcolm first. I maintained this silence through several ensuing days on Hirta, during which each member of our group continued to try to reach some separate peace with all that we had seen and endured. It wasn't an easy time; despite the fact that we successfully avoided discussing the subject with one another, a near compulsion to privately read and view news reports concerning the Moscow disaster afflicted us all, and as the casualty numbers mounted, a common but unacknowledged grief bore down hard. The truth about Dov Eshkol eventually did emerge, but so did reports that he'd had accomplices who'd escaped in some sort of advanced aircraft, at which point apprehension over possible aggressive moves against St. Kilda joined the list of anxieties that were afflicting everyone on the island.

The last of these fears, at least, was allayed when Larissa emerged from two days of ministering to her brother to announce to the rest of us that Malcolm had been in contact with Edinburgh: the Scottish government had refused to reveal anything about Malcolm's purchase of St. Kilda to the U.N. allies, and he had promised more funding for the Scots' war of independence. Relieved that we would be left in peace, at least for a time, the others went back to the business of pondering the recent past as well as the uncertain future. I turned to do the same, but Larissa caught my arm.

"He wants to see you," she said, indicating Malcolm's quarters, which were situated so as to block any entrance to his private laboratory. "But don't let him get excited, Gideon—he's better, but he's not well." She kissed me quickly but tenderly. "I've missed you."

I ran one hand through her silver hair and smiled. "It's been lousy."

She held me tighter at that. "Very lousy," she murmured.

"Larissa," I whispered. "There's something—" I looked into her eyes, wanting to see curiosity but finding only severe exhaustion. "Jesus, you've got to rest."

She nodded, but managed to ask, " 'Something'?"

"We can talk about it later," I answered, believing that we would have plenty of time to do so and still wanting, like some well-heeled suitor, to talk to her brother before I sprang the idea on her. "For now, rest."

She sighed acknowledgment, kissed me again, and strode wearily away, leaving the door to her brother's quarters ajar.

I stepped inside, sure of what I was going to say and hopeful that Malcolm would approve of the plan; wholly unsuspecting, in short, that he was about to tell me what he considered the greatest of his many secrets, a tale so bizarre and unbelievable that it would force me to the conclusion that he had, in fact, lost his mind.

CHAPTER 42

Malcolm's quarters in the compound were even more spartan than his cabin aboard the ship, offering, it seemed to me, few comforts that could not have been found on the sparsely populated Hirta of two hundred years earlier. In the far wall a bay window similar to the one in my room looked out over another rocky, mysterious stretch of oceanfront, and before this window Malcolm sat in his wheelchair, bathed in the soft sunlight of St. Kilda and watching the hundreds of seabirds on the rocks with the same simple enthusiasm I'd seen in his features several times before. It was a vivid reminder that the young boy who had entered that hellish hospital all those years ago had not been completely destroyed by the experience; yet, paradoxically, the very youthfulness of the look should have been enough to remind me of the extent to which Malcolm depended on Larissa and to convince me that any notion of his approving of my running off with her was absurd.

He sensed my presence but made no move to face me. "Gideon," he said in a voice that seemed not so much strong as an attempt at strength. He paused for a moment, during which I prepared to make my case to him; but before I could speak he asked, "Are the materials for your Washington plan still in place?"

The question caught me with my jaw already open; and now that mandible seemed to actually fall to the floor. "I beg your pardon?" I mumbled.

"Your Washington plan," he repeated, still watching the birds. "How soon can you be ready to implement it?"

I somehow managed to collect my wits enough to say, "You're not serious."

Still not turning, Malcolm nodded as if he'd expected just such an answer. "You think that what happened in Moscow means that we should suspend our work. You think it may happen again."

At that instant every ounce of self-delusion somehow drained out of me like so much blood. I took a few shaky steps toward a straight-backed mahogany chair, falling into it as I suddenly realized the folly of my recent plans as well as the extent of Malcolm's commitment to his undertaking. Emotional protests and declarations seemed pointless, given the situation, so I answered him in a voice that was as rational and grave as I could make it: "Malcolm—you yourself have said that there are terrible problems inherent in what you're doing."

"What I *said,*" Malcolm answered, quietly but pointedly, "was that we've done our job too well. Dov Eshkol proved that."

It was an almost incredible statement. "Yes. I'd say that he certainly did."

"And so we learn and go on." He still seemed unprepared to look me in the eye. "As you and I have already discussed, we must make sure that all future projects will be exposed in a reasonable amount of time. We'll plant hints—more than hints, obvious flaws—so that even the most obtuse—"

"Malcolm?" I interrupted, too shocked to go on listening to him but still trying to speak in a straightforward, calm manner. "Malcolm, I can't go on being part of this. What you're doing, it's more than just subversive, it's unimaginably dangerous. Surely even you see that now." He gave no answer, and my head began to grow feverish with incredulity. "Is it possible—are you really going to try to deny it? This business, this *game* of yours, it may seem manageable to you, but there are millions of people out there who have to make sense of thousands of pieces of bizarre new information every day, and they don't have the time or the tools to sort out what's real from what's blatant fabrication. The world's gone too far—people's minds have been stretched too far—and we have no idea what will set the next lunatic off. What'll you do if we carry out this latest plan, and some anticorporate, antigovernment lunatic in the States—and there are plenty of them—uses it as a rationalization to blow up yet another federal building? Or something even bigger?" I paused and then shifted gears, trying to direct the discussion away from the kind of moral and political dialectic of which he was a master and focus it instead on my very real concern for him and the others: "Besides, how long can you really hope to get away with it? Look at how narrow our escape was this time and what it cost us. You've got to consider something else, this isn't—"

I cut myself short when I saw his hand go up slowly. "All right," he said, in a voice choked with sorrow and regret. "All right, Gideon." He finally wheeled his chair around, his head drooping so low that his chin nearly rested on his chest. When he glanced up again, he still wouldn't connect with my gaze; but the grief in his features was apparent and pitiful to behold. "I would have done anything to prevent what happened to Leon," he said softly. "But every one of us knows the risks—"

" 'Knows the risks'? Malcolm, this isn't a war, for God's sake!"

At last those hypnotic yet unsettling blue eyes met my own hard stare. "Isn't it?" he asked. He began to reach around for the crutches that were clipped to the back of his chair. "You think," he went on, his voice getting stronger, "that this method of addressing the problem doesn't work." He fought hard to get to his feet, and though I felt more of a desire to help than I ever had before, I once again refrained. "You think that the world's illness is beyond this sort of treatment. Fine." He took a few steps in my direction. "What would you prescribe instead?"

I simply could not engage him on this level, and I made that fact plain: "Malcolm, this isn't about 'illnesses' and 'prescriptions.' Civilization is going to do whatever it's going to do, and if you keep trying to stand in the way you'll just create more disasters. Maybe you're right, maybe this information society is taking us into a high-tech dark age. But maybe it isn't. Maybe *we* just don't understand it. Maybe Julien's wrong, and this isn't a 'threshold moment,' and maybe there were people like us sitting in some scientifically advanced horse and carriage when Gutenberg ran off his first Bible screaming, 'That's it! It's all over!' I don't know. But the point is, neither do you. The only thing we *do* know is that you *can't* stop change and you *won't* stop technology. There's nothing in the past to suggest that it's possible."

As I was speaking, Malcolm turned, almost with the slowness of a clock, to look out at the birds again. "That's true," he murmured.

Ready as I was to argue on, his statement came as a complete surprise. "It is?" I said a bit dimly.

Malcolm nodded. "Yes. There's nothing in the past to suggest that it's possible—*yet*."

As he roamed back over to the window, I followed, suddenly feeling very nervous. "What do you mean, 'in the past, *yet*'? Malcolm, you're not making sense."

As he attempted to explain himself, Malcolm seemed to grow increasingly unaware of who I was or even that there was anyone in the room with him; and the vacant brilliance that his eyes took on as they stared at the similarly dazzling blue of the sky above the ocean offered the first hint of real mental imbalance. "Suppose I were to tell you," he said, "that through that room"—he indicated an adjacent chamber in the direction of his lab—"and behind a certain very thick door you'll find a device that may be able to redefine, even destroy, both history and time, at least as we currently understand them. That in a very short while it will be possible to move through our temporal continuum and alter the past, so that 'history' will no longer be an unalterable chronological record but a living laboratory in which we will conduct experiments to improve the present condition of our planet and our species."

Had it even occurred to me to take this statement seriously, I might well have fallen over; as it was, I only became steadily more convinced that the man's mind had snapped. "Listen, Malcolm," I said, putting a hand to his shoulder. "Try to understand—as a doctor it's incumbent on me to tell you that you've suffered a breakdown. A potentially severe one. And given what we've all been through, I'm not surprised. You have friends in Edinburgh, and no doubt they'll know of hospital facilities we can use quietly. If you let me run some tests and suggest a course of treatment—"

"You haven't answered my question yet, Gideon," Malcolm said, his voice still betraying no emotion.

"Your question?" I said. "Your question about roaming back and forth through time, *that* question?"

He shook his head slowly. "Not back *and* forth. No one seriously believes that we can create closed timelike curves that could allow a subject to move in one direction and then return to the exact point from which he or she started. At this point it's just not feasible."

"Oh, but going one way *is*?"

Malcolm ignored my sarcasm. "The physical problem isn't particularly exotic or complex," he said. "Like most things it's really just a question of power—electromagnetic power. And the only conceivable way of generating such power—"

"Would be superconductors," I said with a sudden shudder, vaguely remembering an article I'd read on the subject some months earlier. I looked to the floor, still in a state of disbelief but for some reason quite shaky all the same. "Highly miniaturized superconductors," I added, real apprehension beginning to belie my dismissal of his words.

"Sounds familiar, doesn't it?" Malcolm had increasing difficulty controlling his emotions as he went on: "Imagine not being forced to accept the present that's been handed down to us. Having instead the ability to engineer a different set of historical determinants. You say that the contemporary world can't be helped by the work we're doing now, Gideon, that it's beyond such remedies. Well, the same thought began to occur to me over a year ago. But the answer, I saw, wasn't to suspend what we were doing. We needed to adjust the work, certainly—that was part of the reason we brought *you* in. But we had and have to keep at it until the day comes when we can change the actual circumstances of our present reality by modifying the past." He put a hand to his head, obviously feeling the effects of the controlled but no less extreme passion with which he had told me his tale. "That day isn't far off, Gideon—not far off at all."

I sat back down in my chair. The worst insanities often come in ostensibly rational forms; and I told myself that such was the reason I had been momentarily uneasy, even credulous. I also acknowledged that there was no way I could force him into the kind of serious program of rest, medication, and psychotherapy that he clearly needed; nevertheless, I made one final, weary attempt to reach him:

"Malcolm, I wonder if you realize the language you're using. And if it doesn't suggest something to you." He didn't answer, which I took as a sign that he was willing to listen to what I had to say. "You talk of 'engineering the past,'" I went on. "Don't those words strike you as awfully loaded, given your personal history? I don't doubt that you'd like to change the present that was 'handed' to you—you have every conceivable reason. But you need to hear this—" I stood up and walked to him. "You can use the tools your father developed to try to destroy the world he helped build. You can bury society in confusion, deceive the public into believing your version of history, even watch people and cities be destroyed, and you can tell yourself all the while that it's a necessary and noble crusade. But in the end you're still going to be the man you are—you're still going to be ill, you're still going to need those crutches and that chair, and you're still going to be consumed by heartbreak and anger. You don't want to change *the* past, Malcolm—you want to change *your* past."

For several long minutes neither of us spoke; then Malcolm's glittering eyes went narrow and he nodded once or twice, making his way back to his chair. He got himself into it slowly, then looked up at me and asked:

"Do you have anything to offer, Gideon, other than the utterly obvious?"

Insults from patients with grandiose delusions were certainly nothing new to me; but this one, I must admit, stung. "Can you really call it obvious," I answered, trying to sound unfazed, "and still go on with what you're doing?"

He let out a disdainful hiss. "Gideon," he said, shaking his head in evident disappointment. "Do you imagine I haven't been over all this? And through the kinds of programs you're suggesting? In my youth I tried them all: psychotherapy, electroshock, drug treatments, everything—with the exception of further gene therapy, of course, which I think I can be excused for ruling out. And yes, I learned what drives me, how deep the anger inside me runs, how personal as well as philosophical my motives are. But in the end I'll say to you what I said to every doctor I saw." Some of the manic gleam went out of his eyes, to be replaced by undiluted sadness. "It doesn't really change anything, does it?"

"Doesn't really change anything?" I echoed in astonishment. "My God, Malcolm, if you know that you're acting out of personal prejudices and unresolved feelings—"

"Oh, they're *resolved,* Gideon," he answered. "I'm *resolved* that I hate the world that my father and his kind built—a world where men and women tamper with the genetic structure of their children simply to improve their intelligence quotients so that they can grow up to devise better and more convenient ways to satisfy the public's petty appetites. A world where intelligence is measured by the ability to amass information that has no context or purpose save its own propagation but is nonetheless serviced slavishly by humanity. And do you know the hard truth of why information has come to dominate our species, Gideon? Because the human brain *adores* it—it plays with the bits of information it receives, arranging them and storing them like a delighted child. But it loathes examining them deeply, doing the hard work of assembling them into integrated systems of understanding. Yet that work is what produces knowledge, Gideon. The rest is simply—*recreation.*"

"And how," I asked, making no attempt to hide my weariness with his tirade, "does this relate to your awareness of your personal motivations?"

Again shaking his head, he replied, "Gideon—these *are* my personal motivations now. I understand that you think I need treatment, but I've traveled that road—and shall I tell you something? It's led directly back to the point where it started. Admittedly, having made the trip, one knows just where that point is and what surrounds it. But one is still there. So what do you want people to do, Gideon, when they discover their personal motivations? Abdicate? Stop playing a role in the world? What person in history was not driven by his own personal motivations? And how could there have been any development without those drives?"

"That's not the point," I countered. "If you're genuinely self-aware, then your behavior can change."

"Ah, the mantra of the psychologist!" Malcolm's voice was rising disturbingly. "Yes, Gideon, it can indeed change, but change to what? Shall we be Christlike and turn the other cheek to avarice, exploitation, and ruination? Shall we watch the world burn down because we fear that our motives might not be strictly impersonal? I tell you, I'd hurl myself into that sea first! Because you're not talking about change, Gideon—you're talking about paralysis!"

"No," I said, "I'm talking about addressing those problems in ways that don't end up killing millions of people."

"I did not destroy that city!" he shouted, and by the way his body had begun to tremble I could see trouble coming; yet, much as it shames me to admit it, I was too appalled by what he was saying to do anything about it. "I didn't train Dov Eshkol," he went on, "and I didn't turn him loose on the world. Nor did I create a society so obsessed with commerce that it refuses to effectively regulate even the most dangerous forms of trade! But I'll tell you what I *did* do. I suffered through a set of experiences that gave me a unique perspective from which to view—and perhaps affect—that same society. Should I refuse to do so because my motives have a personal dimension that worries people like you? Take my advice, Gideon—worry about the purity of your own motives, and let mine be." He spun his chair around toward the window, raising one fist. "I know why I am what I am—but I will not let those who made me this way enjoy the final triumph of my acquiescence in their effort to make the world a massive *hive,* one in which human beings play with information endlessly for the profit of hidden masters—and in the process learn *nothing.*"

Far more than the conversation, it seemed to me, had ended with that last fateful word. I offered no argument, for there was no point in arguing with such profound psychosis. Some of what he'd said was doubtless true, though I couldn't say how much. All I knew for certain were the same two things I'd been sure of when I'd entered the room: that I could no longer stay on that island or participate in Malcolm's schemes, and that when I left I wanted Larissa to go with me. My uneasiness about telling Malcolm these things had vanished in the face of his mad monologue, and I blurted it all out in a fairly arch manner; yet as soon as I did, his features began to draw into an expression of defiant threat that made me regret my boldness.

"I'm not sure I like the idea of you roaming loose, Gideon," he said in a measured tone, "now that you know all our secrets. And do you honestly think that Larissa would go with you?"

"If you didn't stand in her way," I replied, as bravely as I could. "And as far as your secrets go, what are you worried about? I'm a criminal, remember, I'm in no rush to go to any authorities. And even if I was, who in the world would believe me?"

Malcolm cocked his head, considering it. "Perhaps . . ."

Suddenly he sucked in a rush of air, and his hands fairly flew to his temples. I made a move to help him, but he waved me off. "No!" he said, gritting his teeth and fumbling in his pocket for his injector. "No, Gideon. This—is no longer your affair. Take your tender conscience—and leave—*now*!"

What was there to do but comply? Farewells would have been inappropriate, even grotesque, in light of all we'd been through and said to each other. I simply crossed over to the door and opened it, all anger gone, all compassion numbed. As I stepped out I turned once, to see Malcolm sitting there, huddled with the injector at a vein in his hand, murmuring something to himself through his still-clenched teeth.

I found myself thinking that it was a pity that all his talk of time travel had been so obviously delusional; for when all was said and done there really was very little in the present for such a man.

CHAPTER 43

My only remaining quandary was how much to tell the others about my conversation (if conversation it could be called) with Malcolm. I knew that all of them were immensely loyal to him, though each in a different way, and it was not my purpose to tamper with those relationships. But they had a right to know that his behavior and statements had been such as to make me question his sanity, and so I asked them to join me in my quarters, which they did at sunset. As I related my tale, I sat in the bay window that looked out over the little cove, the omnipresent flocks of seabirds keeping up a chatter during their evening feed that made it difficult for me to speak in the hushed tone that I could not help but feel the situation warranted. I tried not to be biased in my explanation, but I also tried to be frank and complete, stressing Malcolm's consistent refusal to accept any responsibility for the Moscow disaster and detailing in full his apparently genuine belief that he would soon be able to travel through time.

"Did he happen to say," Eli remarked, looking, to my surprise and dismay, very intrigued, "whose configuration he's emulating?"

I had to shake my head hard. *"What?"*

"Was it Gödel?" Eli went on. "Kerr? Or Thorne maybe?"

"Not *Thorne,*" Jonah said dismissively. "Even Malcolm doesn't have the power to create a *wormhole* in his lab—"

"Eli? Jonah?" I was a bit dismayed and let it show. "You're not going to do any good by humoring him about this. It's a fantasy, and a potentially dangerous one, based in a lot of old and new psychological trauma—"

"Do you *know* that?" Thc tone was Malcolm's, but the voice belonged to Larissa. She was sitting near me but looking away, deep concern all over her face; she seemed to have known from the moment I'd begun speaking that she would shortly face a crisis of her own.

"If you do, Gideon," Julien threw in, "then you know more than many brilliant minds who have studied the subject for generations."

"Listen, I've read Einstein and Hawking," I countered. Then I added, with some embarrassment, "Well, I've read Einstein, anyway. But I've read *about* Hawking. And both said that the paradoxes inherent in the idea of time travel forbid it as a physical possibility."

"They forbid one *type* of it," Eli countered, adding, in terminology that matched Malcolm's, "closed timelike curves. But there are other ways to move through time, though they're not particularly appealing—"

"I *think,*" Colonel Slayton said firmly, "that this is perhaps not the moment for an academic discussion of time travel." He eyed me sternly. "Gideon, I'm sorry to have to say this, but you *could* be seen as having personal reasons for calling Malcolm's judgment into question. You're aware of that, I trust—and aware of the fact that *we're* aware of it."

Julien, Eli, and Jonah looked away in evident discomfort; Larissa, however, moved closer to me. "That statement's a little out of line, isn't it, Colonel?" she said. "Gideon's never done anything to warrant suspicion—or disrespect."

"Gideon is fully aware of the respect I have for him, Larissa," Slayton replied. "But he also knows that I have to ask."

I nodded to Larissa, indicating that what the colonel had said was true but trying at the same time to silently thank her for coming to my defense. "I understand, Colonel," I said. "But believe me, no personal interest would ever make me misrepresent something like this. It's not just that it would be unethical—I've considered Malcolm a friend. And it's friendship that's making me warn you about this. There's nothing more I can do. I told him I can't participate in this undertaking anymore, and after a rather dicey moment he agreed that I should depart. So it won't be up to me to deal with the question of his mental health. But I had to tell you that in my opinion it needs dealing with—badly."

Colonel Slayton took this all in with a slow nod and a look that was, for him, very close to being emotional. Julien and the Kupermans, on the other hand, were quite openly saddened. "But," Eli said eventually, "where will you go, Gideon?"

I glanced at Larissa, who did not return the look. "I haven't really decided."

"There will be warrants out for you," Slayton advised. "The U.S. is certainly out of the question, and Europe will be dangerous, too."

"I know." For the first time since I had started to anguish morally over my participation in Malcolm's enterprise, I began to realistically consider leaving these people with whom I had shared so much in such a compressed time; and it tugged at me hard. "I suppose I'll head south," I went on, turning away from them. "Try to find someplace where no one's paying attention to any of this." I attempted to rally and smile. "If anybody feels like coming along, I wouldn't say no."

Slayton, Julien, and the Kupermans tried to return my halfhearted smile, but with as little success as I was enjoying: the moment had arrived for good-byes, and we all knew it. Slayton was the first to approach me, his strong hand extended. "One of us will get you over to Scotland in the jetcopter, Gideon. We've got an emergency reserve of various currencies, you can dip into that. And you'll want some alternate identity documents and discs. But be careful—we can adjust them to match your DNA for the average reader, but if anyone runs one through the universal database, you'll be in trouble. You'd better have a couple of sidearms, as well."

"Thank you, Colonel," I said quietly, shaking his hand.

As he studied my face, his eyes went thin, the one on his right pulling at the long scar that I no longer even noticed when I looked at him. "Try not to be too alarmed about Malcolm. He's exhausted. We'll look after him and make sure he recovers—and once he has, you may want to return, Gideon. I know there are aspects of this fight you don't like, but now that you've been part of it I think you're going to find readjusting to the world you used to know . . . difficult."

"I'm sure that's true, Colonel," I said. "But you shouldn't have someone on your team whom you can't rely on absolutely. And after—well . . . too many questions, that's all."

Slayton touched his scar briefly, then clasped my shoulder. "I suppose you're right. But I'm sorry to see you go, Dr. Wolfe." He began to walk slowly toward the door. "As for me, I've seen madmen burn cities before. Not on this scale, perhaps, but enough to know in my heart where the blame belongs. So take my word for it, Gideon—that's one thing you don't need to burden yourself with while you're on the run."

As Slayton's soldierly step began to resound on the stone walkway outside, Eli and Jonah came over to me together, Eli giving me the same generous smile he had when I'd first faced him in Belle Isle prison. "I owe you one jailbreak," he said. "So if they pick you up and you get a chance to make that phone call . . ."

I chuckled and shook his hand, then glanced from him to Jonah. "None of it bothers you two—the things I've said?"

"About Malcolm?" Jonah answered. When I nodded, he went on, "The colonel's right, Gideon. Malcolm's mental state is exceptionally intertwined with his physical condition—I think you can appreciate how and why as well as any of us. But we've known him since we were teenagers. He comes out of these episodes if he gets enough time and rest."

"But—this time travel business—"

"Fatigue and stress, Gideon, trust us," Eli answered. Then he cocked his head. "On the other hand—"

"On the other hand," Jonah finished for him, "I certainly want to be around just in case. Beats squabbling over tenure at Yale or Harvard." There being nothing left to say, both men removed their eyeglasses at almost the same moment, in the same gesture of uncomfortable emotion. "Well—good-bye, Gideon," Jonah said.

"And remember what Colonel Slayton told you," Eli answered as they turned to go. "Life out there may look awfully strange to you now—say the word, and we can bring you back."

They both waved as they passed out the door, still looking and apparently feeling very awkward. I turned toward Julien, suddenly taking note of a distinct lump in my throat. Fouché stood tactfully and held up a hand, nodding toward Larissa. "I shall warm the jetcopter, Gideon," he said. "It will be dark soon—a night flight always attracts less attention."

Once he was gone I turned to Larissa, who had her arms wrapped around her body as she stood staring out at the rocky cove. Ready to sweep her away with soft, irresistible imaginings about our future together, I smiled and began to approach her—

But just as I did I experienced, with dizzying suddenness, that same feeling that had hit me at the start of my final encounter with Malcolm: a swift loss of illusions that was as chilling and draining as a razor slash through a major artery. The mournful look on Larissa's face told me in the clearest and most brutal possible manner that if I forced her to choose between her brother and me I would lose and that the contest would be only an exercise in cruel futility. All my desperate fantasies had been made possible, I now saw, by a deliberate avoidance and denial of what I knew about their shared past, as well as about the extent not only to which he needed her but to which she needed to live up to their bond. It was that bond that had preserved both of their fragile, limited capacities for intimacy and commitment during their ravaged childhoods and that had kept those capacities alive during the years that had followed. I was therefore not simply being foolish in thinking that our feelings for each other could never supersede such an attachment; I was terribly wrong even to have hoped that she would betray both him and herself so fundamentally.

"It'll be dark soon," she said, looking at the sky. "There isn't much time." She tightened her hold on herself. "Thank God," she breathed, making clear the pointlessness of further talk.

Though it took every bit of my strength, I stayed several feet away from her. "If he gets worse, Larissa—"

"I'll know what to do."

I took a deep breath before continuing uncomfortably, "There was one thing I didn't want to say in front of the others—he made a reference to suicide. It may have been argumentative hyperbole, or it may have been sincere. He really has been worn down to almost nothing."

She nodded. "I'll bring him back. I always have."

The voice that spoke these few words was remarkable: utterly ageless, completely heartbroken. The young girl who had once schemed with the stricken but brave brother who had tried so hard to protect her was trying to crack through the hard, shell-like composure of the woman before me to say that though she could never leave him, she desperately wished I would not go. No sound came out of her, however, for several very painful minutes; and then, just when I thought that the composure would remain intact and the cry would go unvoiced, just as I was about to choke out a good-bye and force myself out the door, the break came. She spun around, rushed at me in emotional ruin and wrenching tears, and buried her face in my chest as she had often done. *"No,"* she said, pounding on me with her fists as hard as she could manage. *"No, no, no . . ."*

I took her wrists gently in my hands, kissed her silvery hair, and whispered, "Please be all right, Larissa." Then I placed her fists by her heaving sides and fairly ran from the room, still able, it seemed, to hear her sobs long after I'd boarded the jetcopter and found myself once more cruising low over the icy North Atlantic.

CHAPTER 44

I went south, all right—I went south in every conceivable way . . .

During the jetcopter ride to Edinburgh's William Wallace Airport, Julien, whose understanding of and sympathy for such loss went beyond the usual Gallic insight into affairs of the heart, tried to assure me that there was no way of knowing what would happen in the future, that at least Larissa and I were both still alive, and that we were far too well matched simply to end things so suddenly and completely. The paradoxical effect of his words, however, was to confirm my despairing conviction that I had lost forever the strange but wonderful woman it had taken me a lifetime to find. When we reached our destination, Fouché climbed out of the aircraft, hugged me vigorously, kissed both my cheeks, and gave me his personal assurance that we would meet again. But when the jetcopter took off and left me standing with nothing but a small shoulder bag containing two hand weapons—one capable only of stunning, the other a lethal rail pistol, both fabricated out of composite resins impossible for any security system to detect—I had to do some very quick breathing and thinking even to begin to suppress the feeling of horrifying loneliness that swept over me. For I was indeed alone now: alone in a way that I once would have considered inconceivable and that made me quickly question the moral principles that had landed me in such an unenviable position.

The days to come were even more confused and bizarre. Everywhere I went—restaurants, bars, hotels—news about and investigations into the Moscow disaster and its aftermath dominated the media, as did reports concerning the mysterious aircraft that was rumored to have been escorting the suicide bomber on his mission. I was believed by various military intelligence agencies and police forces to have been on that aircraft, and my picture—along with those of Slayton, Larissa, and poor dead Leon—flashed onto public video screens with disturbing frequency, making it necessary for me to change my appearance and adjust my identity discs before even departing Edinburgh. It also made it necessary for me to get used to seeing Larissa's face pop up in unexpected places, an additional burden that was almost unbearable. From Edinburgh I took ship to Amsterdam (traveling by air was out of the question, given that airlines were required to run all identity discs through the universal DNA database), and from there I continued south by bus, train, and even thumb as I attempted to melt into the great global background, sticking as much as possible to areas where information technology was not ubiquitous in the hopes of staying unrecognized—and sane.

I succeeded in the first of these goals; as to the second, I cannot say. I still did not know precisely where I was going, and as the days became weeks, the constant need to fabricate new identification, hack into bank databases to secure money (after the bankroll I'd taken with me from St. Kilda had run out), and flat-out lie about almost every detail of my existence twenty-four hours a day began to take a severe mental and emotional toll. This state of affairs was sorely aggravated when one day, during a slow passage through Italy, I passed a small café that had a newspaper vending terminal. On the cover of every front page that flashed by on its screen were headlines containing the word "Washington," as well as pictures of the first American president. I dashed about until I found a place that vended *The New York Times,* then deposited my money in the machine and waited breathlessly for the printout. Swallowing two straight grappas like so much water, I read of my former comrades' apparent return to action: the hoax was playing out just as we'd designed it to, except that Malcolm's hope that it contained fatal flaws was proving a vain one. The story was being accepted everywhere—especially in Europe, where any apparent proof of the moral imperfection of the United States was always welcome—as indisputable.

The shock of the thing was manifold. Just the reminder that I'd not so long ago been involved in so insidious an enterprise was, of course, disquieting now that I was away from it. But even more, I knew that from that moment on any news report I might happen to read or see, no matter how momentous its details, might be a lie; and the flimsy connection to reality that I had carefully nursed during my weeks of hiding began to fall away. I took to drinking heavily, telling myself that it was simply to blend in with and secure the goodwill of the locals so that none of the regional constabularies would think to send my face out over the Net or run my discs through the universal DNA database. But in truth I had nothing else with which to relieve the utter alienation. As I made my way down into the lower part of the Italian peninsula, I descended into severe alcoholic confusion, and when it became difficult to obtain money due to the unreliability of electronic banking in that near-anarchic part of the country, the confusion became degradation. By the time I reached lawless Naples, I looked as though I belonged on its streets; and it was only a chance sighting of a meaningless piece of wall decoration in a decrepit bar that changed things.

In a stupor, I looked up from the redolent table on which I'd been resting my addled head for the better part of an hour one evening to see a yellowing poster that advertised the beauties of Africa. The thing was, of course, some forty years old, a relic from the time when what in recent years the public and media had once again taken to calling the Dark Continent had not been almost depopulated by tribal wars and the AIDS epidemic; but it nonetheless ignited my drunken imagination. Wild visions of a land of lush jungles, windswept savannahs, and marvelous wildlife—all of it uninfected by the plague of information technology, since Africa was the principal island in the analog archipelago—took an iron hold on my debilitated mind in the days that followed, and I even spent one night trying to sober up in order to determine if the idea of going there had any merit at all. I found to my great surprise that it did, although sobriety also brought a realistic appraisal of contemporary Africa's afflictions. But I decided that I would rather take my chances with disease and war than with imprisonment and insanity. I therefore cleaned myself up, took on the identity of a respectable American businessman with a bad gambling habit, and found my way to a notorious Neapolitan loan shark. Thinking me a safe risk who would stray no farther than the local high-stakes games, this man proved more than willing to provide the U.S. dollars I needed to achieve my desperate purpose.

During my weeks as a habitué of the city's worst drinking and drug-dealing dens, I had made the acquaintance of two particularly unsavory French pilots who ran guns to various parts of the analog archipelago and who spent their downtime in Naples because they could get exceptionally potent heroin and hashish on its streets. Returning to one of their haunts, I discovered that they were delivering a shipment to, of all places, Afghanistan, but that they were expected back within the week. Those next days were restless but hopeful ones for me, as I became more convinced than ever that I would soon be in territory that the information revolution had passed over, where all the complex philosophical and social issues that had put my life in such a state of upheaval would not hold sway, and to which continual rehashings of the destruction of Moscow—and the attendant speculation about the mysterious "phantom ship" that had been detected in the area of that disaster—would not penetrate.

As I dried out and began to invest my money in travel books rather than drink, I even went so far as to imagine that I might start a new life in Africa; this despite the constant reminders of those same books that most of the species of wildlife that had once brought tourists to the continent were now extinct and that because of widespread disease and unrest, any foreign travelers who still wanted or needed to visit the area must receive copious inoculations and stay in constant touch with either their country's consulates or representatives of the United Nations. These latter admonitions I could not, of course, heed: the first because it would have meant offering a doctor a DNA sample, the second for even more obvious reasons. Still, desperately attached to my dreams, I proceeded with my preparations with a dedication I can only describe as feverish.

When the two French pilots finally returned from Afghanistan, they were initially in no mood to hear about ferrying passengers to Africa, regardless of how much money I offered. For a time it seemed that my plan would never be executed; but luck, or what I took for luck, soon swung my way, and the men received an offer from a local dealer to deliver a large shipment of small arms to the man whose tribal forces currently occupied the Rwandan capital of Kigali. After stipulating that they would deliver the goods by airdrop only—for no one outside Rwanda, not even other Africans, could any longer be persuaded to touch down in the pestilential ruins of that city, where local forces battled in streets strewn with rotting corpses like dogs fighting over a poisoned bone—the pilots struck their deal. They then informed me that they intended to make a refueling stop in Nairobi after their drop; if I was willing to accept

Kenya as my point of entry into Africa, they would be willing to take me along, provided I still had the large amounts of cash we had earlier discussed.

Thus it was that I found myself two days later lying atop several packed parachutes, which were in turn laid out across a half-dozen crates of shamefully obsolete French weapons. To avoid the interminable savagery of the Sudanese civil war, the plane had flown above the Red Sea as far as the Eritrean coast, where it was safe to go inland: war, famine, and plague had wiped out virtually the entire population of not only Eritrea but Ethiopia beyond. A mad dash across war-torn Uganda was to be the last leg of our inbound flight, a dangerous maneuver for which the two Frenchmen apparently thought they could best prepare themselves by mainlining the large amount of heroin they'd brought along with them. All this would have made life interesting enough; the addition of antiaircraft fire elevated the experience to terrifyingly riveting. The pilots were scarcely up to normal flying conditions by then, much less a fully lethal combat situation, and when we took a direct hit to one of our engines and began to lose altitude precipitously, they began to shout at each other so violently and incoherently that I couldn't see any way the situation was salvageable. The pilots, however, apparently could: one of them seized a pistol, raced back to where I lay, and, holding the gun to my head before I could manage to get one of my own sidearms out of my bag, ordered me into one of the parachutes. Apparently I had been deemed disposable ballast, and though I tried to argue in broken French, it was clear that if I didn't comply the man would simply shoot me and throw me out. Under the circumstances, I jumped.

That my landing near what I later learned were the Murchison Falls cost me only a mildly fractured left tibia was actually miraculous, given that I'd never before parachuted from a plane and had been forced to make my maiden jump over the spectacularly beautiful but utterly treacherous terrain of central Africa. Of course, even a mild fracture of the tibia can be exceptionally painful, and as I gathered both my wits and my few possessions after landing I began to groan with increasing volume: a mistake. Elements of the force that had been shooting at our plane had apparently followed my parachute's decent, hoping for a prize captive. Doubtless they would have been disappointed to get only me, a disappointment spared them by my rather liberal use of the stun pistol that I wasted no time getting into my hand.

Determining my location required some fairly extreme guessing. After stumbling about in fairly high growth for several hours, I suddenly came upon a vast expanse of water; knowing that we had not flown south far enough to have reached Lake Victoria, I could only suppose it to be Lake Albert. I was at the northern end, out of which flowed waters that I thought I could remember reading were among the sources of the White Nile: following them, then, would lead me into Sudan, where I certainly didn't want to go. East and south were the butcher's yard of Uganda, and west? To the west was yet more war-ravaged country, which had been given so many names by so many successive regimes during the last twenty-five years that the rest of the world had gone back to referring to it by its collective ancient title: the Congo. It was into this great unknown that, by process of elimination, I now elected to travel, limping through the Mitumba Mountains with scarcely any idea of where I might be going or what I might hope to do when I got there.

Days passed, and the reports of wildlife extermination that I had read before my departure began to ring true: I saw no signs of any animals big enough to eat and indeed heard scarcely any signs of life at all save for the echo of gunfire throughout the mountains. Insects, rainwater collected from enormous leaves, and analgesic—as well as hallucinogenic—roots became my diet, the last at least keeping my mind off my throbbing leg. But no amount of mental alteration could disguise the fact that I would soon be dead; and when my long trek at last took me back into sight of Lake Albert—for I had no compass, and those who think it's easy for a novice to find his way through a wilderness by the sun and stars alone have evidently never tried it—I simply sat down on a steep incline and began to howl mournfully, keeping up the noise until I finally passed out from hunger and exhaustion.

That I was revived and then carried from that spot by a man who spoke English was, at the time, less remarkable than the fact that I was alive at all. "You are a great fool," the tall, powerful man laughed as he slung me over his fatigue-clad shoulder. "Did you come to see the gorillas, then, and discover that they are all dead?"

"Fool?" I repeated, as I turned my upside-down head around to see several other soldiers walking near us, their camouflaged uniforms faded but their assault weapons gleaming. "Why do you call me a fool?"

"Any stranger in Africa is a fool," the man answered. "This is not a place to be unless you are born here. How is it with your leg?"

In fact my leg was throbbing with every step he took, but I only said, "How did you know—?"

"We saw you jump from the plane. And land. And shoot our enemies! We thought the jungle would claim you. But then you began your womanish wailing. It might have attracted our enemies. So we decided it was better to rescue a fool than become greater fools by letting him be the cause of our deaths."

"Sound thinking," I said. "You speak English very well."

"There was still a school that taught it, when I was a boy," he answered. "Below the mountains."

"Ah." Wondering how long I was to hang there, I asked, "Where are we going, by the way?"

"We will take you to our chief—Dugumbe. He will decide what to do with you."

I eyed the rather ferocious-looking soldiers again. "Is he a compassionate man, by any chance?"

"Compassionate?" The man laughed again. "I would not know. But he is fair, even with fools." Shifting me onto his other shoulder without breaking stride, he added, "It must have been something very terrible."

"What must?" I said, wincing with the shift.

"Whatever drove you here," the man answered simply. "You must have been driven. I know this. Because not even a fool would *choose* this place."

CHAPTER 45

The man's name, I soon learned, was Mutesa; and during the months to come he and his family would prove my saviors, taking me in as something of a cross between ward and pet after their chief, the aforementioned Dugumbe, announced that I could not stay in his tribe's mobile armed camp without a sponsor. Dugumbe fancied himself an enlightened despot: he dressed in an elaborate combination of traditional garb and several modern military uniforms and liked to pepper his conversation with concise denunciations of Western society. His personal code of conduct was based, or so he claimed, on the principal dictate of one of his nineteenth-century ancestors: "Only the weak are good—and they are good only because they are not strong enough to be bad." Yet beneath all this bluster Dugumbe possessed surprising intellectual rigor, even erudition, and in time his attitude toward me would soften. Indeed, because of our shared resentment of the technologically advanced world beyond the shores of Africa, Dugumbe and I would eventually become friends of sorts; but my primary gratitude to and affection for Mutesa, his wife, and their seven children was by then already solidly and irrevocably in place.

Dugumbe made it clear from the beginning that in addition to requiring a family to shelter and feed me while I was among his tribe, I would also need to fill some sort of role in his impressive force of five hundred disciplined, battle-hardened—and, it must be said, ruthless—men. I had no intention, of course, of sharing the remarkable technology that was hidden in my shoulder bag; I had already been fortunate that Mutesa and his detachment had been far enough from the action during my encounter with their enemies that they'd simply thought that I'd killed the men with a conventional weapon. Nor did I much relish the idea of going into tribal battle with an American or European assault weapon in one hand and a crude machete in the other. I asked Dugumbe whether he had any sort of medical officer, to which he said that while of course he had his tribal shaman, he was aware that when it came to the wounds of battle Western doctors could often be more effective. And so I became a field surgeon, calling on my medical school knowledge and even more on the basic tenets of hygiene and sterilization.

We campaigned all that winter and spring in the mountains, where I spent much of my time learning what plants were known to Dugumbe's people to have medicinal properties. Eventually we assembled quite a rudimentary pharmacy, which was fortunate, as there were no longer any "medicines" in the Western sense available to such people: during the height of the AIDS epidemic, Western pharmaceutical companies—after making donations of meaningless amounts of anti-HIV drugs for publicity purposes—had stopped shipping to poverty-stricken Africa not only those expensive products but also drugs that treated the host of other diseases that were decimating the continent: sleeping sickness, malaria, and dysentery, to name but a few. Necessity had, in the years that followed, forced the women in tribes like Dugumbe's to seek new cures in the jungle forest (his shaman continued to rely on spells and absurd potions made primarily from desiccated animal and human flesh), and they had discovered several plants with quite powerful antibiotic and analgesic powers. Some of these, such as the root I had experimented with during my first days in the mountains, had extreme side effects ranging from hallucination to death; but in controlled doses they were quite useful, and it struck me as deeply ironic that the same drug companies that had written Africa off so cold-bloodedly could have made enormous profits had they only shown a bit more foresight.

Dugumbe had decided that the need to stay on the move precluded his participation in the regional slave trade, thus saving me from an inconvenient crisis of conscience. Though never really dead in Africa, trafficking in human beings had in recent years proliferated to an extent that rivaled its ancient heights; and although I often heard Dugumbe describe it as an honored tradition, I chose to ignore such statements, just as I ignored all potentially disturbing aspects of the tribe's folklore, including and especially the ridiculous edicts of Dugumbe's shaman. My satisfaction with the way in which I'd removed myself from the information society that dominated the rest of the world, along with my nightly conversations with Dugumbe about the evils of said society, allowed me to turn a blind eye toward not only the petty squabbling that underlay most of the area's conflicts but also the smaller ways in which purely traditional wisdom hurt these people of whom I was daily growing fonder. It was not until the following summer that their customs and rituals would present me with any serious problem; when it finally came, however, the problem was so serious that I almost lost my life over it.

One evening, I arrived at the series of linked canvas tents that was home to Mutesa's family to find the mood uncharacteristically solemn. Mutesa was striding about with the air of a truly authoritarian patriarch, which stood in stark contrast to the usual way in which he joked and played with both his children and his wife. That good woman, Nzinga, was utterly silent—again very unusual—and while Mutesa's four sons were going through their usual evening ritual of cleaning both his and their rifles, the three girls were huddled in one of the tents. All of them were crying; the loudest was Mutesa's eldest daughter, Ama, who was just thirteen.

I asked Mutesa what evil had come into his house. "No evil, Gideon," he answered. "My daughters weep foolishly."

"And me?" Nzinga called out as she prepared the evening meal. "Do I weep because I am a fool?"

"*You* speak because you are disobedient!" Mutesa shouted back. "Finish making my food, woman, and then prepare your daughter! The shaman comes soon."

"The *butcher* comes soon," Nzinga said as she passed us on her way into the tent where her daughters were hiding. Mutesa made a move to strike her, but I grabbed his upheld arm, although I don't think that he would have followed through with the blow. Nonetheless, he was clearly a tormented man just then—and his discomfort was becoming infectious.

"Why is the shaman coming?" I asked. "Is there illness in your house? If so, I can—"

"You must not interfere, Gideon," Mutesa said firmly. "I know that you of the West do not approve—but it is Ama's time."

All was instantly, appallingly clear. I groaned once as the realization sank in and then tightened my grip on Mutesa's arm. "You must not do this," I said, quietly but with real passion. "Mutesa, I beg you—"

"And *I* beg *you,*" he answered, his voice softening. "Gideon, Dugumbe has decreed it. To resist means the girl's death, and if you involve yourself, it will mean yours, too."

He pried himself from my grip, no longer looking angry but

instead deeply saddened; and as he followed his wife into the next tent to comfort his daughter I stood there agape, trying to determine what in the world I could do to stop the sickening rite of passage that was about to take place. My mind, however, had been dulled by shock; and when I heard a gaggle of old maids start to collect outside the tent, chanting a lot of idiotic nonsense about a girl's entry into womanhood, I began to panic stupidly, rushing outside and screaming at them to keep quiet and go away. But they completely ignored me, making it plain that my status as an outsider made me invisible at such a ritualistic moment. All the same I kept hollering until the shaman arrived, accompanied by several armed guards who looked quite menacing. In the shaman's hand was a vicious-looking knife, and the sight of it, along with a very no-nonsense glare from the shaman, was enough to send me back into the tent, where I now found Mutesa with his arm around the shaking, sobbing Ama.

"Mutesa," I said, realizing with deep dread that there was in fact no way to stop the nightmare, "at least tell the shaman to let me prepare her. I have drugs that can dull the pain, and we must keep the knife and the wound clean."

"Gideon, you *must not interfere,*" Mutesa once again declared. "This is not a subject for argument. It will be done as it is always done." I thought he might even weep himself when he said, "She is a female child, Gideon. The pain does not matter, only the ceremony." At his words Ama began to shriek fearsomely, and Mutesa tightened his grip on her. Ordering her to be silent, he proceeded to drag her out to the crowd that had gathered.

Ama's cries were horrible to hear even before the cutting began; but when the knife went in they became quite simply the most horrifying and unbearable sound I've ever heard. I clutched my head, thinking that I might go mad—and then a thought occurred to me. I ran to where I'd stowed my bag and withdrew the stun gun. If I could not stop the unspeakable act, I could at least ease the child's torment.

I dashed outside to a scene so revolting that it stopped me dead in my tracks. There was no special area set aside for the procedure, not even a blanket thrown on the earth—the regard in which the "female child" was held was amply displayed by the way her genitalia were being cut up in the dirt, much as one would have gelded an animal. With a sudden roar, I brought the ceremony to a halt; and when I raised my weapon the shaman, bloody knife in hand, took a step away from the girl, giving me a line of fire. Instantly I pulled the trigger, and Ama's body jerked a few inches into the air as she painlessly and mercifully lost consciousness.

"She is only asleep!" I shouted, using much of what little I knew of their language and breathing hard; then I quickly directed the weapon at the shaman's guards. "Tell the shaman that he can go on now, Mutesa," I said in English, opening the tent flap and backing inside. "And I hope that your gods will forgive you all."

CHAPTER 46

Needless to say, things were never quite the same for me in Dugumbe's camp after that evening. Oh, I argued the subject with the chief, to be sure, argued it many times on many nights. But for the most part he thought my declarations nothing more than amusing, although on a few occasions they seemed to make him quite irritated. A woman who took physical pleasure from sex, he said, was a woman who could never be controlled, who would roam from tent to tent like a whore—and he would have no whores in his camp. Furthermore, he told me that though he had enjoyed my company and appreciated my efforts on behalf of his people, I would do well to pick my battles more carefully: he could brook only so much impertinence from any man, particularly any white man, and he had no desire to make an example of me. Knowing that his veiled threat was sincere, I finally let the subject drop and elected to surreptitiously do what I could by teaching the mothers in camp how to administer analgesics and, when we could make them, opiates to their daughters before the terrible ceremony. But in truth many of those women, having endured the same torture, seemed to have no inclination to ease the suffering of even their own flesh and blood; and so the mutilations went on as before.

Little came of my use of the stun gun. I knew that the soldiers who had been at the ceremony would report to Dugumbe about it (though the shaman, not wanting to admit that anyone's powers were greater than his, would likely not follow suit); so that very night I went outside camp and drained the weapon's energy cells. When Dugumbe demanded to see the thing, I offered it to him as a gift; and when it failed to produce any effect he tossed it back, declaring that the soldiers were fools and that Ama had simply fainted from the pain. This left me with the dilemma of possessing only a weapon that would kill; and so it became necessary to watch myself carefully, to avoid arguments (which meant avoiding the shaman), and to try to concentrate on my medical duties.

But disillusionment made such a life increasingly difficult, and it wasn't very long before I found myself wondering if by coming to Africa I had really escaped the evils of the "information age" at all. What was the collected wisdom of Dugumbe's people if not "information"? Unrecorded, true, but nonetheless powerful—and manipulable. What had Mutesa done in his tent that night but convince himself of something that he knew in his heart to be utterly false but to which it was necessary to adhere if he were to preserve his place and his faith in the tribe? Could he not have accurately had *"Mundus vult decipi"* painted above the entrance to his tent? Were the evils that I'd sought to escape when I'd boarded the Frenchmen's plane outside Naples not in fact human evils, defiant of time and technology and passed on wherever the human species elected to establish its dominance?

And wasn't Malcolm right in saying that we would never change any of this until we could reengineer the past?

Such thoughts burned in my head not only during my waking

hours but when I was asleep, as well; and when those dreams were one night accompanied by a sound I knew to be the deep rumble that Malcolm's ship produced when he wished to either terrify his enemies or destabilize their structures, I thought as I began to awaken that it was only my subconscious making an appropriate association. It wasn't until Mutesa shook me to full consciousness and told me the rumors about a strange aircraft that was making its way toward the general area of our camp from the northeast that I realized the sound had been real.

"It is said that they look for you, Gideon," he told me urgently, "and that if they are attacked they destroy entire fields, whole parts of the forest, even villages, by increasing the power of the sun."

I sat up on my cot, trying to grasp it. Clearly the ship was coming, and clearly it was coming for me: the line of approach indicated that it was following the same route I had used to get to this place. My movements through Europe and then into Africa could not, of course, have been difficult for my friends aboard the vessel to track; and at first the fact that they had, given my recent feelings about life in Dugumbe's camp in particular and the analog archipelago in general, seemed a good and welcome thing. But as my mind cleared, other thoughts brought a pang of deep dread:

Why were they coming? My falling-out with Malcolm had been virtually complete, and I knew him too well to think that he'd ever accept someone who had expressed such severe doubts about his work back into the fold. Nor, for that matter, would the others, whatever our mutual affection; even Larissa had expressed no desire to have me stay if I couldn't believe in what they were doing. Why, then? I had no special technical knowledge that they needed—their successful deployment of the Washington materials had proved that. What did they want?

All possible avenues of explanation led to only one conclusion: Malcolm had told me sincerely that he wasn't at all certain he wanted me "roaming loose" if I knew his secrets; and that vulnerability must have begun to gnaw at his unstable mind so much that he was now coming to put an end to at least one of his worries—permanently.

During the following the two days—which is also to say the *last* two days—as the thunderous rumbling has continued to reverberate through the mountains and the reports from villages on the lower slopes have become more numerous, I have tried but failed to come up with another, *any* other, interpretation of the situation. I don't know why Larissa or the others would participate in my death unless Malcolm—persuasive as he can be—has managed to talk them into it. Perhaps he's even fabricated evidence to prove that I've betrayed them. Whatever the answer actually is, I will likely never learn it; all I know for certain is that I can't risk seeing these people who have sheltered me become collateral victims of this continued madness. I must move on.

Dawn is just breaking, and I can hear Mutesa assembling his kit outside my tent. His insistence on escorting me to the coast is, I think, partly the result of our friendship and partly due to the gratitude that he has always shown in his eyes, but never acknowledged in words, for my having eased the suffering of the unfortunate Ama. It will be hard to say good-bye to him and his family, but I shall miss little else about this place. Dugumbe's occasional pearls of wisdom—especially his admonition that information is not knowledge—cannot, I must regretfully record, rationalize his actions; and though, as I say, I'm grateful that he is concerned for my safety, I can declare in the privacy of these pages that on balance his own definition of knowledge is no boon to his tribe or to the world. I've told him that when the ship comes he must neither engage it in battle nor hesitate to tell those who fly it where I have gone, and I hope that he will heed the advice; but his belligerent pride may make him incapable of doing so.

Mutesa is whispering my name through the canvas; I must go. If we make the coast, I have decided, I will post this document somewhere on the Internet, for the little good it will do. After that, I have no illusions: I can and will try to run, but if Malcolm and the others truly want me dead, chances are I already am.

CHAPTER 47

OFF THE COAST OF ZANZIBAR, 3 A.M., TWO DAYS LATER

Quick as I have tried to be about telling this tale, I can be quicker still in bringing it to a close—for events during the last twelve hours have suddenly made it certain that no one will believe what I have written. All of us live in a different world from the one that existed just fifty-odd hours ago: the one that I inhabited when I first sat down to record my account. Just *how* different this world is I do not yet know; I have seen only a small piece. But if that piece is any measure, those of us aboard this ship may well be the only humans on earth who are aware of the startling transformation that has taken place. Everyone else cannot help but accept this new reality as the way things have always been, and therefore the record I have written will seem not only implausible but insane.

I say "aboard this ship" because that is, somewhat surprisingly, where I am: aboard the great electromagnetic vessel that until yesterday morning I considered Malcolm Tressalian's most remarkable invention. Larissa sleeps next to me on the bed in my quarters as I write, exhausted, as are we all, by the task of trying to comprehend what has happened. That task has not diminished the joy of being with her again, of course, nor of discovering that in fact my friends were not out for my blood. But it is consuming enough to have made this happy time take on the trappings of unreality, and I expect at every moment to wake up back in Chief Dugumbe's camp, to the sounds of food being prepared and weapons being readied. Perhaps that is why I cannot sleep—why I *will* not sleep—until I have made a record of this last episode: for if indeed this new world still exists when next I wake, I may need to refer to these pages to remind myself of how it came to be.

Mutesa and I lost the few men who were in our party not twelve hours after leaving camp. The sight of Malcolm's ship, when it finally did appear on the horizon behind us, was simply too much for them to bear, as it nearly was for me; but Mutesa was as stalwart as ever and, finding us shelter in the hollow of a giant baobab tree, prepared to help me make what was presumably going to be my last stand. At his insistence that I arm myself I reluctantly took out the rail pistol, incapable of fully comprehending that I might have to turn it against Larissa and the others and wondering if it might not be better all the way around to simply surrender myself.

This I decided to do, much to Mutesa's dismay. As the ship approached the tree in which we were hiding, he insisted that he escort me out onto the grassy patch of flatland that surrounded it, to make certain that I was not simply shot down like a dog. How exactly he intended to prevent this was unclear, but I welcomed his company on what I genuinely thought might be my final walk across any part of this Earth.

Mutesa's bravery took on a bewildered quality as the ship slowly descended in our direction until the bottom of the hull brushed the tips of the waving grass. Then the little green lights began to flash amidships and the hatch flew open, revealing Fouché and, behind him, Larissa. My heart leapt at the sight of her, terrified though I was: she seemed more beautiful than ever, so beautiful that I didn't at first notice that she was screaming to me over the din of the ship's engines in a voice filled with desperation. It took several more minutes to make out just what she was saying, and when at last I did my smiling face went utterly straight:

Malcolm, she was saying, had vanished.

As Larissa and Fouché continued to wave me aboard the ship, I tried to make some kind of sense out of the situation. But sense was waiting on board the vessel, not out there on that grassland. I turned to Mutesa to say good-bye and found him already smiling: I had told him about Larissa (though not about the ship), and, having now seen her, he had apparently reached the conclusion that I was going to be all right. I hugged him tightly, and he told me that I mustn't feel at all bad about returning to my world, for his really wasn't any better—a fact that he suspected I had already learned. I smiled and nodded, then ran for the ship, leaping inside and into those arms that had for so long formed the stuff of my waking and sleeping heartaches.

After getting an additional hug and nearly as many kisses from Fouché, I headed with the pair of them to the nose of the ship, where Colonel Slayton and the Kupermans were waiting. More warm greetings were exchanged, my relief that my suspicions about them had been so wrong growing by leaps and bounds. But before we could enter into any serious discussion of what had happened, we needed to hide ourselves where we would be safe from the weapons of the various tribes of whom my friends had inadvertently been making enemies in their efforts to find me. Lake Albert seemed the obvious spot for such asylum, and soon we were beneath its surface, surrounded by all the military, human, industrial, and animal wastes that had been discarded there during the long years of Africa's decline. Night soon fell, mercifully taking this dismal panorama away; and we did not turn on the ship's exterior illumination as we talked at the conference table, partly for fear of being detected and partly to avoid the ugliness around us.

With Larissa's arm tightly entwined in my own, I began to listen to the story of Malcolm's disappearance, though the telling did not take long. The success of the Washington scheme had apparently driven him into a deep depression. Convinced that the hoax would be quickly exposed and finally force widespread acknowledgment of the dangerous unreliability of modern information systems, he had been stunned to watch it become, throughout the winter and spring, just another source of media fluff and academic revisionism. During the summer he had first stopped eating regularly, then at all, and he had come out of his laboratory so rarely that the others had begun to wonder how he was surviving. Finally, after he'd been locked away for three solid days, Larissa had taken her rail pistol and shot the door down.

Inside the lab was an apparatus such as none of the rest of the team had ever seen. It was impossible to tell what the original design might have been, for it was badly mangled: the result of either a furious destructive rampage or some kind of explosive malfunction. Whatever the case, there was no sign of Malcolm, nor of his body nor indeed of any blood; and this fact brought my warning about the possibility of Malcolm's attempting suicide back into Larissa's thoughts. For the next few days she and the others used the ship and the jetcopter to search the sea for any sign of him, and for several more days they wore out their wits trying to think where else he could have gone and how. Finally accepting their inability to solve the mystery, Larissa decided it was time to find me (a task that took them all of a week) and see if I might have any ideas as to where her brother's desperate mental state could have led him.

Shocked but not entirely surprised by all this, I tried my best to come up with some alternatives to the blackest option. But the attempt was hopeless from the start, and as this became increasingly apparent the others began, one by one, to beg off and go to their quarters to absorb what seemed the only possible conclusion: that Malcolm, despondent over not only the Washington hoax but also the failure of his last technological creation, had smashed the device to pieces and then thrown himself into the sea. That no evidence of the suicide had been found was not surprising: the waters of the North Atlantic were vast, so vast that even the elaborate detection equipment on Malcolm's remarkable ship might have failed to find his body before it was torn up by predators or simply drifted down into some abyss.

Larissa, of course, had suspected that this worst possible conclusion was unavoidable; but given the unique and poignant nature of her shared background with her brother, that suspicion did little to ease the blow when it finally fell, and I was grateful that I could be there to soften it, if only a little. Such was perhaps not the romantic reunion that I had spent so many months unsuccessfully trying to keep out of my thoughts—indeed, we never left the conference table throughout the entire night—but as she drew steadily closer to me, I at least began to sense that she would survive the loss intact and that we did indeed have a future together. The approach of dawn found us both in that hazy, tearful state of exhaustion that often accompanies grief; and then, before either of us was really aware of it, something very strange began to happen:

The sun came gleaming clearly into the ship.

The waters of Lake Albert had been somehow cleansed of the filth that had been horribly evident the night before; and the sight was so miraculous that both Larissa and I could do little more than stand up, move to the transparent hull, and smile in wonder for several minutes. Then the others came barreling in, not one by one but in a noisy herd, shouting the news and asking—rather dimly, I remember taunting—if we'd seen what had happened. There was absolutely no rational explanation for the event: we had heard no sounds of machinery at work during the night, and besides, the technology to do such a thing didn't exist anywhere in Africa—quite probably in all the world. It really did seem nothing short of a miracle; but the shocks were just beginning.

After engaging the holographic projector, we rose back up above the surface to see that the western shore of the lake was utterly free of any signs of conflict. Moreover, animals were visible: the same species of wildlife that I'd read and then observed to be extinct in Africa were everywhere, making the area look much like the yellowed old poster I'd seen in the miserable bar in Naples. None of us could find anything to say, though this was not our usual horrified shipboard silence: this was, for once, a quiet delight, occasionally broken by laughter and quick, astonished cheers.

The question of what to do next arose comparatively slowly. I offered the suggestion that we make for the coast to see if, along the way, we couldn't find some clue as to what was going on. But the journey that followed was only more bewildering. Prosperous villages and towns now dotted the landscape where days before there had been only ghostly ruins left by war and plague. Still more wildlife abounded, along with an occasional luxury bus full of tourists. As we neared the coast, the signs of prosperous civilization grew thicker and more impressive, until finally we broke through to the sea to behold:

Zanzibar. The impoverished island of Zanzibar, in bygone eras a center of the slave trade and in more recent times a decrepit, disease-ridden relic of that evil past. But now? Now what loomed before us looked more like Hong Kong, or rather what Hong Kong would look like had it been designed by people with not only money but taste. A gleaming city stood at the center of the beautifully landscaped island, made up of high-rise buildings that accented the colors of the sea, the mainland jungle, and Zanzibar's pristine white coral beaches. It was, in short, an oasis of enlightened industry and beauty—one whose existence was impossible to explain.

Our ship now lies beneath the waves off that oasis. We still have no definite answers, of course, nor have the ship's communications and monitoring systems been of much help. We seem to be having trouble establishing and maintaining satellite links, and even when we do, we hear strange reports from around the world that make as little sense as what we've seen in East Africa. There are occasional tales of conflicts in parts of the world where there should be none, along with even more frequent and remarkable stories that indicate many previously war-torn parts of the world are enjoying peace and prosperity. All of it supports a seemingly impossible but no less obvious theory:

That Malcolm has actually succeeded in his quest to conquer time.

If this is indeed so, then his mechanism must have self-destructed after completing its task—indeed, it may have been designed to do so—and we therefore have no idea where, or rather when, he has gone. The list of possibilities is infinite, as we discovered when we tried over dinner this evening to determine precisely what place and point in history one would have had to reach, and what one would have had to do once there, in order to produce the effects we have witnessed and heard about. Nor have we yet determined the full range of those effects; assuming that the incomprehensible has in fact happened, we must now travel the world as Larissa once proposed to me that we do, living by our own law and observing what may well be the many signs of our departed friend and brother's handiwork in a further effort to unravel the riddle of his destination. But time and history are infinite webs, and the slightest touch on any of their innumerable filaments can provoke change beyond imagining; thus the truth may ever elude us.

If he *has* managed it, did he leave any clues? Notes? The others could find none, but certainly we must return to St. Kilda to search again. Yet even if we should discover such documentation, will any of us be able to understand it enough to repeat his experiment? Would we want to? More questions without answers. The one thing we can be sure of is that, whatever has happened, Malcolm will never come back. Nor do I think that he would wish to—even if he were dead. Improved as this new modern world may be, it is still the modern world, and it would likely suit Malcolm no better than it did before. Throughout his life, his terrible physical and emotional wounds made him a man to whom Time could offer no comfortable moment. Perhaps now he has returned the favor by destroying the very concept of Time; and perhaps in so doing he has experienced, if only for a fleeting instant, the kind of ordinary human contentment that so consistently and tragically eluded him in this reality.

As for the rest of us, we have all taken heart from even the possibility that Malcolm has achieved his final dream—no one more so than Larissa. She will of course miss the brother with whom she shared more secrets and sorrows than anyone should ever have to bear. But she knows that whether he has broken Time or been broken by it, he is finally at peace; and the torments that seemed to him so unending have been revealed as the transitory vexations of a troubled world—one that he may, in the end, have helped to make less mad.

ACKNOWLEDGMENTS

This book has been dedicated to my literary agent, Suzanne Gluck, not simply because she has handled my career with enormous skill and compassion, but because, when asked by Walter Isaacson and Jim Kelly of *Time* magazine if she could suggest an author to write a serialized novella about the near future, she put my name forward. During a remarkable meeting that followed, many of the ideas that were eventually embodied in *Killing Time* were worked out, and as the first parts of the story were being written for *Time*, Walter and Jim provided much insight and encouragement, for which I am deeply grateful. Also of great help at *Time* were Teresa Sedlak and Barbara Maddux. But Suzanne remained the person who ultimately made everything work, as she always does; and this book is truly almost as much her doing as it is mine.

Despite the appearance of its first chapters in *Time*, publication of the book remained a gamble, one that I am thankful that my editor and publisher, Ann Godoff, was willing to take. Ann remains the most daring single person in her business: the extent of her success should surprise no one.

I am also indebted to Hilary Hale for her friendship, advice, and stewardship of my work in the rest of the English-speaking world.

Many authors' ideas about what the future will be like have affected my own opinions, either by challenging or reinforcing them.

In the realm of scientific speculation I must mention Michio Kaku, Lawrence M. Krauss, and Clifford Stoll. Books and articles by Robert Kaplan, Benjamin Schwartz, and David Rieff helped me refine my thoughts on what world politics and society will be like in the years to come, as did conversations with my good friend and mentor, James Chace, who took the time to study the manuscript. I learned a great deal about the history and impact of hoaxes from the work of Adolf Rieth and Ian Haywood. And my ever-incisive friend David Fromkin helped me speculate as to just what historical frauds would have the most impact on the world.

Thoughts on the story itself, as well as personal support, came from Hilary Galanoy, Joe Martino, and Tim Haldeman. For helping to keep me going I must thank my parents; my brothers, Simon and Ethan, and their wives, Cristina and Sara; Gabriella, Lydia, Sam, and Ben (the last three especially for their creative input early on); my cousin Maria and her husband, Jay (and Nicholas); John, Kathy, and William von Hartz; Dana Wheeler-Nicholson; Jim Turner and Lynn Freer (and Otto, of course); Bill and Diane Medsker; Ellen Blain; Lindsey Dold; Michelle McLaughlin; Jennifer Maguire; Ezequiel Vinao; everyone who "survived" at Oren Jacoby and Betsy West's house; and Perrin Wright.

Debbie Deuble, the best of friends and my West Coast agent, has endured my ranting without giving in to the temptation to break my arm. She knows how much it's meant to me.

Special words of thanks go to Tom Pivinski, Bruce Yaffe, Ernestina Saxton, and Vicki Hufnagel, all of whom have never stopped trying to get me well.

The difficult home stretch was gracefully illuminated by Laura Bickford, whose arrival was well worth the wait.

ABOUT THE AUTHOR

CALEB CARR was born in Manhattan and grew up on the Lower East Side, where he still lives. He is the author of the bestsellers *The Alienist* and *The Angel of Darkness,* along with several volumes of nonfiction. Carr writes frequently on military and political affairs and is an editorial adviser to *The World Policy Journal* and *MHQ: The Quarterly Journal of Military History.*

ABOUT THE TYPE

This book was set in Galliard, a typeface designed by Matthew Carter for the Merganthaler Linotype Company in 1978. Galliard is based on the sixteenth-century typefaces of Robert Granjon.